THE STUART LEGACY

The
Stuart Legacy

ROBERT KERR

STEIN AND DAY/*Publishers*/New York

First published in the United States by Stein and Day/*Publishers*/1973

Copyright © 1973 by Robert Kerr

Library of Congress Catalog Card No. 73-81732

Printed in the United States of America

Stein and Day/*Publishers*/Scarborough House, Briarcliff Manor, N.Y. 10510

ISBN 0-8128-1631-5

Contents

Part I

Part II

Part III

Part I

'Ten-tenths of the law'

The tall young man named James Stuart put one hand on the ship's rail and leapt ashore. It was only then, when he was standing on the quay, that his height and his breadth at the shoulders became noticeable to anyone who happened to be watching. Several were.

They would notice, too, that he was careful to come down on one foot and that he walked with a perceptible limp. The mate lifted a bundle from the deck tied up with leather thongs and threw it after him on to the quay.

'The skipper's compliments,' he said.

Stuart made him an insolent bow.

'My grateful thanks to the skipper,' he said, 'and tell him the next time he brings a woman aboard to keep a closer eye on her.'

'You bastard,' said the mate, quietly but with feeling.

Stuart shook the glistening blond curls that fell to his shoulders.

'No,' he said pleasantly, 'it was my father who was the bastard. Through no fault of his own, mind you. But I was born in holy wedlock. Although who can ever be sure? You might care to debate that question with the skipper. That's to say, when his head is better.'

'Goldilocks!' said the mate, spitting emphatically on the quay. 'By Jesus, we're well rid of cargo like you.'

Stuart shook a reproachful finger at the sour face above him and grinned like a wolf. Then he turned to the port baillie who stood beside him glowering up into his face with the question, 'Papers?'

Stuart tucked under his arm the sword he was carrying. He

9

unfastened his doublet at the throat and pulled out a small leather bag that hung there under his shirt. Loosening it, he slipped out a missive, folded three times and carrying a seal.

The baillie studied it with nervous concentration. Stuart noticed that he seemed to feel the heat. Beads of perspiration had broken out all over his forehead. That was odd because the weather was not really warm. It could be the mental effort of understanding the document Stuart had handed him.

'Henricus Rex ... Jacobus Stuart ...' It was at times like this that the baillie was sorry he had not paid more heed to the Latin master at the High School of Edinburgh.

James Stuart filled in the time by looking at the scene before him: the Shore of Leith; the packages of merchandise stacked on the quay; the thin grey houses with steep red roofs above their crowstep gables; and, on the farther side of the quay, two men who were standing there in shabby black clothes. It seemed that they had nothing better to do that morning than loiter idly there.

This was it then—his country. The only country he could call his own. For the first time in his life he was not a foreigner. It ought to be a comforting thought. He remembered what his father had told him with so much emphasis, 'Remember, boy, when you go there, you are *returning*. Even if it is for the first time.'

He ought to feel a throb of pride or, at least, of proprietorship. But that, no doubt, would come. At present, he confessed to himself, he was conscious only of curiosity. It was different from what he had expected, which had been ...

But already, as the seconds passed, the imagined country was being swept out of his mind by the real one.

This was the country his father had come from. 'Don't expect much of a welcome, boy. Then you won't be disappointed.'

He was though. He could not deny it, but he was. Somehow he had thought it would be different.

For a moment his glance wavered back to the two men on the other side of the quay, looking at them, associating them tentatively with the horses that stood nearby, tethered to rings set into the front of a quayside house.

Two men in black—serious men with closed, important faces.

10

One of them had a square-cut black beard and an air of authority. His fingers played nervously with the hilt of a short sword he was wearing. They were studying the heavy sky and the sullen sea beyond the pier end. Out there an island rose like a sharp carved strip in the water half-way across to the land which at that point in the Firth is six miles or so distant. The bearded man suddenly stopped fingering the hilt of his whinger. He was looking along the cobbles between the houses and the water where, at that moment, two horsemen had come into sight.

One of them was small and slimly built, wearing a doublet of brown velvet. He had a finely curved nose and an assured manner that went with it. One who had a social position and intended that it should be respected. Behind him rode a groom with a led horse. The first man would be about the same age as Stuart who, as the rider approached, unrolled the belt of his sword and buckled it round his waist.

His present business was with the port baillie.

'You don't look like one of us,' the official frowned fretfully. Stuart grinned and nodded.

'Sunshine does that,' he said.

It might have been so. His cheeks were tanned and the curls that blew about his face had been bleached by the sun. But his clothes, too, were unusual in those parts. His doublet of dark blue quilted silk was buttoned only at the throat. His breeches were tighter and longer than they were usually worn in Scotland. His light brown hat of soft felt had a red ostrich plume fastened by a jewelled brooch to its band. These were styles picked up somewhere abroad.

'And you don't talk like one of us,' said the port baillie.

'This French accent of mine will wear off very quickly.'

'But it says here that you *are* one of us,' said the baillie irritably. 'Scots, it says. Student. Armiger. That means nobleman.'

He still looked unhappy.

Stuart nodded. He doubted whether he could properly be described as a nobleman but there was no harm at all if this official thought so.

The port baillie furtively considered this new arrival whom winds and waters had brought to the Shore of Leith.

Class: gentry. That was clear enough even if there had not

been a document to attest it. Distinguishing physical mark: a limp. Chief characteristic: impudence. Profession: adventurer? The kind that more often leaves this country than arrives in it. Which brought the baillie to his next point. Probable reason for coming: some crime committed in foreign parts?

In short, just the kind of man who would cause trouble if he stayed. And trouble was expected. That was obvious enough from the special watchfulness which the Palace had enjoined on him a few days before. For some reason, His Majesty was anxious.

Knitting his brows heavily, the baillie looked again at the new arrival. He thought: Better if this young man were rounded up and given the choice between a damp cell in the tolbooth and service in the wars ... The sort of man Captain Sinclair could use ...

'Nobleman? Now does it. Your Latin is better than mine.'

'Stuart,' the baillie said.

'That's a name my father left me. He didn't leave me much else, God rest his soul.'

'There's nothing wrong with the name. You'll want me to sign this?' The baillie had still an aggrieved tone.

The young man made a submissive gesture and hitching his bundle to his shoulder, limped across the quay in the wake of the officer. They were watched with attentive curiosity by the men in black.

'You're lame,' said the baillie.

'I am,' Stuart admitted. 'Have you any treatment to suggest?'

The baillie ignored the question.

The young horseman in brown velvet dismounted further along the quay, handed the reins over to the groom and strolled over to the water's edge. There he stood looking seawards. Stuart thought that he must be expecting some vessel to put in.

In the booth which the baillie used for business, there was a small desk, a stool, a pen and an inkpot. There was not room for much more. Before signing Stuart's passport, the baillie hesitated, uneasy.

'You're lame,' he said again.

'I still am,' Stuart agreed.

'You got that at sea?'

'Yes. At sea.'

12

It was true. He had.

The baillie gave up the topic. 'What is your reason for coming here?'

'To attend to some family business.'

'Ah! Property?'

'That depends.'

'On what?'

'On whether someone else hasn't got at the property first.'

The baillie grunted. This off-hand way of talking about a serious matter made him impatient.

'Let me give you a piece of advice,' he said. 'In this country possession is *ten*-tenths of the law, so—keep away from the courts.'

Stuart bowed politely.

'Much obliged. Now,' he said, 'can I ask *you* some questions?'

The baillie nodded.

'Tell me,' said Stuart, 'who are these friends of your outside? The two gentlemen in black.'

'No friends of mine,' said the baillie shortly. 'What's more, I've never set eyes on them. Not in all my life until this day!'

'So they've come from some distance.'

'It seems so.'

Stuart showed him a silver coin in the palm of one hand. Then another. And a third. They seemed to interest the baillie. He cleared his throat.

'If you were to ask me—' he began while he handed over the passport, signed and dated.

He was looking thoughtfully across the quay at the ship from which Stuart had landed. The *Mary of Danzig*.

'—my guess would be that they have come here on Council business.'

'Council business? Business of state? Do you really think so, baillie? And the other gentleman, the one in brown? What about him?'

The baillie shrugged his shoulders.

'I can't remember ever seeing him before, sir.'

'A stranger. Like me. He seems to be expecting a visitor.'

'The ferry will be here at any moment. From across the water.'

Stuart turned away from a topic that had been sufficiently

explored. 'By the way,' he said, 'is there a surgeon hereabouts? Somebody on that ship was hurt last night. An accident. Cracked his skull, I should say. A rough night at sea.'

'Here it was calm enough.'

'No doubt. But in the open sea squalls can blow up all of a sudden. You would be surprised. Anyhow, there is need for a surgeon aboard that ship,' he said. 'Now what kind of business would bring them here, the gentlemen of the Council? What is your belief?'

'God only knows, Mr. Stuart.'

'Well said, baillie. Well and piously spoken. Goodbye then, or as they say in France—adieu.'

'Fare ye well,' said the baillie.

Stuart put down the three silver coins on the baillie's desk and went out. Another three would have got him the name of the brown rider. But would it have been worth the money?

While he had been talking to the baillie, a broad-beamed, un-decked boat had come into sight between the two wooden piers which, like lobster's claws, reached out from the town into the deeper water. The boat's crew had let down a sail and were working their craft to the quay with their oars.

The man in the brown doublet walked down a flight of stone steps that led from the quay's edge to the water. On the boat stood a young woman in a green riding costume. The man handed her ashore and bowed low over her hand. One of the men in the boat handed something up to her—a large hooded bird which perched on the lady's wrist.

Then it seemed that an unrehearsed incident occurred. Perhaps the young man who had greeted her said something that the new arrival resented. At any rate, she drew back sharply. Her chin went up. The man leant forward, making gestures of suppli-cation. The young woman shook her head angrily and—if Stuart saw aright—stamped her foot. Then she ran lightly up the steps and leapt on to the horse which the groom had been holding. The young man in brown velvet followed her, frowning.

Stuart watched the episode closely until the pair, with the groom at their heels, trotted past him on the cobbles.

The lady was worth a look. Dark blonde curls and a profile like the outline of a flower cut in the air by a diamond; skin of ivory, flushed with the faintest rose. The bird which she bore on her gauntleted wrist was a superb white Greenland falcon wearing a scarlet hood. There could be very few birds of that quality in Europe.

These, thought Stuart, are the nobility. She is a lady of rank and he is her—husband, lover, brother?

He acted as he had been taught to do at his school in Paris when meeting persons of beauty, wealth and position. Her glance lingered on him for an instant, long enough for her to admire, if she had a mind to, the grace of his bow, the sweep of his plume to the stones. She said something to the young man beside her, who looked back at once at Stuart and grimaced. They broke into a canter.

At that moment Stuart was easing his shoulders into the burden of his bundle. Just for a moment he followed the riders with his eyes. Then he looked at the two men in black, first at one, then the other. Two distinct glances emphasised by a slight but perceptible jerk of the head. Then he lurched southwards, along the banks of the little stream that flowed into the harbour, winding between wooded banks. He was humming a simple tune he had known all his life.

Two miles or so away he could see a town, sitting darkly on its rocks; a fume of smoke above a packed congregation of houses.

As he turned to go, the figure of a woman had appeared for a second at the fo'c'sle of the *Mary of Danzig*. She was sturdily built with fine white shoulders boldly displayed by a low-cut smock. In her gleaming black hair was a Spanish comb. A white arm rose in greeting; Stuart gave her a cheerful wave in return.

The men in black were sauntering with heavy nonchalance towards the port baillie who had come out of his booth and was looking after Stuart.

'Not like one of us,' the baillie was saying to himself, 'but someways like a man I've seen a while back.'

The puzzled frown was still between his eyes as he heard the question asked by the foremost man in black, 'What name did he give, Fleming?'

The sword-slipper's trade

Jean's Sandy Donaldson looked uneasily at the tall, fair-haired young man who had just engaged a room in the lodgings, the chamber on the third floor that was always hardest to let, being just under a patch of the roof where the rain came in. The young man had taken it readily enough. And now Jean's Sandy was wondering if he should have let the room so cheaply.

Something about the newcomer was faintly disquieting. He was foreign and yet not foreign: tough—but with easy manners. Too easy? There was a smoothness about him that suggested the trickster rather than the gentleman. A student. That was what the passport said ... Student of what? He was quiet—too quiet— quiet enough to be dangerous. From lodgers of this sort one could have trouble.

'That's all then, is it not?' said Stuart curtly. 'You see me. You have been paid. There's nothing more, is there? Except that you still have to show me the room.'

'Aye,' said Jean's Sandy. 'Just so.' Rubbing the hard stubble on his chin, he led the way to the spiral stairs ...

The room was cleaner than Stuart had expected. It had the essentials. A bed. A basin and jug. Water? Donaldson had brought up a kettle and a rag; fairly clean.

Stuart put down his bundle and went over to the window, to look at the town of Edinburgh.

Roofs mounting each beyond the other. As the town climbed the ridge of rock to which it clung, somewhere beyond, just hidden by the slopes of tile and slate, would be the castle, climax of the whole architectural scheme. Perched on its cliff, clad in

16

masonry and iron, it held the city under the threat of its cannon with their undeniable claims to power and authority. After a steep climb through trees, he had emerged from the ravine cut by the river and there suddenly it was, bold and dominant upon its pedestal cliff, like a clenched fist lifted against the sky. Its walls bristled with artillery. Its windows were few and heavily barred. It embodied power and secrecy. In this brooding citadel, the threads of state and policy were drawn together. A menace? At least a reminder.

As he had stood there, admiring it, a man had stopped beside him. Nodding towards the Rock, he had said, 'Nobody has ever escaped from it.'

Stuart looked at him.

'One of my family did,' he said.

'You must come from a clever family,' said the man with a touch of sarcasm.

'I do. What's more, he grilled the gaoler over his own fire.' And Stuart had gone cheerfully on his way entering the town by a gate on the steep southern slope.

Now from the third floor window, he looked out at the roofs and streets of Edinburgh. His hat lay on the bed beside him. He unfastened the jewelled brooch from his hat and put it in the small leather bag which hung round his neck under his shirt. Now his plume was held in place, none too securely, by a single pin. In a strange town it was just as well to show nothing that was too valuable and too conspicuous ...

Immediately beneath him was a close, still unvisited by the morning sun. A sword hanging over one door showed what went on inside. 'Damasker, sword-slipper and cutler to the King,' read the inscription. Near it, was a tailor's shop and a printer's.

Leaning out, he thought he caught sight of one of the men in black he had seen earlier in the day. But in that he could have been mistaken.

Stuart was whistling thoughtfully to himself as he clumped back down the stairs. He nodded to his landlord.

'Are your eyes good?' he asked the landlord.

'Good enough.'

'Can you see a police spy when he comes into the close?'

'There are no police spies in this town,' Donaldson said primly.

'Who would they want to spy on?'

'A fair question, billy. Who is in Edinburgh today that was not here yesterday? It can't be you who brings them into the close, can it? And for that matter there's nothing to find out. See you remember that, Donaldson.'

Stuart left the lodging and walked across the close to the sword-slipper's. No sign of the spy. The booth was two steps down and, as he stooped to go in, a bell rang and the high scream of a grindstone tapered into silence.

Stuart threw his sword on the counter.

'Sharpen,' he said, 'if you please.'

An elderly man wearing a leather apron peered up at him and then down at the sword. He drew it out of the scabbard and ran his finger along the edge of the blade.

'A wheen broader in the blade than they are made nowadays. I haven't seen its like for years. A relic of the old days, the old feuds. All over now, thanks be to God.'

'If all feuds were ended,' said Stuart, 'what would become of the sword-slipper's trade?'

The old man shook his head.

'You may ask! We sword-slippers are a dying race, sir,' he said. 'The gun rules where the sword was once the master. Soon the only trade left to us will be to sharpen tailors' shears ... Initials!' He was looking closely at Stuart's sword. 'Cut by one who knew his trade ... J.S.'

'An heirloom,' Stuart told him.

'Strange. I saw one like it once. In Lord Orkney's hands. He was a Stuart, of a kind.'

'It takes all sorts to make a clan,' said Stuart.

'And some are better than others,' said the slipper. 'If you'll excuse me, sir. You would like me to sharpen it?'

'I would that.'

The grindstone started screaming once again. The business was soon over.

'Tell me, gaffer,' said Stuart, 'what would be a good house to eat in hereabouts?'

'Monypenny's,' the old man told him after a moment's thought. 'Not good, but you'll hardly do better in these parts.'

When Stuart found it, just five minutes later, he agreed. It was not very good, but his appetite was in no mood to be fastidious. He could eat the mutton. He could have eaten it if it had come off a horse.

And a woman serving the food had rich red hair and pale blue eyes that roved over him with a bold appraisal. She touched his hair. 'Bonny,' she said, her glance softening.

'A wig,' he said. She pulled and he caught her wrist.

'You liar!'

'Go on talking. I like to hear that accent,' he said.

'Where do you come from, handsome?'

He ran his hand along her arm to the elbow.

'Soldiering,' he said.

She pulled her arm back. Her voice lost its softness.

'Another waster home from the wars with fancy clothes on his back and no money in his pocket. I know your kind.'

'So you don't like fighting, beautiful!' he said, and reached again for her arm.

She blazed at him. 'Don't you know what's meat for your betters, soldier boy?'

Stuart smiled broadly at her and nodded. She turned away indignantly.

There was a disturbance at the door and, in a moment, a wild-looking crew came pouring noisily into the tavern. They had bare legs, none too clean, with brogues held on their feet by thongs wound about their ankles. They shouted an incomprehensible greeting to the serving woman who evidently knew them well.

In their belts were bare swords which they pulled out and thrust noisily between the flagstones of the floor so that they stood upright in a row. Old-fashioned weapons, yet they looked as if they had seen some recent use.

The newcomers threw glances of fierce enquiry over Stuart and then, with some words that sounded contemptuous, paid no further heed to him. They were chattering earnestly in some language he did not recognise. Occasionally they threw a word to the woman.

Stuart thought he knew what they were. Men from the wild tribes of the Highlands. He remembered what his father had said of these people. 'Mountainy men and as touchy as gunpowder. Treat them with caution, boy. Caution and civility.'

A few minutes later a huge man came into the house. About six feet by four and the outline well filled in. Fair haired, sunburnt, vast but moving lightly, he wore a buff jerkin cut rather long in the skirt which, with the light blue sash round his ample belly, gave him a vaguely military appearance. Stuart thought he looked like a huge brown egg with a smaller pink egg perched on top of it.

On one of his shining, pock-marked cheeks was a long diagonal scar. His moustache was blond and had an arrogant upward sweep. He was about a dozen years older than Stuart and had filled those years with the kind of hard living that does more to sharpen a man's wits than to smooth his manners.

After nodding abruptly to the Highlanders, he came over to Stuart.

'Sinclair,' he said, touching the broad, drooping brim of his hat. Stuart nodded and said nothing.

'Do you insist on talking to yourself? Or may someone else join in?' asked the fat man.

Stuart jerked his hand towards the wooden bench on which, with the greatest self-assurance in the world, Sinclair was already making himself at ease. This was a man, it seemed, with no excess of sensibility. In fact, thought Stuart, an impudent rogue —like himself.

'You have newly arrived here? ... Don't ask me how I know. Your first visit?'

Stuart nodded.

'A mistake,' said the fat man sadly. 'Some people make it. Not many. Why did you?'

'My father suggested it.'

'Fathers should be more careful what they say. Did he give any reason?'

'He told me the country was beautiful.'

Sinclair gave a series of inclinations of the head which, if they had been less majestic, might have been called nods.

'Did he suggest how you were going to live on beauty?'

Stuart grimaced.

'I expect not,' said Sinclair. 'Only one way of living on beauty is known to me. Your father wouldn't be likely to recommend

it. But here you come ... I should say from Europe, from somewhere South. I should say from France. Yes? An easy guess.
Accent—and clothes, my dear sir. The French style launched by
the greatest captain of our times, Henry of Navarre. You have
served with him? No. Too young? What a misfortune! You
missed a great experience.'

'Maurice of Nassau was the better general.'

'Matter of opinion.'

'My father told me that. He served with both. And he said
moreover that there was no sound in all the world like the
trumpets blowing the charge at Ivry.'

'By God, your father was right. I can hear them now. What
was his name?'

'The same as mine,' said Stuart with a pleasant smile.

'That often happens,' said Sinclair, unperturbed. 'So you've
just arrived. And I am just leaving. For where? Would you guess.'

Stuart shrugged his shoulders.

'Give up?' said Sinclair, interrupting himself long enough to
signal to a potboy for drink. 'Think of somewhere far away,
uncouth, barbarous and, without boasting, a trifle dangerous.'

'Hot?' Stuart's curiosity overcame his new and unnatural
reserve.

'Cold. Cold as the Arctic snows. Cold as the frozen steppes.
In fact, the frozen steppes! Muscovy! What do you think?
That I must be mad? Mad is what I am. Sinclair. George. Captain
in the service of his royal Majesty, the King of the Swedes,
Goths and Vandals—and at yours ...'

'Muscovy?'

'Muscovy. The fantastic domes of the Kremlin sparkling across
the blinding wastes of snow! The trouble about this country
of ours, Mr—'

'Stuart.'

Sinclair bowed. 'I did not hear the Christian name.'

'James.'

'The trouble is, James, that this country can imagine no use
for the brains and muscles of its best sons, gentlemen of breeding
and mettle like our noble selves. Sad, sad! Even sadder, the
confession must be made that for our part we vastly prefer killing
to working.'

21

There were noises at the other end of the room. The mountain men were pulling their swords out of the floor and leaving.

'Do you see those fellows?' asked Sinclair. 'In a week's time they'll be fighting in Ireland.'

'Ireland?'

'There's trouble there. The Earl of Tyrone has risen against the English Queen. Most of the people are with him. And many men go over to lend a hand, like those gentlemen.'

'With that old iron?' Stuart flicked a thumb towards the swords.

'Until they can pick up something better.'

'And which side will they fight on?'

Plainly Sinclair thought this was of minor importance.

'Tyrone has Spanish money. In the end, England should win. Our friends will act as the tactical situation suggests. I tried to persuade them to come with me to Moscow. But no! They had notions of their own. Stubborn cattle! But what brings them as far south as this? That is something I'd like to know. The usual route for them is by boat out of the Western Isles. Half a day's rowing and they're in the glens of Antrim—and the war can start! But for some reason they're travelling this way.'

'Maybe to buy better arms.'

'And maybe it's plain Highland daftness.' Sinclair dismissed the matter from his mind. 'The trouble, my boy, is that we are a nation of wastrels, spendthrifts, dreamers. No escaping from it. When Gabriel blows his trumpet, we'll be there in the front rank, poor as rats and plaguing the colonel for our back pay. Allow me to present myself—Sinclair, George, Captain. I've said that. Youngest son but one of the Earl of Caithness. We are an old family and a restless one. And you are Stuart, James. Anything else?'

'Formerly student of Paris, scholar at the Academy of M. de Pluvinel, first equerry of Henry IV, King of France and Navarre.'

'My respects, learned and noble sir. M. Pluvinel had an apt pupil.' He lifted his hat with an ironical sweep which irritated Stuart a great deal. 'I remember Navarre at Coutras. He was a boy then.'

'My father was at Coutras.'

'Was he indeed? When the Prince de Condé was unhorsed that day, I gave him mine.'

'He was unhorsed twice then.'

'I never heard it.'

'My father gave the Prince *his* horse,' said Stuart.

'There is a difference between us of memory,' said Sinclair, losing his smile.

'My father had an infallible memory,' said Stuart in a soft voice.

'You puzzle me,' said Sinclair with a perceptible change of tone. 'You look lively but you act quietly.'

'I'm dozing,' Stuart replied. 'Don't wake me.'

Sinclair looked sharply at him. With an air of nonchalance, he pulled a dagger from under his doublet, holding it loosely between his fingers and making it vibrate on the table. All the time he watched Stuart closely. Stuart appeared to be lost in thought. His eyes seemed to be watching something far away.

'You have only to say,' said Sinclair, 'and I'll go.'

Stuart looked surprised.

'Do you want to go?'

The knife quivered on the table, faster and faster.

'I am not used to persons who contradict me,' Sinclair remarked casually.

The expression on Stuart's face was one of deepening mental confusion.

'I don't understand you,' he said.

The fat man surveyed him with marked dislike.

'When you've had time to sort your thoughts out,' he said, 'just let me know.'

The dagger continued to vibrate on the table.

'I don't understand you,' Stuart repeated in a dreamy voice.

It seemed that a kind of nervous tremor had attacked his right hand. It caught Sinclair's eye.

'What are you shivering for?' asked Sinclair. 'Nothing to be afraid of.'

Stuart looked bewildered.

At that moment it happened. With the side of his left hand, Stuart struck the dagger from Sinclair's fingers and with his right he caught it before it fell.

23

Sinclair rose. His hand flew to his sword. But by that time, Stuart held the dagger to his heart.

'No, gallant captain, no,' he said softly. 'I beg of you. I have a temper which frightens me sometimes. I have to watch it.'

Sinclair's eyes softened. His body relaxed. He sat down.

'That was clever,' he said respectfully. 'You didn't waste your time in that dancing academy.'

'Fencing academy.'

'Call it what you like. Now, it's your turn to order the drinks,' Sinclair pointed out. 'This gentleman wishes to buy wine!' he called. 'Now let us talk.'

It was Sinclair who talked.

'Maybe I was wrong,' he said, thoughtfully. 'Maybe this country does have a use for you after all....'

'Maybe I have a use for it,' said Stuart. 'One question I'd like to ask if I may.'

'Ask, boy.' Sinclair made a gracious sweep of his arm.

'Where can I find the Earl of Gowrie?'

Something crumbled in Sinclair's face. Some deep, indefinable change occurred. The only expression left alive was a profound alarm.

Stuart was about to repeat the question when Sinclair said hoarsely, 'No. No!' He had some difficulty in getting the words out. With rapid flapping gestures of his hands he imposed silence. Then he rose, looked round, went to the door leading to the kitchen, closed it and came back.

'What the devil made you ask about him?'

'Curiosity,' said Stuart.

'About some things it's dangerous to be curious, boy. Speak in a whisper and don't use that name again where anyone can overhear. Listen. The man you spoke of is dead. *Dead*. Understand? So is his brother Alec. You knew them? You didn't? So much the better for you. Now forget you ever heard of them.'

'But why?'

'Listen, Stuart. These two—the man you mentioned and his brother—tried to murder the King's majesty a few weeks ago. To make it worse, the deed was done in their own house in Perth. Tried and failed. Then they were killed by the King's servants. So perish all traitors, say I.' Sinclair raised his hat and threw his eyes piously upwards. 'Their estates have been given to other men. Their name is blotted out. It must not be spoken on pain of treason. Be warned. Now you know why I may have appeared nervous just for a moment.'

'But why—?'

'Keep your voice down, man.'

'Why?' Stuart whispered, 'did they attack the King?'

'Wickedness,' said Sinclair. 'Treason. What else? That's the story—the true story—unless you think the Privy Council of Scotland is telling a pack of lies. Be content with what I've told you. Look on anything else as moonshine. And ask me no more.'

'Maybe I can ask someone else.'

'And maybe you can end on the gallows! That can be arranged! But you didn't come to Scotland to do that did you? What's that man to you or you to him?'

'Only a question, that's all.'

'Then leave it so, unanswered.'

'It seems that I must.' Stuart made a gesture of resignation but kept his eyes fixed on Sinclair's. The fat man suddenly thrust his face into Stuart's and spoke quickly.

'Find a man named Andrew Freeland. Ask him your question. He'll be hidden somewhere in the town. You'll know him by a little red mark on his cheek. But be careful. Few will know where to look for him. And fewer can be trusted. What you want for this kind of work is—'

At that moment, the door leading to the close opened and a man entered. Sinclair nodded to him and rose to his feet.

'My business has arrived,' he said, with a shrug. 'Just one thing before I go. What you want is a caddie. In this town a man needs a caddie more than he needs a horse. To do his business. They are all scoundrels. Some are worse than others.'

Stuart remembered hazily what his father had told him of the breed: 'A secret society, boy, and very powerful. Eavesdroppers, procurers, spies. Most of them come from the mountains. They talk to one another in a tongue civilised men don't understand. A great advantage. All cities have this affliction. In Edinburgh they are called caddies.'

Sinclair went to the tavern door and shouted, 'Donald!' Three times the shout was repeated, then came an answering cry.

'This one is the biggest rascal of them all,' said Sinclair reassuringly. 'But *you* can trust him with your life—and even your money. I abetted a felony once by saving him from the gallows.'

From the close outside a ragged figure with a red beard and a crimson-veined nose peered at them from tiny blue eyes under swollen eyelids. A Highlandman.

'Donald Gregory! What his real name is I won't tell you. Maybe you can guess. A broken clan. Thieves to a man. Donald, this is Mr. Stuart. Look after him, eh?'

The Highlander looked Stuart over, his little eyes screwed up, his mouth pulled down at the corners with cunning and calculation. Then he answered.

'I will that, Captain.'

'Wait outside then.'

Sinclair held out his hand to Stuart. 'He'll take you to Freeland if any man can—and if you still want to go.'

'Thank you. I'm fairly warned.'

'We'll meet again,' said Sinclair with conviction. 'Two men like us. The world is not wide enough to keep one from the other. If you want to take cover suddenly, as can happen, send word to me through Gregory.'

Stuart nodded.

'Oh, and a word of advice,' said Sinclair. 'Whatever you do, give no drink to the caddie. When he takes a drop too much—'

He spread his hands wide and was turning away when Stuart said with a thin smile, 'You may be needing this, Captain Sinclair.' He held out the dagger he had snatched.

Sinclair took it with a frown of annoyance. Then he turned to the newcomer, a small, white-faced man with a shifty grin. Stuart went out to inspect his new servant.

'Good morning, my lord,' said Gregory with a bow.

Never in his life had Stuart set eyes on a more untrustworthy face.

'Do you know where to find a man named Andrew Freeland?' he asked.

The caddie gave him a searching look from his little screwed-up eyes.

'Freeland was not always his name, my lord, if that's the man you mean.'

26

'With a red mark on his cheek,' said Stuart.

'That's the man, sir,' said the caddie. 'I'll find out where he is hiding and tell you. But—this could be chancy work, my lord....'

'Life is chancy,' said Stuart. At that moment, over the caddie's shoulder, he caught sight of a black figure slipping down an alley.

The concert is over

Stuart spent a long time in his hired room sitting on the bed and easing off one of his boots. When the job was done, he was white in the face. For a few minutes he remained quite still. Then he got up and poured hot water from a kettle into the bowl.

Round his ankle was a stained roll of cloth which he began to unwind. He was engrossed in the task, cursing softly, when a small noise made him look up.

A slight elegant figure stood at the door looking down at him with an expression of cool but concentrated interest. A young man wearing a brown velvet doublet.

'That's an ugly mess on your ankle, Stuart,' he said.

Stuart looked down at it dispassionately. A wound ran horizontally on the inside of the leg just above his left ankle. It had been there a long time. Now it was healed for the most part, although there was still some discharge that was staining the bandage yellow. When at last it dried up, it was going to leave a deep dent in the flesh.

'Yes,' he said.

'How did you get it?'

'Kick from a horse. Waggon wheel ran over my foot. Tombstone fell on it in a graveyard. I was trespassing at the time.'

The intruder sneered.

'Your pet shark took a friendly nip one day,' he said.

'How did you guess?' Stuart asked.

He lowered his foot into the basin of hot water and began bathing it gently.

'You know my name,' he said, without looking up. 'That was clever. And you took the trouble to climb three stairs to visit me. That was polite.'

'Not clever,' said the other man. 'Just a few questions in the right places. No trouble at all. As for polite, I'm usually polite when I'm on business.'

Stuart surveyed him. Slender, olive-skinned, with delicately moulded features and dark brown hair. Age? Somewhere in the early twenties. The ease of manner which can be more offensive than rudeness.

'And now,' said Stuart, 'suppose you go on being polite and climb down those stairs you have just come up. Adieu, Mr—'

'The name is Bannerman. Rory Bannerman. And it would not be adieu. No. Au revoir, at most.' A faint smile touched the corners of his eyes but did not visit his lips.

'Adieu, Bannerman,' said Stuart.

The man in brown velvet changed the weight of his body from one foot to the other. He seemed to be in no hurry to go.

'That depends,' he said easily, 'on whether you want to be at liberty—I will not say alive—by tomorrow morning.'

'Accidents may happen to anyone,' said Stuart.

'It would not be an accident. You have come to a country where some people are interested in you. Don't ask me why. Unfortunately they can make your life disagreeable or even short. Somebody is going to cut your throat one day, Stuart, unless I am much mistaken. It happens,' he sighed. 'Even in this enlightened and beautiful land, it happens. Unless, of course ...'

'Unless?' asked Stuart without looking up.

'Well, that mess on your ankle will be of interest to many people. They may wonder how you came by it. No doubt there will be different theories. My own belief is there may also be a small mark on one of your shoulders, probably the left, something looking as if it had been made by a hot iron.'

'Where does that take us, do you suppose?'

'Isn't it obvious? To save themselves from the trouble of putting a dagger into you in one of the dark alleys of this town, those friends of yours may decide to ship you back to the place you have come from. Don't you think that would be reasonable, from their point of view?'

29

'I think,' said Stuart, evenly, 'it would be reasonable for you to shut that door with the handle you will find on the outside.'

His ankle was responding to the warmth of the water. The intensity of the irritation had faded. Now he would put a fresh bandage on and some of the salve he had brought from Amsterdam. In a few minutes, he felt that he would be able to deal with Bannerman. 'And if it's money you're after ...' he began.

Bannerman interrupted him with a musical laugh.

'You misunderstand me. No, Stuart, what I was about to propose was something quite different. Here you have no friends. However, you have assets. You are a gentleman. You have looks. Presence. Insolence. A talent for action. And so on. Above all, you have nothing to lose. Nothing.'

'Nothing?'

'Nothing.'

'My good name?'

Bannerman smiled and pointed.

'The name of a man with that wound on his ankle?'

'My life?'

Bannerman agreed.

'Just at this moment, I would not give much for it. Three days maybe.'

'Three days.' Stuart was winding the fresh bandage round his ankle. The task called for all his powers of concentration.

'Three days,' said Bannerman, 'at most.'

'A lot can happen in three days.'

'It can. One way or another. The question is, which way? Good or—' Bannerman drew a finger across his throat and with his teeth clenched, drew in his breath noisily.

'What do you suggest I do?'

Bannerman smiled coldly.

'Come and see me, Stuart. I have a mission to suggest which would take you away from this town for a little. Oh, an agreeable mission. Most agreeable. To escort a charming lady who has urgent reason to visit the North country.'

'Why don't you do it yourself if it is so agreeable?'

'Because—there is a reason I can explain. A reason of state. When you come to visit me, I can tell it. Incidentally, Stuart, your looks reminded my sister of his late Majesty, the King's grandfather of blessed memory. No doubt a coincidence. We can talk about it when you come to see me. Here is the address. Bannerman's Lodging. The last close on the right before you reach the Palace. Any time. But better after dark. Remember. Bannerman's Lodging. Last on the right. Try to keep alive till then.'

He was closing the door behind him when Stuart called 'Hey' and he turned.

'Just one thing, Bannerman.'

'Yes?'

'The right shoulder, not the left,' said Stuart.

Bannerman looked puzzled for an instant. Then his face cleared and, with a quick nod, he left.

By the time Stuart reached the foot of the stairs, he decided that his ankle was, at last, getting better. With luck, he should be able to inspect the town.

'Donaldson!'

The landlord appeared.

'If anybody should come asking for me, tell him that I'll be back before midnight, without fail. Should I be a few minutes late, you can order the prayers for the dying.'

'For the—'

'They won't be prayers for me, Donaldson.'

The landlord stared.

Stuart strolled out to the wide street which was tilted steeply down towards the east.

The afternoon sky was clear all the way from the salmon-pink flush beyond the castle to the shrill green that faded into a purple fume downhill.

Stuart stood for a moment at the kerb watching a file of soldiers who had been on a guard at the palace trudge up to their barracks.

They were tall, well-built fellows, if somewhat wanting in polish, he thought.

He turned to saunter down towards the east where in the Canongate, he would be likely to find what he was seeking, a tavern where the smells would not be too offensive.

Stuart was aware of those strangers, his fellow-countrymen who passed him on the pavement. Bigger than the French and bonier than the Flemings, there was about them an air of sedate truculence which, he thought, could become slightly disagreeable. Among them, there were strongly contrasted individuals. The racial mixture here might be much as he had known it elsewhere, but the bottle had not been so thoroughly shaken.

In one respect, humanity was the same as elsewhere. It was composed of two sexes. Glances of frank appraisal; cheeks reddened by some rudely amorous wind; lips that invited inspection and made no promises; in short, a familiar traffic which made his homeland less foreign, less hostile than at first it had seemed.

He went on, cheered, and found a tavern where he could contemplate the world with a jug of wine before him. But he thought he would not risk the food there. After a time, he rose and resumed his stroll downhill.

Suddenly, at his shoulder, there was an insinuating croak.

'Not that way, my lord. Not that way at all.' It was the caddie.

'You! At last! By God, you don't believe in hurrying, do you.'

'It was harder than I thought to find Freeland. Indeed, it was near impossible,' said the Highlander with a smirk. 'And hurrying would hardly have helped. You're taking the wrong direction, sir. You should go uphill and—'

Directions followed in a flood of words, and Stuart, after listening intently, turned on his heel. His caddie walked some distance behind him.

Stuart bore southwards, leaving the great market place at the corner Gregory had pointed out to him and taking a steep street that twisted downhill under the Castle Rock. Soon he was in a run-down quarter of the town.

Shops that had given up the pretence of being in business. Women standing in doorways who no longer expected that anyone would buy whatever it was they were selling. Heaps of ordure. Dogs.

He passed through a tunnel-like archway—a pend Gregory had called it—which burrowed into a row of houses and arrived in this gloomy little yard. Houses stood all round, five or six storeys high. In the middle, a well. Facing him across the close, a lintel above a door with the motto carved in it, 'Nisi Dominus Frustra 1542'. Just what he had been told to look for.

Walking rapidly towards him across the court was a handful of men, one of whom carried bagpipes and another a drum. They gave him a sharp look but passed on without speaking. Now there was nobody in sight but one old woman sitting at a first storey window looking out.

Stuart crossed the yard and entered below the carved lintel. He was about to climb the stair that faced him inside when he heard footsteps coming down, with the tripping three-time pace of somebody young and in a hurry. Stuart stood on one side. A tall man passed him, throwing up his forearm at the last moment so that his face was hidden by a cloak.

Stuart heard the stranger's steps diminish quickly across the cobbles of the close and fade away. He mounted the stair, one step at a time to spare his ankle. He was going to the fourth floor. After a few steps he was aware that a smell of burning was growing stronger. Arriving, he pushed a door open.

A cloud of smoke billowed out at him like a curtain in a gust of wind. Crouching, with his nose pinched between his fingers and his eyes screwed up tight, Stuart went in. The room was full of evil-smelling smoke. Against the wall, a table was turned over on top of a mattress under which some sticks were burning. There was no sound of crackling; the flames had not yet caught the woodwork. But soon they would.

Stuart lurched forward with his hands held out in front. Crossing the room, he threw up a window. Then he gathered up the burning mattress and bundled it out. He stamped on the sticks that were alight on the floor.

After a moment he stopped coughing and blinking, and could see what there was to see. It was not much.

A man lay on his back with his arms stretched out on the floor. He had four days' growth of fair beard and a small red scar shaped like a new moon on his cheek. His lips were twisted in a violent grimace. His bulging bloodshot eyes stared at the ceiling. Just below one eye a stick was burning with a triangular yellow flame. Either the flame would burn out in a few seconds or it would reach his eyelashes. The man was not likely to care one way or the other.

Stuart lifted the stick and threw it into the fireplace. He bent over the prostrate man; touched something wet; felt a wrist.

One of the riding boots the man had been wearing lay on the floor beside him. The hose had been ripped up and something had happened to the foot. It lay at a strange unnatural angle to the leg and there were deep purple weals on the instep. There was some blood but not much.

Stuart went over to the window and looked down. The mattress he had thrown out lay smoking on the roof of a two-storey house which abutted on to the one he was in. The cover of the mattress had been slit down the sides.

He turned to look again at the man on the floor. With that broad wound below the breastbone, Andrew Freeland was not going to tell him the true story of Lord Gowrie's death. Whatever he might have said, he would say no more.

Stuart went thoughtfully down the stairs. When he passed across the close, the old woman was still at the second floor window. 'The concert is over,' she screeched at him, rocking to and fro in a wild fit of laughter. Stuart hurried on, through the pend.

He found Gregory a hundred yards up the street.

'That journey was wasted,' he said. The caddie looked a question out of his little red-rimmed eyes.

'Somebody got there before me,' said Stuart.

'God save us!' said the Highlander with no obvious sign of surprise.

'He hasn't saved Freeland.'

'You weren't there, my lord, at the time?'

'How could I be there,' said Stuart irritably, 'when I haven't even been in this part of the town?'

'True, my lord, true. But Freeland dead—'

'I didn't say that, did I?'

'You did not. But supposing anything has happened to him —that will be another of the name who has gone.'

'What name, Gregory? What name?'

The Highlander leant forward and whispered hurriedly, 'What name did Freeland have before he became Freeland? Think, sir! What was the name of the two boys who were killed in Perth?'

34

Brown-eyed deceiver

Darkness was closing gradually round the town with the long-drawn melancholy of the northern summer and the town assumed a secrecy that was not wholly friendly. From the closes came whispers, shouts, the noise of water splashing from a height. Lurching feet, the clatter of a man falling. Stuart felt for the sword that the slipper had sharpened.

The architecture of the street made a powerful impression. There were plenty of crevices in this dark cliff of masonry where disorders of every kind might be lurking. Closehead after close-head he passed, each like an embrasure in a fortress wall, each opening into the darkness of a court where a murky light flickered, or on steps going steeply downwards into a black abyss.

Now and then his eyes caught the wink of lights on water. Down there to the north, not so far away, was the sea he had crossed.

Stuart glanced into each close as he passed, taking in deep draughts of the cool and powerful impregnation which the wind carries from a few hundred miles of salt water ...

At the sound his ears had picked up, Stuart came to a sudden and quiet halt. His eyes roved this way and that. He had heard a sharp intake of breath which might have been the beginning of a cry. It had been smothered.

It had come from the dark entry that opened beside a turn-pike stair which thrust its half-circle of masonry into the plain stones at the side of the cobbled street. He peered into the entry, standing motionless, hardly breathing, attentive. Silence? No.

A shuffling as if someone's feet—the feet of someone in there—

were trying to hold on a surface of slippery stone.

The sound he had heard the first time was renewed, more briefly, urgently.

By the time Stuart had composed the impressions of his senses into a woman's sob, he had moved cat-footed into the black close.

He entered from the street with a forward roll of his left shoulder and a twitch of his fingers towards the knife hilt at his right haunch, ready to meet the surprise which might be waiting. It was.

He grappled with an adversary before he saw him and took a fierce blow on the chest from an elbow. Somewhere before him was a man. Beyond that, dimly outlined, a woman.

But a quick flash of grey reflected light low down was vastly more important and quite familiar. A dirk.

Stuart threw himself at it, both hands reaching. A vicious pain tore along his left forearm but he held a wrist and, wrenching with all his strength, forced a grip to give up the dirk. It clattered on the cobbles. He took a step back and drew his knife.

Knees bent, body balanced and drawn into itself, flattened as far as he could against the left-hand wall, he moved forward to the attack.

The odds were against him. Inevitably, he would be silhouetted against the light coming from the street outside. No time this for the tricks of his fencing masters. No room for pretty foot-work. But he had surprise on his side. Keep that advantage, boy! Make a quick end of the enemy in the shadows.

Stuart could see him better now, as his eyes grew used to the darkness. A strongly-built, middle-sized man who was pulling out a rapier. This was the moment! Before the rapier—too long a blade for close fighting like this—was drawn.

With a shout, he struck hard—once, twice—at the other man's sword-arm with the flat of his blade. He heard a grunt of pain. He had hit the forearm where the bone was nearest the skin—with luck the hand would be numbed! Yes! It had dropped from the rapier hilt.

Stuart dived, groping for the dirk on the ground between them. His adversary, holding his helpless arm, waited for the finishing thrust.

Giving him no time to recover, Stuart spun him round and pushed him roughly against a wooden door which he could dimly see behind. Then he thrust with the man's dagger. It was a blow with all his power behind it, aimed at the cloth of the doublet just on the shoulder line.

An angry yelp sounded in the close. Somebody's shoulder had been scratched. Looking at the man pinned to the door, Stuart decided the account was balanced. He pulled the man's rapier from its sheath and tucked it under his arm.

A slim woman stood there still looking at him in the darkness. 'You are a terrible fighter, aren't you?'

It was a youthful voice, speaking with the beguiling local intonation.

'Ma'am,' said Stuart, 'I do as well as I can. We'll leave this close, if you will allow me.' He put his arm round her shoulder and pulled her out of the close into the open street. 'What were you doing in a place like that?'

'You might have killed him,' she said, standing back.

'He might have—'

But Stuart thought that he should not carry the retort any further. Besides, he had something else to think about. This scratch on his forearm. His shirt sleeve was wet through and he could feel the blood already in the palm of his right hand which he was pressing to the wound.

'You couldn't fetch a rag, I suppose?'

She came forward, nearer. She was dark, he thought, and young. But still he could not make out her features.

'You're hurt?'

'No. But—'

Now they were in the street, where there was more light.

'Let me see.' But a second later she had seen too much, the blood running along the back of his left wrist to his knuckles. She swayed forward against him and he took her in both his arms.

Stuart looked down at the fainting girl. Something turned over in his breast.

What he held in his arms, forgetful of the scarlet liquid which was staining her clothes, was about fifteen—sixteen?—years old and the most beautiful girl he had seen in his life ...

37

'What a fool I am! How I hate myself for doing that!'

She was standing before him, steadied by his hands.

'You are sure you feel well now? Nobody likes to see blood for the first time.'

'It isn't the first time. I am always like this.'

'You'll grow out of it, that's sure.'

'And now you must be nearly dead. So much blood you've lost.'

Stuart shook his head. In fact, he thought that the blood had already stopped flowing. The cut was no more than a surface scratch that would ache for a day. And his shirt sleeve was acting as a bandage. If it were quickly washed and bound he would be better by morning.

'If you could show me a surgeon's shop.'

The girl shook her head. In this fading light he could not be certain if her hair was black or dark brown. And at the moment, nothing seemed as important as that, except the colour of her eyes.

'My mother will dress it for you. It is only a step from here to the house.'

'You're sure that your mother will not feel ill when she sees blood?'

'She has grown out of it. But you will not tell her about that man. My mother is a very stupid woman in some ways. She'll make such a fuss—want me never to visit my grandmother again. Such nonsense! So—do you promise?'

'If you will agree never to stay out after dark again. Promise!'

'Do you trust a girl's promise?'

'I could trust yours.'

'You must be mad!'

'Very likely I am.'

'Girls with brown eyes are all deceivers.'

'I can't see what colour your eyes are.'

'Deep, deep brown!'

'Tell me, Mademoiselle Brown, how are we going to explain this to your mother?'

'Leave that to me, Monsieur—'

'Stuart.'

'Like the king?'

38

'Just like the king except that I spell it with a "u". How am I to call you?'

'Beaton.'

'Beaton.' Stuart uttered the name as if it was very important that he had heard it aright.

'Mary Beaton.'

'—Mary Seton, Mary Carmichael—'

'—And me!'

Stuart found her laugh fresher and more musical than any girl's laugh he had ever heard.

'Do you belong to the same family as—?'

'As the Queen Mary. Naturally. In Scotland everybody belongs to the gentry. I expect you think that you are a member of the royal family. You are probably called James.'

'How did you guess?'

'Oh—because—James Stuart! It's natural.'

'So is Mary Beaton!'

'You are French, though.'

'Scots—with a French accent. The worst kind.'

'Thank you for the warning, monseigneur. We have arrived.'

It was a house like any other in the High Street of Edinburgh although with the air of being better looked after than most. The house of a well-to-do shopkeeper of some kind. On a carved stone above the lintel he could see initials and figures picked out in colour.

He followed the girl up a turnpike stair, noticing that the treads were freshly cut. He was in the house of someone with money to spare.

'This is Mr. Stuart, mother. He has had an accident.'

Stuart met the grey eyes of a gauntly handsome woman whose hair had been blonde and was now streaked with grey.

'He has that!' she exclaimed with a shrewd glance at his arm and an upward gesture of her hands.

'Tell me, Mr. Stuart,' she asked, 'what mischance befell you?'

'Don't trouble him mother. I'll tell you the whole story.'

While Mrs. Beaton became busy with hot water and clean rags—'Let me help you off with that shirt, Mr. Stuart. Tch! What a mess!'—Mary Beaton answered the question her mother had put to him. She described in the most vivid detail an

39

adventure which, it seemed, had just befallen him.

Set upon by two thieves, he had defended himself gallantly until, providentially, the girl had arrived on the scene and called loudly for the Watch. One of the thieves had tried to shut her mouth. James Stuart, forgetting his own danger, had gone to help her with such fury that first one and then the other miscreant had made off. One had dropped his rapier as he fled.

Used to telling his own necessary lies, Stuart was impressed by the drama and verisimilitude of the invention. He was grateful that neither woman asked him to explain the brand on his shoulder.

Mrs. Beaton punctuated the narrative with exclamations of horror.

'And the Watch—did they come in time?'

'Mother!' Mary tossed her head. 'Have you ever known them to come in time?'

'Go and fetch a clean shirt of your father's, Mary. It will be too small for Mr. Stuart, but he might get it over his head. And I can ease it under the arms. Certainly he can't wear this again until it has been washed. It's a fine shirt, Mr. Stuart. You didn't buy it in Edinburgh.' Then, after Mary had left the room, 'That was a good story, Mr. Stuart. Two thieves, one dropping his sword. I won't ask you what really happened?'

'Thank you, Mrs. Beaton.'

Her grey eyes met his in an even steady gaze. She shook her head. 'That lassie! What *did* happen?' she went on in an urgent whisper. 'I wish I knew. Things are going on that I don't understand.'

'Any more than I do, Mrs. Beaton.'

'Until two months ago, the beginning of the summer, I thought I knew everything about my children. Now—' She wore an anxious frown.

'Children, Mrs. Beaton?'

'Son. Daughter. Now the boy has vanished. Doing what? God knows! The lassie, his sister—she knows. But will she tell!'

'Children grow up. Take their own ways—'

'Things I don't fathom all round me.' She wrung her hands. 'I am glad you were there, Mr. Stuart,' she said.

'I, too, Mrs. Beaton.'

'You'll stay and have a bite of supper with us.'
'Madame, you are too kind.'

At the door, as he left, the girl whispered : 'Mr. Stuart—'
'Jamie.'
'Jamie!' ...
'You should be more careful where you go at night,' he said.
She nodded, possibly in agreement. 'Sometimes you can't be careful.' He looked at her hard.
'I'll come back for my shirt,' he said. But already the door was shut.
Her eyes were a dark and beautiful blue. He had looked very carefully.
Stuart was frowning as he walked westwards up the street, his arm in the sling. 'It will prevent other gentlemen from jostling you,' Mrs. Beaton had said.
'Or it will remind you to keep it still,' her daughter had added.

Only the Devil knows

'You dealt with that one brawly, my lord.'

Stuart turned to the voice that sounded suddenly at his elbow.

'Where have you been?' he demanded. 'I thought it was your duty to see nothing like that happened to your gentleman.'

'You were so quickly at him, my lord,' said the ingratiating voice beside him. 'I had no time. Then I saw you with a lady.' He smirked.

'Perhaps you can tell me who he was?'

'It was pit-mirk in that close. How was a body to see him? The town is full of rascals.'

'Look,' said Stuart, holding up the rapier he had taken. 'Have you seen this before?'

'Never in my life. There are letters cut on the blade. Well-worn. I doubt if you could read them in this light. A weapon of a good class.'

'Yes,' said Stuart. 'The gentleman will want his property back. How do I give it to him?'

'I'll ask here and there in the town. If all else fails, we can pin a paper up at the Cross.'

'Be sure he comes to me to ask for it.'

'Have no fear about that.'

'And find out who he is, in the meantime.'

'I will that, my lord.'

'Now lead me to Captain Sinclair,' said Stuart.

He was sprawling astride a bench, enormous, perspiring and

at his ease, when Stuart, stooping to avoid the beams, made his way towards him through the dusky tavern.

'Ah ha!' cried Sinclair, pointing to Stuart's arm sling, 'you've been in the wars? Already? Somebody who was quicker with the knife than I was,' he added with a cunning look, 'and was maybe named Freeland.'

'Not Freeland.'

'No?'

'No. It was done by the man who owned this.' He held out the rapier. Sinclair took it, peered at it, frowning.

'He lent it to you?'

'You can say he lent it.'

'But it wasn't Freeland?' Sinclair put the rapier down on the table.

'Freeland is dead,' said Stuart.

Sinclair's arm, raised to beckon, remained in the air for a second.

'Dead! You didn't—?'

'No.'

Sinclair's eyes roved over Stuart's face for a moment.

'Speak, friend,' he said.

Stuart sat down. He talked rapidly for five minutes. Sinclair listened, his brows drawn together. At the end, he called for drink. When he spoke again, it was in a lowered voice and after making sure nobody was within earshot.

'Did I not tell you it was dangerous to be called by that name?' he demanded. 'Two boys die who bear it. Their servants are executed. Now another of the family goes. It can mean only one thing, Stuart. The threat to the King is still alive, or was until today when Andrew Freeland was killed.'

'What threat?'

Sinclair brushed the question aside.

'They killed him after asking him questions. The drum and pipes were there to drown his screams when they put the Boot on him! All that is clear enough. What we don't know is what they asked him and what he answered.' He frowned.

'There is something else we don't know,' said Stuart.

'What is it, boy?'

'We do not know who they were.'

43

'No. But we can guess they were jackals sent by the Council and paid by the King ... Did you see the man who came down the stair? Would you recognise him another time?'

'I think not. His face was hidden by that cloak.'

'But he saw you?'

'I think he saw me.'

'A pity,' said Sinclair. 'Better if he hadn't. Look out, boy! You may be charged with arson and murder. Two capital crimes. It's a sinful world, Stuart. The pity is that it isn't always the sinners who are punished ... No. The murder was done. The fire that was meant to cover up the deed was put out. By you. Very imprudent of you. The court will want to find someone to hang for the murder. And you were seen at the spot. You are a kenspeckle lad. You can't be mistaken for somebody else. Not with those clothes. That hair. That limp. People will remember you.'

'The limp is not so bad as it was.'

'But bad enough to be noticed.'

Stuart laughed. 'So I arrive in the town this morning and kill Freeland before nightfall! That would be quick work, would it not?'

'It will impress the judge. It will make him think all the worse of you. This, he will say, is the work of an expert, a hired assassin sent from the Continent.'

'But what motive will they imagine for me?'

'God knows, man. Perhaps to shut his mouth. Perhaps you had heard that he was ready to reveal to the Council where they could lay hands on more of those traitors who used to be called you-know-what. He was going to turn what they call King's Evidence. So you killed him. Motives are no trouble for a lively imagination.'

Stuart grinned.

'Who will believe a tale like that?'

Sinclair snorted with derision.

'Everyone who believed that those two boys planned to kill the king. Maybe that isn't so many. But a judge and jury will believe it. And that will be enough.'

'A jury?'

'Oh, you'll have a jury. Never fear. This is a civilised country

44

you've come to, Stuart. A jury will be empanelled and sworn for its eagerness to believe in your guilt. But very likely you'll have made a confession long before then. You've seen what kind of mish-mash the Boot can make of a man's foot. A very civilised machine, you'll agree, for making the sinner repent. It won't make your limp any better.' He laughed harshly.

'Damn you, Captain Sinclair,' said Stuart coldly.

'Thank you, Mr. Stuart. When I asked why you came all this way to find a certain nobleman, you answered, "Curiosity". Would you care to improve on that?'

Stuart shook his head. 'Not yet awhile, Captain. It will wait until I can give you a better answer. If ever I can.'

Sinclair expelled his breath noisily.

'It's your business, boy. You know what you are doing. Now this'—jerking his thumb towards Stuart's arm sling—'How did you come by it?'

'I was walking down the High Street with the evening light behind me,' Stuart began.

'A scandal!' Sinclair exclaimed when he was finished. 'Letting a good-looking lassie of her age be out at that hour of night! I'd like a word with her father. What do you think she was up to? A lover, most likely.'

'It seems she has a brother who has disappeared. The mother doesn't know what he is about.'

'But the girl does, eh? Do you suppose the girl is carrying messages to the boy?'

'That's what I think, Captain.'

Sinclair surveyed him sympathetically.

'You had better come with me, Stuart. To Russia. This place it too hot for you. It's time for a change of scene. The domes of Moscow, boy! The palace of the Tsars! Don't they tempt you? Listen, plunder is waiting for good soldiers. Gold. Jewels as big as pigeon's eggs. Sables to wear. Women. Gorgeous Slav women with broad cheekbones.'

'Snow. Frost. Filth. Slavery,' said Stuart.

Sinclair drew his brows together.

'For a young man, you are damnably low-spirited, Stuart,' he said. 'And not very clever, in my opinion. Still, the offer stays open.'

'Thank you, Captain.'

'But can you stay alive long enough to make use of it? That's not so certain. Consider! Those men in black—the Council is shadowing you, God knows why. Maybe *you* know. You don't say. All right. A man is entitled to his secrets. Secundo, you are seen leaving a house where Andrew Freeland has just been murdered. Tercio, you make a mortal enemy of a man who seems to be a professional assassin. Three good reasons to expect an early end. Let me warn you. If you stay here, you'll last no longer than a week.'

'Bannerman gives me three days.'

'Who the devil is Bannerman?'

'Rory Bannerman. A man I've met.'

Sinclair shot him an odd look.

'I've heard of him,' he said. 'He may be right. He will know more than we do. They say he is tied up in some business at Court. Some ploy with the King. Anyway, three days or seven—what does it matter! On the other hand, make up your mind to go with me to Russia and I can hide you in safety until it's time to sail. It's the best hope you have.'

Stuart shook his curls and said nothing. Sinclair resumed irritably.

'You are damned stubborn, Stuart. You came here to see—that man. To ask him a question. Now he's dead. His secret is dead with him. So why stay?'

Stuart looked him in the eyes.

'Because I haven't come all this distance to leave here on the day I arrive. Besides, is it so certain that the secret behind the business at Perth is dead? The man I must not name dropped a word about it to one who was a comrade of mine for a while. The man he told was killed in a fight at sea. I know. I was there. But Gow—'

Sinclair's fist crashed on the table.

'Careful, idiot!'

Stuart went on.

'So he had dropped a hint to one man. To one man only, do you think? The man who talks once talks more than once.'

Sinclair thrust his red chin forward.

'And why should it be so interesting to you, Stuart?'

'Why not? It's interesting to the King and the Council. Why not to me? After coming all this way, I mean to find out the secret if I can.'

'Well, if you run into trouble, shout for help. Somebody might hear,' Sinclair sneered.

'If you reach the Kremlin, go into one of those old churches and say a prayer for me.'

Sinclair looked at him steadily for a minute out of straw-fringed, angry blue eyes.

'I'll not forget,' he said.

'Talking of that, what have you done today, noble Captain?'

'Enlisted four lucky young men for the King of Sweden's service ... Lucky? You think not? Listen. One thief, one murderer, one seducer with the girl's brothers hard on his heels. And one who has no more wits between his ears than the average horse. But soldiers they are now, all of them, and I mean to see them in battle yet.'

'Good luck to them,' said Stuart. 'This calls for another round.'

He lifted a hand to signal.

But the serving boys' attention was fully taken up with a new incursion from the night outside. Half-a-dozen of them, dressed with a kind of shabby extravagance and walking with more swagger than assurance.

Stuart's eye ran over the costumes: darned stockings creased round the ankles, worn shoes that gaped in places between sole and upper, stained velvets that might have been looted from an old clothes stall.

Vagabonds of some sort. Thieves, perhaps. Jugglers? Acrobats? A troupe of some kind?

At their head was a man on whom the years had conferred a paunch but no solemnity. A man with bold black eyes, black hair faintly dusted with grey. As he advanced into the cellar he was singing in a rich, well-managed baritone:

> Sweet violets
> Sweeter than the roses are
> Covered all over with marmalade
> Covered all over with—

Within a yard of Sinclair, he broke off.

'Good evening, gentlemen, good evening,' he said, sweeping his battered hat off with a grandiose bow. 'May a wandering minstrel join you?'

Comedians. And from the sound of their speech, English.

Looking them over, Stuart had no difficulty in assigning parts: ruined nobleman, jovial innkeeper, intriguing statesman, saintly priest—and the boy with long bleached hair? A player of women's parts, surely. A heroine. One could even suspect traces of carmine on his lips from the performance of the night before. A good-looking lad, and one who with skilful lighting and plentiful paint would make a seductive enough woman mincing in a skirt on an ill-lit stage.

Whatever Sinclair had been going to say, probably insulting, he suddenly changed his mind.

'Long time since I heard that song,' he said. 'Not that it's a good song. But it takes me back. Sit down.'

Rubbing his second chin, he looked meditatively at the other man, who turned abruptly to his companions.

'Sit over there, my boys. At that other table. This one is for your betters.'

They obeyed.

'You have them in hand,' said Sinclair.

'Discipline! The gift of command. Can't be learned. Is born with a man, or not at all.'

He sat down, looking about with an air of truculent cunning.

'What will you drink?' asked Sinclair.

'Sack—as you are so kind,' said the actor.

'In this town the sack is fit only to poison dogs,' said Sinclair. 'Make it Bordeaux.'

'Can't bear the stuff. Sack—if I may be obstinate.'

'You may be as obstinate as you like.'

Stuart beckoned to the boy and gave the order.

'That song—' Sinclair said. 'If only I could remember—What's more—I have seen you before.'

'No doubt,' said the actor. 'Many have. In one of my famous parts.'

'No,' said Sinclair. 'I don't go to the play. I was brought up strictly.'

The actor made a gesture of gracious benediction in his direction.

'Repent, repent! While there is time.'

'It will come back to me. Just go on talking,' said Sinclair.

'Tell us what you are doing here,' Stuart put in.

'A missionary enterprise, sir,' said the actor unctuously. 'Spreading the light among those who dwell in darkness. Not that we have had anything but civility from the natives. At least, they understand what we have to say on the boards.'

'And what,' asked Stuart, 'is the name of your comedy?'

The actor made splendid play with his eyes.

'No comedy, sir. A most doleful tragedy of star-crossed lovers written by a young man whose name I have forgotten. Not that it matters. The players make the play.'

The wine arrived and Stuart said courteously, 'But what of your friends, Mr. — I don't think I know your name.'

'Fletcher. Sergeant Fletcher as I was called in Flanders.'

Sinclair's fist hit the table as if a keg of gunpowder had been exploded under him.

'Fletcher. Sergeant Fletcher! By all the gods of war. Of Black Jack Norris's regiment!' He jumped to his feet.

'And Morgan's company.' Fletcher stood up, too.

'In the trenches before Flushing!'

'In the barbican at Brill! But who are you, sir?'

'Who am I!' roared Sinclair. 'Do you remember the night of the camisado at Sluys when everybody was running from the Spanish foot—and two men stopped the rout, standing shoulder to shoulder in a muddy lane of the town. Who were they, I ask?'

'The immortal Lawrence Fletcher!'

'And the heroic George Sinclair!' Their hands met with a smack like a pistol-shot.

'By Hercules, your Scots accent was thicker in those days, old comrade.'

'And your belly not so thick.'

'Age and careless living, Colonel.'

'Captain,' said Sinclair, primly. 'Meet Mr. Stuart. His father fought in our wars.'

'The son of an old comrade! Your hand, sir.'

With an inward groan, Stuart recalled the times when his

49

father had fallen in with some battered, garrulous veteran of the charge at Ivry.

Sinclair called for drinks for the bedizened vagrants at the next table.

'Let them drink with us, Sergeant,' he said. 'As your superior officer, I order it.'

'Your worship does them too much honour.'

'Come over here and sit down. And,' to the serving boy, 'bring five more of your horrible sherry.'

'No, Captain, no,' Fletcher protested. 'It's not so vile as that.'

'Introduce your company,' Sinclair commanded. 'My God, a more underfed, pox-ridden platoon I haven't set eyes on, not for years. Do you eat all the rations, Sergeant? Boys, give up the theatre and follow the drum. I'll see you are fed.'

A gloomy, cadaverous man among the actors spoke up.

'Fed to the cannon, guv'nor, that's what you mean, ain't it? Fed to the bleeding cannon.'

Sinclair looked him over with contempt.

'Whatever has come over old England? Where is the spirit of Agincourt?'

'You ought to hear us in Henry V,' piped up the boy.

'And what part do you fill in that drama, little man?' asked Sinclair.

'He's the French King's wife ... Peregrine Wroxall, better known as the Virgin Queen for reasons I decline to mention.'

'You're a liar, Fletcher.'

The drinks for the other ranks (who had already been drinking on their own account) now arrived; the long-haired boy turned to Stuart, 'Do you know there are only two of us here?'

Stuart was somewhat surprised by the remark.

'Meaning what exactly?'

'We are the only two here with shoulder-length hair with a wave in it.'

'I was born that way.'

'You're lucky. The amount of trouble mine gives me—curling irons and so on—you'd be surprised.' Ignoring Stuart's glare, the boy went on, unabashed, to tell how he been framed on a false charge of shop-lifting in Whitechapel.

'The Sergeant keeps on that it was something else—you know

'—but it wasn't.' He ran away from home. Then, by accident, he discovered that he had this gift for impersonation.

'There's just one trouble, mate,' he said, leaning forward and lowering his voice.

'What's that?' asked Stuart.

'I can't tell you here.' He looked round nervously. 'If we could slip outside.'

'No, thank you,' said Stuart.

'Oh, just for a minute—'

Stuart looked at the boy's thin, anguished face.

'Very well. One minute.'

'I knew the moment I set eyes on you that you were the sympathetic kind.'

'I am not,' said Stuart irritably.

He led the way to the door. Someone gave a low, derisive whistle.

In the close outside a yellow light gleamed feebly from two lamps. It was enough for Stuart to see a squat figure with a beard like a badly made bird's nest. He heard a voice borne on the wings of aquavitty.

'My lord.'

'You'll have to wait, Peregrine,' said Stuart. 'What is it, Gregory?'

'That man you pinned to the door.'

'What about him?'

'He didn't like it. He didn't like it either that some women helped to unpin him.'

'Shame was added to defeat,' said Stuart smoothly.

'Just that, my lord.'

'He knows what he can do. You told him where he can claim his sword?'

'I didn't—I thought I'd better tell you something first.'

'Tell me what? Who is he? The King?'

'For God's sake, no! He is Kennedy. A gallowglass.'

'What the devil is that?'

The door of Monypenny's tavern had swung open and Sinclair stood behind him, enormous and indistinct.

'So you are still here,' he said. 'You ask what a gallowglass is. I'll tell you. A gallowglass is a particular kind of Scottish-Irish

51

gentleman rogue who has the vices of both nations and the virtues of neither. He is usually a Highlander of too gentle birth to drive a plough. So he goes over to Ireland and hires his sword to some chieftain with a family feud on his hands. Sometimes the gallowglass comes back to Scotland. That's Scotland's misfortune. This one, Kennedy, would long since be decorating a gibbet but for one useful fact. He is protected by the Earl of Orkney. You can say he is one of Orkney's kept murderers.'

'Tell him how he can get his sword, caddie,' said Stuart.

Sinclair laughed.

'You don't think he'll come when it suits you to invite him, do you?'

'I am in no great hurry myself to see him again.'

'You will see him,' said Sinclair, 'when you're alone and he has some friends with him. Boy, you have enough troubles as it is.'

'Listen to what the Captain says.'

'Do what I tell you, Gregory.'

The caddie disappeared into the shadows, and Sinclair turned to the door of the tavern. For a moment he stopped there with the door open. Light and noise spilled out together. English voices singing.

> For the drums did go with a rap-a-tap-tap
> And the pipes did loudly play.
> Saying, Fare you well, my Polly dear
> I must be going away.'

Somebody was beating time on a table with a flat of an iron hand. Sinclair went in and the door shut behind him.

'You were going to tell me something, Peregrine,' said Stuart.

'It's like this,' said Peregrine gratefully. 'I have to play this girl. There's one big speech I do. From a balcony.'

'And you have a bad memory.'

The boy shook his head violently.

'I have a wonderful memory. Look. Here's the speech.'

He held out a crumpled piece of paper. Stuart looked at it. Poetry.

'So what's the difficulty?'

'I can't read! I used to have a mate who would read it to me.

But he quarrelled with old Fletcher and ran off.'

'So?'

'If you were to read the stuff once, I'd remember it.'

'Let's see it.'

' "O Romeo, Romeo! wherefore art thou Romeo?" Who wrote this?'

'Dunno,' said Peregrine. 'Some bloke. They sit around in public houses and make up that sort of thing.'

Stuart read out the whole part, more and more amazed at the extraordinary language.

It was very late that night when Stuart left the tavern. As they parted, Sinclair said, 'Take my advice, boy. Leave the town Go into hiding until you can walk without that limp. You are making it too easy for them to pick you out.'

'Thank you, Captain,' Stuart saluted.

'Idiot.'

Stuart walked back to his lodgings three yards behind Gregory. The street was steep and oddly tilted. It seemed to lurch unsteadily beneath him.

It must be the effect of his recent spell on the North Sea, he explained to himself.

The moon had not yet risen and the caddie lit the way with a lantern swinging from a forked stave at his shoulder.

Stuart was addressing to himself some reflections of displeasure on his conduct earlier that evening. Hardly the behaviour of a gentleman, although understandable enough after a successful scuffle. As for that, it did not appear quite the glorious victory it had seemed to be before ...

'You were lucky. That's the truth. You took him unawares. And the light was as much in your favour as his. Also, it was not necessary to humiliate him as you did. Own up, Jamie. You wanted to show off to that girl ...'

At the time, he had thought her a shade cool about his gallantry. Now, looking back, he decided that she had been secretly amused.

This thought distressed him.

He swept his mind clear of the unpleasant thought and began to think of other things. He had a great deal else to think about: a murder of which he might yet hear more; a disdainful great lady with a white falcon on her wrist; her companion who had contrived to be helpful and threatening at the same time; the English boy actor and the magic lines he had spoken.

'My lord!'

Gregory swung the lantern from his shoulder and closed its shutter. His voice was hoarse and urgent.

'Into that entry, sir! Make haste!'

It was a minute or two before Stuart, standing in his dark corner, saw why.

Two men approached and passed, walking with a ponderous tread. A faint grey light gleamed on helmets and breastplates. On their shoulders were muskets. They bore themselves with a slight swagger. Others like them followed. Stuart could hear a crash of heavy boots moving together. He was not, however, prepared for the appearance of the next passer-by.

This was a tall man walking alone, cloaked to the chin and, it seemed, talking to himself. Another lunatic? When the newcomer came opposite the dark passage where they were standing Stuart realised his mistake. Beside the man trotted a black cat, very slim and elegant, with which he was carrying on a lively, whispered conversation. The cat was answering. Stuart could not hear the man's words any more than he could distinguish his features.

At an interval after this strange apparition came other men, marching two by two, making the reticent noises of the heavily armed as they passed. The sinister little procession moved through the deserted alleys of the town, looming up out of the darkness and returning to it once more.

Gregory waited until the sound of their footsteps had died away before he answered the question that was written on Stuart's face.

'That was Lord Orkney.'

'And Lord Orkney's cat,' said Stuart.

Gregory nodded.

'The cat goes everywhere with my lord. He talks to it all the time. Do you know what folk say?'

'I can guess.'

Gregory nodded and crossed himself.

'The only doubt people have is which of the two is the Devil.'

'I didn't see his lordship's face.'

'May you never see it!'

'Lead the way home,' said Stuart curtly. Lord Orkney, Kennedy's protector—like man, like master. But his ankle was hurting him now. It was time for bed.

'A fine rose, preferably red'

The morning came in pale splendour.

From the window of his lodging, Stuart gazed spellbound over a vast expanse of shaven land and sunlit water northwards of the city.

He had wakened from alarming dreams of cats with an infernal irritation in his left forearm. He looked cautiously under the bandage. A long scratch with a rim of inflamed skin round it. But it seemed to be healthy enough. More important, his ankle was free from pain and more supple than he had known it for a long time. Gingerly, he put his foot to the ground and was encouraged. He called down the stair for a can of hot water and, while he waited, resumed his survey of the scene outside.

It possessed a kind of beauty which he did not know. A town, an old, worn, capital city, with the qualities of an outpost, crouching on its rock, armed and watchful. The colours were spare and subtle, as if some agency other than the weak northern sun had drained the landscape of assertion and richness. The shapes, on the other hand, were arresting and, in places, fantastic. Westwards, as if in revenge for the puritanism of the lower country, mountains broke out in blue and purple recessions of tone. At one point, high up and far away, the sunlight shone back, brilliant as a flame but cold, cold. A river? A slope of wet rocks? More likely a patch of snow.

A boy entered Stuart's room carrying the hot water. He shaved with more than his usual care. Yesterday he had seen two beautiful girls. Fortune was smiling on him ... No ... a repetition of that luck was more than a man could reasonably ask from life.

56

Scraping at his chin, he peered into the few inches of polished metal that served as his mirror. What he saw did not encourage vanity.

A long nose and thin lips. Small blue eyes with an expression in them that was either humorous or cynical, as you chose to see it. Those weeks on the rowing bench of the galley had done his looks no good ... But did looks matter? There was something more important, something which, when he scrutinised it honestly, brought him even less comfort than his appearance did. Still scraping, he addressed words to himself which he did not speak aloud:

I know you. You are enamoured of that girl. So you are content to be here. But for how long, James? Tell me that, if you please. How long will the devil of restlessness leave you alone? You know how it has been before, in Paris and in Flanders. One morning you wake up and nothing will do but you leave at once, by the first horse or ship you can find, for God knows where, anywhere.

You have an agitation in the blood, Stuart. It is like a fever. It will attack you again. You know it will. And not all the blue eyes in the world will hold you. You are not the man to settle down with a woman. Be an honest man, Jamie, and do not see this girl again ...

His chin was smooth now, and he was glaring savagely into the reflection of his eyes in the glass.

'Except, of course,' he said aloud, 'that you must fetch your shirt, boy.'

Stuart jingled his way cheerfully downstairs. Ahead lay the beautiful unknown. To begin with, he would send Mary Beaton a rose and an elegant message.

In the close, just outside the door, bonnet in hand, stood Gregory, looking more shifty than ever. But since so far as Jamie could judge, he was likely to be doing some business with rogues, there was no harm in having one rogue on his side. After a nod of greeting, he asked,

'Has Kennedy come looking for his rapier?'

'Not a sign of him. And the paper I put up at the Cross has gone.'

'Meaning what?'

'That somebody has read it,' said the caddie. 'But if you were to ask me, you'll not see Kennedy this day.' Gregory leant forward to speak with lowered voice. 'They're up to something, that lot. Lord Orkney called his captains to him at first daylight. Since then they have been busy dragging men out of the dram-shops. All men of Orkney's. Twenty or more. Kennedy among them. Now they've gone. Vanished! God kens where.'

'How do you hear this?'

'From a cousin of mine who is in the way of hearing such things, my lord.'

Stuart gave Gregory a long, hard look. And Gregory gave a long, hard look back.

'What's afoot, do you think?' asked Stuart.

'What I might think is neither here nor there, my lord, begging your pardon. But I say, when that bees' byke is stirred, let husbands look out for their wives, men look out for their lands and the King watch over the peace of his realm.'

Stuart grinned.

'Coming from you, that's a warning to heed!'

'Lord Orkney has bad blood in him,' said Gregory, 'and bad blood whiles grows worse. Before we are many hours older, we should ken more.'

Stuart thought it quite likely.

What kin of his—in blood if not in law—this Earl of Orkney might be he did not know. Like himself, a Stuart. But what else? Cousin? Uncle? He should have paid more attention when his father explained the family tree.

Gregory was speaking casually—too casually.

'That English player ...'

'You mean Sergeant Fletcher.'

'That's the man.'

'What about him?'

'Just that he was seen having words with one of Orkney's captains this morning early.'

Stuart looked sharply at him. Gregory's eyes avoided his.

'A coincidence,' said Stuart.

'Very likely indeed,' Gregory agreed.

'After all, what would a man like Fletcher, a comedian, want with a captain of cut-throats?'

'An Englishman is always English,' Gregory pointed out. 'All the more when he is in Scotland.'

'What the devil has that got to do with it, man?'

'Nothing at all, my lord,' said Gregory, placidly. 'And now what might be the orders for the day?'

But it was a second or two before Stuart remembered what had seemed the most urgent business when he came down the stairs.

'Do you know where I can buy a fine rose blossom, preferably red?' he asked.

Gregory blinked twice before answering.

'There's a man keeps a bit of garden in the back Canongate—red? I wouldn't ken.'

'Buy a rose, Gregory, then find me. Meanwhile, I'll go and choose a new shirt for myself. Where do I find one?'

'The Lawnmarket, my lord. Turn left when you leave the close. You'll see the booths in a few minutes.'

'Look for me there.'

'And, sir, keep your eyes open for black beetles.'

'I do one thing to black beetles, Gregory.' He stamped his foot hard on the cobbles.

'Be careful, my lord!'

The caddie left the close for the busy main street. Stuart followed him at a more leisurely pace.

On his way to the shirtmaker's he felt the warning, which came as a pricking sensation in the finger tips. His fingers touched the hilt of his sword.

For no reason at all, but in response to a sudden thought—no, it was slighter than a thought. Out of the corner of an eye he had been aware that somebody in the crowd had turned sharply towards him. But when, with many precautions, he had looked round, no one was taking any interest in him.

Stuart dived through the first archway off the street and found himself in a labyrinth of alleys one of which took him into a narrow courtyard. Storey above storey, the houses elbowed nearer to one another on their upward flight. Ahead of him, a low, uneven tunnel offered escape into deeper darkness.

He heard a woman's voice above, saying—but perhaps he was mistaken—'Bonny!' The voice was heavy with emotion.

Leaning out of a window three flights up was a woman, amply built, with glossy black hair undone and flowing over one shoulder. She was resting her bosom on her forearms, and she did not trouble to hide its dazzling whiteness.

'Dearie,' she said.

Stuart sketched in the air his admiration of her ripe beauty.

'Why don't you come up and talk to me—a lovely boy like you?'

'*Cherie*,' he said, 'I am too weary to climb all those stairs.'

She was as coarse-looking a queen as he had ever bartered nonsense with.

'A Frenchman,' she said, softly, 'who can't climb stairs? Darling, take a deep breath. At the top, there's a bed for you.'

'The Auld Alliance! Some other day, we can renew it.'

Stuart was still looking upwards when a third voice, a man's, intruded on the talk.

'The Frog, by Jesus! Jock, Patty!'

Stuart sprang round, but not fast enough.

Through the tunnel into the close came three men in black, armed.

They were on him before he could draw.

'Cowards!' A woman was screaming from somewhere overhead. 'Three men fighting with one. Murderers!'

'Hold your tongue, you fat cow,' shouted one of the men in black. The other two laughed.

Stuart's arms were pinned to his side. He brought a knee up viciously. Somebody squealed with pain. While they wrestled there was a woman's cry of 'Gardez-loo!' above. One of the men in black looked up. Too late. On his head fell an earthenware pot and smashed in pieces on the pavement. It had been filled with all sorts of odorous horrors. Above, women were shrieking with laughter ...

If only he could pull the sword out. If only— But at that moment one of the black-clad assailants swung a fist gauntleted in steel. Stuart felt himself falling a long way through darkness. Pain swelled intolerably in his head. A brilliant light exploded, then dwindled to nothing.

The captain's lady

Later, he had a vague recollection of a journey in a hard and uncomfortable vehicle—a cart?—first over ill-laid cobblestones and then over a stony road. How long it lasted he did not know. Suddenly the journey ended. He was lifted roughly and half-dragged, half-carried into a building. He knew because the light was suddenly reduced and the sounds had an added resonance.

About this time, Stuart became aware of several puzzling circumstances. His head hurt, his hands were manacled and he was standing, or swaying, in front of a heavy oak table. But more interesting was what he saw sitting at the other side of the table facing him. The figure of a man he had seen before. Wearing a black doublet, and with a beard cut square. On the Shore of Leith! Almost the first man he had seen on arrival. His welcome to his native land.

He became aware then he was being addressed.

'Your name is Stuart. James Stuart. For what reason have you come to Scotland?'

Stuart made an attempt to answer but it was not very successful. His second effort was better.

'Because it is my country. My father was born here.'

Black Beard grinned unpleasantly.

'If everyone whose father was born here came back to plague us ...' He did not pursue the thought.

'Why did you kill Andrew Freeland?'

'I did not kill Andrew Freeland or anyone else!'

'Don't lie. You had scarcely landed in Scotland when you went to Freeland's lodging, murdered him and then tried to make away with the evidence of your crime by setting the house on fire.'

'If you know so much, why do you ask me about it?'

'Because I want to know *why*, Stuart. I mean to know why. And one way or another, you are going to tell me why.'

Stuart did not see that there was anything for him to answer in all that. It was time for him to give the talk a new direction.

'Who are you?' he asked with a jerk of his head which he instantly regretted. It produced a sudden sharp increase of pain. 'Where is this? Where am I?'

Black Beard answered irritably.

'Who I am is no business of yours. Where you are? In His Majesty's Castle of Edinburgh. You are in the house of the King of Scots.'

'I don't remember being invited.'

'You don't! Probably you won't remember leaving either. Usually, men don't. You've seen the Rock from below? There is room for a graveyard on it.'

He paused.

'What did you hear in Paris or elsewhere that led you straight to Andrew Freeland's rooms on the day you came to Scotland? You can tell me now or later. But let me warn you, Stuart, later will hurt more. Much more.'

Stuart was standing more erect now. The colour was coming back to his cheeks.

'I will tell you nothing. But I might tell the King.'

Black Beard frowned irritably.

'Talking to me you will be talking to the King,' he said. 'The King does not talk to vagabonds like you.'

'Oh?'

'What can you tell the King that you can't tell me?'

'Secrets. Family secrets.'

For a whole minute, silence hung in the room. Black Beard broke it.

'Take him and lock him up. Put someone in the cell with him. I want to be sure that he's alive in the morning.'

Stuart was taken across a yard to a crenellated wall which seemed to be part of the inner defences of the Castle. Until he reached it, he could see nothing of the world around but a faint outline of distant mountains to the north. They were two score miles away, he reckoned.

The wall was pierced at one point by the opening of a stairway leading steeply down. Here he could see the ground far below and could guess the sheerness of the rock. A dozen steps down the stairway there was a heavy door. One of the two men who were leading him knocked. It was opened by an elderly, grey-bearded man who wore a belt from which hung a bunch of heavy keys.

A few yards along a stone passage, another heavy door stood open. Two steps down was a large bare stone room with barred windows. In the middle of it stood a table, with ink, pen and paper. Stuart turned to the gaoler who had come into the room with him. They were alone now.

'If you want me to write, you must take these off,' holding out his fettered wrists.

'All in good time, sir,' said the gaoler.

'What is this place?'

'The state prison. Cell number one. And, let me tell you, the best room in the castle.'

'I'm honoured.'

'It's meant for gentlemen who have committed serious crimes.'

'What crime have I committed? I'd like to know.'

'Usually it's treason.'

The gaoler selected a key from his bunch and unfastened the handcuffs.

'Now you can write your confession. Much good it may do you.'

'Thank you.'

'If it were me, sir, I'd have a rest first.' He pointed to a heap of straw in one corner of the cell.

It seemed that an idea had occurred to Stuart, not suddenly but rather like the first pale shaft of sunlight struggling through a mist.

'Do you like wine, gaoler?' he asked.

The man with the keys smirked.

'I might do when I can't have aquavitty.'

'But what if you can have both? How about that? Look. What time do you go off duty? Three? Now say you were to call at Monypenny's Tavern. Do you know where it is?'

'Everybody knows that, sir.'

'I expect so. How about asking there for three bottles of Bordeaux wine for us two and a gill of aquavitty for yourself? That dunt on the head has given me a terrible thirst. I'll give you the money. But only if it suits you to do it.'

'I'll do it, sir. Why not?'

'All open and above board,' said Stuart earnestly. 'Oh, and another thing. You might see a man named Donald Gregory—'

'The caddie, sir?'

'The caddie. He is often to be seen at Monypenny's. If you could give him a message for me ... Tell him I want a powder for my bad head, something to make me sleep tonight. Any apothecary will know what I need. But don't let Gregory have any drink. Remember. He's a terrible man for the whisky bottle. Now about money ...'

Stuart slept on his heap of straw. For how long? When he woke he was aware that the light in the cell had changed. It was softer and it came from a different direction. Also someone was rattling a key in the door. The gaoler had returned with the wine in a basket and a small paper packet which he held out.

Jamie was pleased to find that the man, whose exemplary stupidity he had noticed at once, had already been at the whisky bottle. He opened the sealed packet which the gaoler had brought. It contained a white powder and, on a thin paper folded small, a note in a hand he did not know:

'They dare not try you and will not hang you. Kennedy will do it. Tomorrow is the night. Waste no time.

'The rose is bonny. If I were one of your foreign sluts, I might wear it behind my ear. But I am instead, your M.'

It was in a shapely Italian hand and the spelling (so far as he could judge) was correct.

Gregory must have gone to the girl and, together, they had concocted it.

He spoke to the gaoler:

'Will you be kind enough to bring me a glass of water. I

want to take this powder for my headache. It is nearly time for a drink.'

But not yet, he thought. The evening light would linger awhile on this height above the town. He had an appointment with the dark. On the other hand, he had a great deal to do in the next few hours. It was a nice question of timing. And he must not/ be in a hurry.

The man returned with the water.

'Ah, there you are, gaoler. What's your name by the way?'

'Jamie.'

'Like mine. Brothers, in a sense. Do you know my head is feeling easier already. But I'll take the powder. Just to be sure. And then we'll taste the wine. The wine! The wine! You'll have to be careful, brother James, that I don't get drunk. Remember, I have to write this damned confession. What crime should I plead guilty to? Rape, arson, highway robbery, murder, treason?'

'It's usually treason, sir.'

'Yes. You've said that already. Treason. Very grave offence. Ends one way only.' He seemed to have a new idea. 'But look, there is only one chair in this beautiful room. Why don't you fetch in another? For yourself. Or make it two. Why not? I expect we'll have visitors here before the night is over.'

Over the second bottle of wine, conversation grew easier. Stuart professed that his head had improved remarkably from the powder. A sentry who had been on duty outside was invited in by Stuart. 'I insist, I insist, man. There is enough wine for the three of us.' The talk grew free. Stuart laughed at some anecdotes told by his companions.

'By God, that was a funny one. You'll have another glass, Sergeant. Help to cheer up a poor man who is going to be hanged.'

They consoled him.

'You're no' deid yet, man,' said the sentry, patting his shoulder amiably. 'Have some more of your own wine.'

'There's one thing I want,' said Stuart. 'If it is to be my last night on earth—and I'm not likely to find it in the Castle.'

'What's that? We have most things in the Castle.'

'A girl. Have you a girl?'

His two companions were overcome with mirth.

'A lassie!' said the sentry admiringly. 'On your last night on

65

earth maybe! God, you're a gallous bugger and no mistake.'

'There is only one man in this place who has a lassie to visit him every night,' said the gaoler. 'He is a wicked old man and he is the captain of the Castle.'

'Perhaps he'd lend her to me. Or maybe one of your gentlemen could ask her in for a friendly glass on her way to the captain.'

They shook their heads.

'We're not supposed to ken that she comes.'

'It's a secret. A great secret, and everybody knows it.'

'Have another glass, man,' said Stuart. 'I insist. A man with your head. I only wish it were cognac and not this watery stuff.'

But he was pleased to see that the wine was having an effect on those whisky topers. Heads were beginning to loll, and eyelids becoming heavier.

'This woman of the captain's,' he said. 'Nobody sees her?'

'It's like this,' said the gaoler, who was by far the drunkest of the three. 'Along at the far end of the Rock, that way, the outer wall dips to the south side and there is a postern half-way down. A bit gate you would barely notice from the ground. She comes in there, the strumpet.'

'She has a key?' Stuart asked.

The gaoler nodded. The sentry shook his head.

'No,' he said. 'The captain's man goes down after dark— soon!—and unlocks the door for her.'

'Ah! It's time to open the third bottle.'

The sentry rose to leave. 'Duty!' he said

The gaoler seemed to be trying to focus on some object in mid-air. Stuart opened the third bottle and poured into it the white powder the apothecary had sent him. Outside he heard sentries challenge and counter-challenge. 'God the Father'— 'Christ His Son.'

He saw the gaoler's chin was beginning to sink towards the table.

'Have a drop from the new bottle.'

'No, no.'

'Come on, man. If I can, you can.'

'What is this stuff?'

'Wine, wine. Beautiful, friendly wine.'

The gaoler gave him a look in which a small worm of suspicion stirred.

'I dinna like it,' he said.

'This bottle is better. Try it.'

Stuart poured some of the wine into his own glass and drank a sip, hoping that his head was better than the gaoler's.

'Good health,' he said.

'You treasonable bastard, why should I drink with you?'

'Drink by yourself then. Drink up.'

The gaoler rose to his feet with dignity.

'Down with all traitors,' he cried and emptied his glass.

Stuart thought bitterly, 'He is all right. He has a better head than I have, damn him.'

The gaoler got up suddenly and walked across the cell, holding himself with extreme care. He fell with a crash on Stuart's heap of straw. In a few seconds, he was snoring loudly.

Stuart counted a hundred slowly before unfastening the gaoler's belt and slipping off his bunch of keys ...

Up there, on the bald rock, the wind blew freshly. Stuart had climbed the twelve stone steps leading upwards from the state prison building to an uneven platform of rock, edged with a low sturdy wall. Nature and military engineers, working together, had created a fortress of spectacular strength indeed. He waited in the shadow of a wall for his eyes to grow accustomed to the darkness.

It was a night of brilliant stars, the sky like a steel breastplate fretted with diamonds. Hanging on a peg outside his cell door he had found his sword. Now he buckled it on. It was old fashioned—too broad, too short. But it had a king's monogram on it. And it had been a good ally more than once.

He was able to fix directions from a faint wash of pink on the horizon. West! He wanted west by south. He moved forward slowly and with infinite caution, for the ground was devilish treacherous. The rock seemed to have worn into an infinite number of small, sharp and slippery pyramids. Soon he had passed the angle of the Governor's house: he was clear of buildings and was uncomfortably aware that, somewhere ahead and probably quite near, the rock fell abruptly a hundred feet or more. He went ahead at a slower pace, searching the darkness for the outline of the outer, curtain wall of the castle.

The rock began to slope downwards. In a few minutes, the descent grew steeper. He lowered himself, feeling in the darkness for each foothold, knowing that an unlucky step might release an avalanche of stones and betray his presence. Suddenly, he came to a dead halt.

Below, about fifty yards away, a lantern was moving, swinging as it went. A sentry was going his round. The lantern gave the weakest of lights but it told Stuart where the wall lay.

It was little more than waist high on the inner side where, to judge by the sound of the sentry's boots, there was a flagged walk. Then a turret. A few yards further on, another turret with a low building beside it.

He waited until the sentry had disappeared round an angle of the rock. Then he scrambled down to the uneven terrace of which the wall was the boundary. Turning to the left, he went swiftly along the walk and down a short flight of steps.

Reaching a turret which marked a corner of the wall, he found a narrow turnpike stair inside it. Instinct—or hope—suggested that this might lead down to the postern he was looking for, the inconspicuous way out of the castle, which had only one regular user. He was about to go downstairs when he heard a sound and shrank back to be hidden by the curve of the turret.

Somewhere below, a door opened. Then he heard it slammed. A key turned softly in a lock. Someone carrying a light was climbing the stair inside the turret.

Stuart pulled his sword two inches out of its sheath. This would not be one of those occasions on which his opponent would be given the chance to fight on equal terms. The person carrying the light emerged from the turret. A figure in silhouette appeared.

By God, a woman. The captain's girl?

As she moved away from him along the flagged walk, something dropped from her hand. It was not a moment for fine manners but Stuart's curiosity was aroused. He picked up what had fallen. A glove.

'My lady!'

She turned, startled, holding up her lantern. She was masked but, being an optimist in these matters, he imagined her handsome.

'Your glove.

'Thank you. But—'

'Only one question. Have you the key of the postern? The captain bade me ask you.'

'It is left in the door, sir, as usual. I am a creature of habit. The captain should know.'

'I have picked up your glove, madame. Now will you reward me? Just for a moment, take off your mask.'

'Impudence!' She laughed, and snatched the mask away. Stuart looked.

'Lucky captain!' he said. 'I must flee. The sentry is coming.'

'Don't you know he has orders not to see me?'

'I should have guessed. Goodnight, madame. Au revoir. Another time. Another castle.'

He bowed over her hand.

The key was in the door below. The lock was well-oiled.

The path ahead of him twisted dizzily into a black abyss. But beside him was a rope, fastened to rings in the rock-face. And he could see the beginning of a flight of steps not far below. His ankle was aching damnably—but he would be all right ...

Within the hour, Stuart was lurking in a dark corner of the close outside Monypenny's Tavern. Before long, he would be sure to meet Sinclair or Gregory—somebody at least that he knew. He waited, listening to the sound of men talking in the tavern.

Suddenly the windows shook. A heavy cannon had been fired, not far away.

'A traitor has escaped from the Castle.'

Stuart turned sharply.

'Donald!' he said.

'By God, it's good to see you, my lord. Damn few men come free out of that place. But what now? You'll need the luck of the Devil himself.'

'I have it. I have it! Don't you know that I am the only Stuart that was born lucky?'

Gregory crossed himself.

'I hope That One didn't hear you, my lord.'

69

'Don't fret, man. The Devil looks after his own. You asked what now? A few visits, Donald, duty and pleasure.'

'The lady who likes roses?'

'The same. Do you know if she's at home?'

'The streets aren't safe this time of night. Where would she go?'

'I'll see you tomorrow, Donald. And thanks for the wine.'

'Be careful, sir.'

A rare quarry in the hunting ground

After leaving the caddie, Stuart walked carefully downhill, keeping to dark alleys and the shadowy side of closes. He was suddenly and desperately tired. His ankle was hurting damnably. As he reckoned he needed three things, one, a hot bath, two, a few hours of sleep in a comfortable bed, and three—

A few minutes' walk, and Stuart remembered the missing ingredient. He turned left down a familiar road. After a few yards, he saw the bulge of the house intruding on the pavement, the doorway he had entered the night before. He knocked. After a minute the sound of footsteps within. The slam of a bolt. Another bolt. The rattle of a chain. And then the glimmer of a candle.

'Mary!'

'Jamie! What are you doing here?'

'I've come to thank you for my freedom.'

'You won't enjoy it long if you aren't more careful. How did you do it? You'll come in.'

He shook his head.

'The story will keep. It has to do with a lady.'

'I'm sure it has! But you can't stand there, Mr. Stuart.'

'No. I have somewhere to go. An appointment.'

'Oh. Another lady?'

'No. This time a gentleman. I must go now. They are looking for me and mustn't find me here. But—thank you, Mary. And Au revoir.' And he leaned forward to kiss her.

'Madman!' she said, avoiding his embrace. 'Goodnight,' and the door was closed.

71

He ran downstairs and stood for a moment sorting out where he was and where he wanted to be. Then he resumed his way downhill. Through courts and closes, past houses and garden walls, he came out after a bit on a narrow, paved, winding street, a branch of the main artery of the town. Before him was a doorway, wide enough to admit a wagon. Above it, carved in the stone and showing a sheen of gold, was a coat of arms. A lion waving a flag. Bannerman's Lodging.

Stuart opened half of the door. Now he was in a small yard. He crossed it. Under a turnpike stair jutting into the yard was a small iron grille. It opened to his touch.

He went in. No light. No sound. He went quietly up the dark stair. At the end of a corridor he thought he could see a glimmer of light. He moved towards it, on tiptoe.

The door swung open more quietly and more easily than he had expected. He stumbled down a step he had not seen and found himself in a small panelled room, heavy with the smoke of some aromatic wood and warm with the light of candles. The shutters had been drawn. What he saw startled him a great deal and delighted him even more.

He was looking across the room at a naked woman.

No. A half-naked woman. She was sitting in front of a small dressing-table and, in the urgency of her toilet, had slipped out of her bodice and was naked to the waist. She turned round on her stool and thus sat looking at him, intently but without alarm. Probably she had thought that a maid or a footman had come into the room. In any case, she had seen Stuart before.

And he who had thought her beautiful a day earlier when she rode past him on the Shore of Leith thought her even more beautiful now.

The colouring of pale gold, which had been ivory and rose in the sunlight, was lovely on her small insolent face, and glowed upon her shoulders and her breasts with their heavy dark flowers.

Jamie's first natural impulse was to spring forward and take that image in his arms. He restrained himself.

'Madame,' he exclaimed, 'Mes excuses.'

'An intruder,' she said, her eyes watchful but unconcerned, 'with a French accent. What is your name, monsieur?'

'James Stuart, madame.'

The former pupil of M. de Pluvinel's academy for young noblemen bowed gracefully over a small pale hand on which one
majestic diamond blazed. If that had been all the lady's fingers
held, Stuart's gesture, which began so well, might have been
completed more elegantly than it was. But as matters turned
out, he straightened himself in some confusion.

It was the first time he had kissed a hand that was holding
a pistol.

Without any change of expression, she put the pistol quietly
down on the dressing-table. It was a pretty little thing with
a carved ivory handle inlaid with mother-of-pearl. She put it
beside another strange object on the table, a crystal ball.

'James Stuart,' she said, coolly. 'Do you usually walk into
a lady's room without knocking?'

'Experience has shown me that a man who knocks may lose
a great deal.'

In the most nonchalant manner imaginable, she slipped her
arms into the sleeves of her dress. Stuart took a step forward.

'Shall I help with the fastening?'

She kept her eyes levelly on his.

'I have a bell here,' she said. 'If I ring it, ten gentlemen will
come in and cut you to pieces.'

Stuart grinned.

'Ten gentlemen outside have been trying to do that for the
last hour or so. It seems to be a custom in this town.'

For a few seconds there was silence in the perfumed little
room. Stuart scrutinised her with an intensity that equalled her
own.

Her face was a subtly moulded triangle exceptionally wide
across the eyes. Her nose was delicately modelled, her lips were
dark and sharply defined, her eyes green and shaded by long
curving lashes. Her dark blonde hair was cut short and clustered
about her head in shining curls.

The expression of her eyes was secretive, distrustful and calculating. One corner of her mouth curved up almost imperceptibly.

A blonde Spaniard? He had seen one or two French women
whose looks might belong to the same family—and once, in
Paris, a Greek ... No.

Her appearance was more complex than anything within his

73

experience. So that the first glance had inspired him with an overwhelming curiosity, a passionate interest. This was a rare quarry in the hunting ground.

His second glance, as his lips rose from her hand, brought him a chillier message. She was—or he misread an expression in her slanting eyes—more mature than her age seemed to warrant. There was something in her that sent out a warning signal. A signal that meant danger. This girl with the pale lustrous skin was not merely *looking* at him. She was *watching* him.

'James Stuart,' she said, thoughtfully. 'My brother, Rory, said you would come. He said you would be sure to. He had the idea you could be useful to me.'

'Can I help with that hook?' he offered a second time. 'It is hard for you.'

She said nothing but turned her back so that he could.

'I doubt it myself,' she continued.

'I am sorry to hear that. Although, frankly, at the moment, I am more anxious to know whether *you* could be helpful to me.'

'Of course I could ... whether I shall or not is another matter.'

'Your brother mentioned a journey ... what did he mean?'

'First tell me about yourself. You are in some sort of scrape, I imagine.'

Stuart had completed the fastening of her dress.

'Forgive me,' he asked, 'but where is that wonderful white falcon you had the other day?'

'I keep it to kill important prey. Have you any to suggest?'

'I think so.'

'We will talk. But first you must have a bath and a change, Mr. Stuart. You have brought the smell of mud and sweat into my room. Exciting, no doubt, but—'

'I have no manners.'

'You stink,' she said shortly, and smiled, a dazzling smile.

She rang a small silver bell on her dressing table. A servant appeared.

'Prepare a bath and lay out clean clothes for this gentleman. See that all the doors and windows of the house are barred. And have the gentlemen-in-waiting armed, awake and sober. No one is to enter the house without my knowing it.' To Stuart, 'Will you stay to supper, Monsieur Stuart?'

Stuart smiled.

'The alternative is not an empty stomach but a slit throat. What do you think?'

She called after the servant.

'And understand—nobody has come into the house today. Remember! Not a soul.'

'Yes, my lady.'

When he had bathed and shaved, a valet came and helped him to dress in the clothes which had been put out for him. When he was ready, the valet said that my lady would be supping in her own apartment in another part of the house. 'Lead me,' said Stuart.

After traversing narrow and twisting passages, he emerged into what seemed to be a small, richly panelled anteroom. The valet bade him wait.

Stuart had time to look round. Over a carved stone fireplace a picture was set into the dark wood. A startling picture, the portrait of a youth, a boy of sensuous, almost womanish, beauty. The boy's too-full lips were shaped into a half-smile in which there lurked promise, enticement, and refusal all at once. About his melancholy face tumbled a mass of gleaming pagan curls.

As if to add deliberately to the equivocal character of the portrait—Stuart was convinced that this was the image of an individual and not the amorous fancy of an artist dreaming of Ganymede—the boy was painted wearing a shirt which provocatively bared his white young throat.

Who was he? Stuart could see no signature of the artist, no name of the subject. Although he was no connoisseur of these matters, he thought it might have been painted by an Italian.

In this room in a northern city, surrounded by the dark firelight shining on armour and weapons, the painting was arresting, even disturbing. A wanderer from a sunlit, luxurious, sensual world far to the south. What was it doing there?

'Who is he?'

The valet of whom Stuart asked the question looked at him fixedly for an instant. Stuart thought he shook his head in the faintest gesture of denial. He could not be sure. Without speaking, the servant bowed him into the room beyond.

75

Who was the youth? The question would have to wait ...

He entered in time to witness a disagreeable little scene. My lady had just struck a red-haired maid on the side of the head with her open hand.

'Get out, you clumsy slut. And don't come back until you've learnt to keep your thieving fingers out of my jewel box.'

In tears, the girl shot her a venomous glance, and fled from the room. She was followed by a volley of furious words: 'Half-wit. Peasant. I'll send you back to that old whore, your mother.'

Then my lady turned to her guest with only the slightest softening of her expression.

She looks at me, Stuart decided, as if she were measuring a condemned criminal for the rope.

She wore a loose evening gown of some heavy material which had the tendency to fall from one shoulder and then the other. Between her breasts hung a small gold locket.

They were to sup alone. A steward and a page served the meal. In the intervals, when there was no one else in the room, they talked.

'You have a name that belongs to this country,' she said, 'but you speak with a foreign accent. And your manners are foreign. To say nothing of your clothes. Where do you come from, Mr. Stuart? France, I suppose. Tell me about your life, what have you done?'

'Do you mean the truth, madame, or the version I tell beautiful ladies who are my hostesses? By the way, my name is James.'

'The truth would be better, James.'

He told her the version for beautiful ladies who were his hostesses. She listened with a faint smile.

'And may I ask your name, madame?' he asked.

'Madeleine.'

'Tell me, Madeleine, why did your brother think I could be useful to you? Where is he, by the way?'

'He is at court. He has some business there. I expect him later.'

'Ah. I see. But why choose me, of all people? To escort you?'

'Because Rory trusts only desperate men and he thinks that you are desperate.'

'Desperate, yes! And why? Because I have not been one minute in this country before I am watched, followed, hunted

76

and thrown into prison. For what reason, please? Perhaps I am mistaken for another man. And perhaps there is another reason.'

'And perhaps you know what it is,' she said, calmly.

'What do you expect of me?' he asked in a subdued voice. 'You are as desperate as I am. Don't deny it, madame. I am not a fool. Tell me.'

After a moment's pause, she began to speak, in a curious, light, detached voice as if she was telling some frivolous story.

'Your namesake, the King, who is probably some kind of relative of yours, takes an interest in me, James. In fact, he proposes to have me burnt as a witch. Oh, don't think it is a laughing matter. Our Sovereign Lord takes witchcraft seriously.'

'Are you a witch, Madeleine?'

'Some people think so. People will believe almost anything. What do you think, James?'

He remembered the crystal ball he had seen on her dressing-table. 'It could be,' he said. 'It could be. In those few minutes in my life when I have thought about witches, I imagined them as rather like you. But I am told there are ways of proving it.'

'Don't worry. The King will see to all that.'

'So?'

'My brother has a plan. I came to the town against his wish. Rory said I was putting my head in a noose. I was. I had my reasons. Then Rory had the idea that I could escape the stake by becoming the wife of a nobleman of so ancient, respectable, illustrious a name that the King would not dare to put a hand on his wife.

'Oh, the creature exists! He is called the Earl of Cluny. To make things more enticing for me,' she went on, 'he is an old man who devotes his time to the second of our national sports. He hunts the deer on the highland hills.'

He nodded and for a moment was silent. Then he asked,

'You said the *second* sport. What do you reckon is the first?'

'Treason, of course.'

'Treason ... is that your favourite sport, Madeleine?'

She nodded and, with her lips, said 'No.'

After a pause, he took up the questioning again. 'And what was I expected to do? What does escorting you to the north have to do with this scheme?'

She shrugged.

'Now it is out of the question. They are scouring the town for you. The taverns and the brothels are being combed.'

'Wanted for murder,' he said. 'I have read the bills.'

She nodded. 'Everybody is on the look-out—and thinking of the money they would get for taking you! But Rory's idea was that you, being what you are, would escort me to Lord Cluny's place in the north country.'

'Why couldn't Rory go himself?'

'Because it might compromise his position at court. Rory is playing a subtle game.'

'A double game?'

'It's possible. So—he thought of you. But now—no.'

He would have liked to ask her more about herself and, above all, about the reasons for the King's vendetta, but in the circumstances it seemed impertinent and in any case it was she who asked the next question:

'Why *have* you come to Scotland? Tell me the truth this time.'

'You will have heard what the placards say about me. That I came to murder a man named Freeland. It isn't true. That I tried to kill a man named Kennedy. That isn't true, either. That I am an escaped convict. That is true. Look at this.'

He pushed back his chair and slipped off his doublet. Loosening his shirt at the neck, he bared his right shoulder. He was aware of Madeleine's eyes on the leather pouch which hung about his neck.

'Do you see these letters?' he said, pointing at a row of small red weals on the skin. 'What do they say?'

She looked intently for a minute, reached out, touched gently.

'G.A.L.,' she said. 'Gal.'

He nodded.

'Correct. Gal. Galerian. Done with a branding iron. Very painful while it lasted. I am an escaped slave from the King of Spain's galleys. Do you know why men are sent to these bloody ships, Madeleine? Because they have committed a serious crime. Murder. Treason. Or piracy. In my case, piracy.'

'A pirate!'

'So the Spaniards said. The truth is less picturesque. I was a passenger in a Dutch merchantman bound from Amsterdam to

La Rochelle. It was going to pick up a cargo of salt. I was going to land there.

'In the Bay, we were surprised by two Spanish frigates. They were fast boats and well-handled, with plenty of culverins. After a while we were sinking. The Spanish troops—regulars—swarmed aboard us. So—what do you think? I was knocked down and put in irons.

'In due course, I was tried as one of the crew of a pirate vessel. The Spaniards think all Dutch boats are pirates. They are not always wrong. And they need all the rowers they can get for their galleys. So, to the galleys I was condemned. On one of them I spent half a year living on dry beans and foul water, living in stink and ordure, sleeping on the bench I was chained to.

'Then one fine day off Gibraltar, our galleys were caught by a Dutch fleet sailing home from Alexandretta. My galley was rushed by the Dutch and captured. The man who had shared a bench with me—a Scotsman in fact—was killed by a musket shot. I was freed and went to Holland which I had left nine months before.'

He paused, did up his shirt and put on his doublet.

'So,' he said, 'As you see. They are quite right. I am an escaped convict. You are running a grave risk, Madeleine, when you give me shelter.'

She filled his goblet with red wine from a handsome glass jug.

'To piracy!' she said, lifting her glass.

He grinned and drank.

'One thing you haven't told me. Why did you come here?'

He wrinkled his brow and was silent for a moment.

'Because on the ocean, a man may be picked up by a current which carries him, like an empty bottle, to a shore he had never thought of visiting.'

She moved her head in a tiny gesture of impatience.

'You are talking in images, Jamie,' she said.

'Now may I ask you a question, Madeleine? Why does King James want to have you burnt? Let me guess the answer. Because he is afraid of you. There is something about you the King fears, isn't there?'

'He is a very timid man, this King of ours. Everybody knows that!' she said lightly. 'And if it comes to that, he seems to be

79

afraid of you as well as of me. I might ask why?'

In the silence that had fallen on the room, he heard a muffled sound. Somewhere in the house somebody was knocking on a door.

Three knocks well spaced out in time. Then three knocks in rapid succession.

Very still all of a sudden, Madeleine listened, a distant expression on her face. A servant appeared at the door and whispered in her ear. Her face cleared. She nodded and said something to the servant, who vanished.

Rather marry than burn

The door was thrown open. An orange glint where the candle-light fell on armour. A jingle of spurs.

A servant announced, 'Sir John!'

'Uncle!'

'My beautiful niece!'

The man who had been ushered into the room was ugly and impressive; short and corpulent and uncommonly broad across the shoulders. Stuart judged he was in his fifties. He had a head of grey hair, growing close and cropped short, and intensely piercing black eyes under long black eyebrows. The lips which kissed Madeleine were moist and rather pendulous.

Stuart gathered that he was Sir John Bannerman.

'A distant relation of this girl—she calls me Uncle. She refused to marry me because one is forbidden to marry one's uncle.'

'And because my uncle is married.'

All this time his suspicious eyes were taking Stuart in, surveying him east and west.

'This is James Stuart,' she said. 'If he looks a little damaged it's because he has been fighting.'

'A bad habit,' said Sir John. 'So you're the boy they are after. That is bad luck. You have no chance of escape, young man. Look at you. Height. Shoulders. And hair. Why the devil don't you cut it? Fashion? You'll wear ribbon in it next.'

'Why not?'

'Or dye it. No. Useless! They would recognise you just the same. Nose. Cheekbones. And the limp and the swagger in your

81

walk. I noticed it just now. You can't help it. No. You'll have to leave. Go back where you came from. A pity, no doubt, but better Paris than the Pearly Gates.'

'I have a mission here, a tryst to keep,' said Stuart. There was something forced, something guarded about Sir John's joviality that made him uncomfortable. 'But how did you know I came from Paris?'

'News gets about. Besides there's the way you speak. I recognise it. But take my advice. Don't lose that accent. It's an asset. I spent three years of my life at the Sorbonne. Three ill-spent years, boy. Shame, shame! I hope you were wiser.'

He laughed, but his eyes remained shrewd and watchful; he turned to Madeleine.

'I've ridden into town in case your ladyship needs help from the family,' he said, clashing the steel cap he was carrying against the corselet he wore.

'Uncle John, there was no need.'

'Maybe. I heard differently. Two or three more to man the fortress never come amiss. I've brought half a dozen. Good fellows. But rough. Keep an eye on your women, Madeleine.'

'You've been kind. I'll see to them. And I'll warn the girls. The servants will take the wine into the other room.'

She led the way there.

Someone had lit a fire, for the chill of the night air had seeped into the room. There she left the two men.

Sir John stood in front of the fireplace, under that strange portrait. He gave Stuart a sharp look.

'Which of us talks first?' he asked.

Stuart tapped his chest. 'Privilege of a guest.'

'I am the older man. But go on,' said Sir John, with a quick frown of irritation.

'Why does he hate your niece so much—the King, my namesake?'

Sir John looked at him hard before answering.

'Because he thinks she's a dangerous young woman. What do you think yourself?'

'An hour or two ago I had not met the girl,' he protested.

'First impressions are always interesting and sometimes correct. Dangerous, do you think?'

'I'd say she could be dangerous if roused.'

Sir John gave a short laugh.

'If instinct tells you that, instinct is not far out. What you don't understand, young man, is how a single girl, without a husband, without even a lover, so far as I know ...' he shrugged. 'How Madeleine can be dangerous to a king, the lawful son of a queen ...'

Stuart waited.

'Some men are frightened of their own shadows,' Sir John continued. 'Some are frightened of the dark corners of their conscience. One day something might jump out at them. They have things they want to forget, secrets they want to keep hidden, mouths they want to shut. That is true of all men. It is especially true of kings.'

Bannerman's voice faded. He was frowning. Then he broke out almost indignantly,

'You ask me what secret Madeleine knows. If she knows it, she is hiding it. That's all I can tell you.'

His gaze was direct and candid enough, yet it reserved something or Jamie was much mistaken. A residue of doubt, suspicion? It was impossible to be sure.

'And now,' said Sir John, 'I think it is my turn to ask the questions.' Stuart inclined his head slightly. 'Why are you in Scotland?'

'That's simple. I came to find the Earl of Gowrie.'

'Gowrie? ... A name not to be bandied about.'

'I thought he might tell me something. But Gowrie is dead and called a traitor. I was told that if I found a man named Andrew Freeland, he might be able to give me more news of the business. I found him. *He* was dead. Now I am charged with his murder. And that's all.'

'I think not,' said Bannerman simply. 'Not all. Not a half.'

Stuart smiled suddenly. 'Did *you* tell me everything, Sir John? After all, why should you—to a dubious piece of driftwood washed up on the Shore of Leith! Shall we make a bargain then? The whole truth for the whole truth?'

'One truth at a time. And this time I ask first.'

Stuart shrugged, then nodded.

'Ask,' he said.

'What led you to imagine Lord Gowrie could tell you anything of interest?'

For a second Jamie fumbled for words, as if he did not know where to begin; he liked this man, and yet who could tell where his real interest lay?

'You are speaking to an ex-convict, Sir John. A man who has escaped from the Spanish royal galleys. Few galerians survive and fewer escape. Count me as lucky.

'Rowing in the bench next to me was a man from Scotland, there because he was a heretic—a Protestant. He had met Gowrie in Paris and had got the story from him. Later he was killed in a sea fight—head blown off by a musket shot. That was the fight when I got my freedom.'

'What was his name?'

'Forsyth. Quentin Forsyth.'

Sir John knitted his brows for a moment, and shook his head. He had not heard the name before.

'I promised I would find his family if ever I got free.'

'So you came to Scotland—on a wild-goose chase ...'

Sir John had turned his back on Stuart now, and was brooding, as it seemed, over the portrait above the fireplace.

'After all,' said Stuart, 'it's my country.'

'Yes ... Your father ...' Then with a sudden animation and a jerk of his thumb at the picture above the fireplace. 'Bonny, is he no'?'

Beautiful and ambiguous, the portrait looked down, with the hint of mockery more noticeable than before.

'Bonny? Yes. Who is he?'

The door opened abruptly. Stuart blinked and stopped talking. A boy more beautiful than the image in the picture stood there in the doorway.

'Madeleine!'

She had put on a discarded hunting suit of her brother's because, as she said, 'We live in troubled days and it will attract less attention ... and I have always wanted to wear it anyhow.'

'By God,' said Sir John, 'if the King catches sight of you, he'll have the biggest upset since—since many a day.'

He broke off in embarrassment.

The hunting suit was of green English cloth with silver piping. Her legs, to mid-thigh, were covered in fawn-coloured leather gaiters. Her eyes sparkled. The ivory of her cheeks was flushed with rose. It was as if the *mignon* of some loose-living monarch had come into the anteroom.

'Do you expect trouble, Madeleine?' said Stuart.

She nodded. 'Listen.' She held up a finger.

Silence. The gentle noises of wood burning in the grate.

'I hear not a sound,' said Sir John, irritably.

'Exactly. Too quiet. None of the usual noises from the street.'

Suddenly while they listened, there was a sound of voices outside. Stuart judged that it came from the cobbled yard that separated the house from the street. A few seconds later, came the sound of urgent whispers somewhere below.

Sir John pulled his rapier an inch or two out of its scabbard.

There was a knock at the door.

Madeleine said, 'Come in.'

A servant, who looked round uncertainly.

'My lady,' he said, 'one Donald Gregory to see a Mr. Stuart.'

'My caddie,' said Jamie. 'I'll talk to him.'

'Bring him in,' said Madeleine. 'If he is like other caddies, he has something to say.'

The servant disappeared. A minute later, Gregory was at the door. He looked unusually untrustworthy, Stuart thought.

'If you have news for me, Donald, speak out, man.'

'They know where you are, my lord. They are coming here to catch you.'

'Who are? The Law or Lord Orkney?'

'Maybe one, maybe the other. Who is to say, my lord?'

'Why not both of them?' said Sir John impatiently.

'Why not?' said Gregory. 'Although those two are not often found on the same side.'

Madeleine broke in, 'Orkney has been watching this house all day!'

'For what reason?' asked her uncle.

'He has the notion I will leave the town one day soon and would like to intercept me.'

The door opened. Rory Bannerman came into the room in time to hear Madeleine's words.

85

'Lord Orkney,' he said with a smile, 'would like my sister as his wife.'

Sir John broke in indignantly, scarcely nodding at his nephew, 'But Orkney *has* a wife,' he said.

Madeleine shrugged her shoulders.

'Lord Orkney is not the man to let a trifle like that stand in his way. He is used to having his will. Unfortunately, he does not appeal to me.'

'That's good,' said Sir John grimly. 'As far as it goes.'

'And now they have found out that Mr. Stuart is here,' said Madeleine. 'How, God only knows.'

Gregory looked at her through the reddish fringe of his eyelashes. His hand clawed at his beard.

'Would you have a lassie, here, my lady, that might talk when she shouldn't?'

'Red-haired?' Madeleine asked, sharply.

'I wouldn't say no, my lady.'

'Effie! She's done that to be even with me. By God, I'll pay her out if it's the last thing I do. I'll have her whipped three times round the yard and thrown into the street. Send the steward to me,' she called to a servant standing behind Gregory. 'I'll give the orders now before I forget.'

'Yes, my lady.'

She turned on Stuart, her eyes blazing, her face dark. 'Little bitch! First thieving and now treachery!' She was shaking with anger.

'And now what?' asked Sir John. 'What do we do?'

'Only one thing is plain,' said Stuart. 'I must leave at once. Hide as best I can until darkness falls, then trust to luck!'

Madeleine shook her head.

'No, no,' she cried. 'You mustn't do that. We must find some better way.'

'If I stay here—which is impossible—I bring them all down on you.'

'Madeleine, you should not be found here,' Sir John broke in.

'No,' said Rory. 'She must go to Cluny.'

'To that old man?' Sir John retorted. 'I have a better plan, Madeleine. I have horses. If we saddle now and ride, we can be clear of the town before they know it.'

'And where should we fly to, uncle?'

'To that bonny little tower I have above the river in Tweeddale, no more than half an hour's ride over the Border into England. If the King hears you're there, he can't move fast enough to catch you before you are safe on foreign soil.'

'What of the marriage feast?' she asked with a hint of mockery.

Sir John gave an impatient shrug.

'The marriage feast!' he cried contemptuously.

'Why not let Mr. Stuart try his hand after all?' Rory interjected smoothly. 'His need to escape is great. Why not escort my sister to Cluny as he flees the King's soldiers?'

'Because the King is no fool. He will have them followed there and that will be the end,' Sir John exploded.

'Mr. Stuart can take care of himself,' said Rory.

Jamie grinned.

'Mr. Stuart can do that very well,' he said.

'I'll have the horses made ready,' said Sir John. 'One for each of us, Madeleine. Two grooms. And two beasts for the baggage.'

He left the room with a clash of steel.

'And Mr. Stuart—' said Madeleine, 'what of him?'

'I have a grey horse in the stable that will suit Stuart very well,' said Rory. 'I'll see to it now.'

Gregory looked from Madeleine to Stuart. Then he went out.

When the room was empty, Madeleine took his wrists in her hands.

'Did you think I was going to ride to the Tweed with my uncle?' she asked. 'And not be able to live in Scotland as I like? What do you take me for! No! I'm going to be Countess of Cluny. And you, Jamie Stuart, are going to ride with me to the wedding.'

She stood very close to him, her cheeks flushed a little, her body trembling slightly, her extraordinary eyes glowing as if they had been dusted with gold.

'Jesus!' he exclaimed. She smiled and moved closer to him.

'What we shall do is this,' she said. 'I shall ride out with my uncle and his lances southwards over the shoulder of the King's deer park. Then at a moment when the pursuit seems to be gaining on us—I shall arrange to be lost. Don't be afraid. My horse will be faster than theirs and I know the country. You will take another road.

'Go north first, from the lane behind the stables, cross the highway—you will see a tennis court. Keep it on your right and ride fast. When you are clear of the houses turn the horse's head towards the west. You will find a loch under the Castle Rock. Beside the water's edge, close to it at the western end, stands a ruined chapel. Wait for me there, Jamie.'

'And then?'

Her face relaxed, visited by a smile in which there was humour and lasciviousness—or was it pure mischief?

'What do you think! We shall ride to the wedding. What else?'

A slight figure stood in the door, wearing a satirical smile. Rory Bannerman.

'Yes, sister,' he said. 'Remember what St. Paul said. Rather marry than burn ... The grey will be ready in the stable, Stuart.'

'Sir John thinks I'm riding with him to Tweeddale,' Madeleine said to Rory, but still looking at Stuart, who couldn't tear his gaze from hers.

'You're going to Cluny, Madeleine,' he said fiercely. 'To Cluny and the altar.'

'I always obey my brother.' She turned and leant forward kissing Rory lightly on the lips. 'Don't I?'

Part II

The Queen of Elfland

Madeleine had left with her uncle and his mosstroopers. Jamie was leading the grey horse out of the stable into the quiet lane that ran behind Bannerman's Lodging. He was about to mount when a sound made him wheel round. Suddenly a hand fell heavily on his shoulder from behind. At the nape of his neck, he felt the cold ring of a pistol muzzle.

The light was good enough for him to recognise in front of him the man he had seen in the Edinburgh alley, the tall man with the cat.

Lord Orkney peered at him from under eyebrows which, in that light, seemed to have no colour.

After a minute of silence, Orkney spoke to him in an odd, high-pitched voice.

'What's your clan, boy?'

'None of your business,' Jamie answered. 'But as it happens, your own.'

'What do you mean?'

'The bastards,' said Jamie.

Orkney waved a hand. 'Bastard,' he said. 'Bastard of what name?'

'I told you, cousin. Your own.'

'Oh-ho! A Stuart. The country is full of bastards of that name. One of them would never be missed.'

His yellowish eyes roved over Stuart's face.

A small black cat came out from between his feet. Orkney looked down at it.

'Would he, Mawksie? Would he be missed? What do you say?'

He took the cat up in his arms. It looked at Stuart and mewed.

'Do you know what that means, Stuart? It means Mawksie is asking me to kill you. Why do you want me to have Mr. Stuart killed, Mawksie?'

The cat mewed again. Orkney frowned.

'Because he is an impudent rogue who meddles with what is no business of his? And he ought to go the same way as others who cross our path? You think so, Mawksie, don't you?'

With the cat in his arms, Orkney came closer, and Stuart found himself looking into two pairs of eyes, the cat's green and the earl's yellow. Without warning, the cat struck out with its paw. Stuart flinched and shut his eye. Just in time. Four stinging red lines were drawn down his cheeks.

Orkney laughed, a high-pitched laugh.

'Mawksie, Mawksie! Not like you to miss. You don't like Mr. Stuart, do you? And why? Because he doesn't like you ... You should like cats, Stuart. Take my advice. They can read the secrets of the heart. Even the blackest heart.'

'They have plenty of practice,' said Stuart.

The man holding him said, 'Don't talk to his lordship like that, scum.'

'What do I do? Kiss his lordship's arse, or do I leave that to you?'

'Don't lay a finger on him!' Orkney spoke to the man behind Jamie. He laughed and stroked the cat.

'You may be glad to do that yet,' he said to Jamie. 'You may ask to do it as a favour.'

Stuart uttered a one-syllabled French word he had picked up in Paris. It had a wealth of derogatory meaning.

At that moment, the rhythmic crash of marching feet sounded on a causeway close at hand.

'The King's men! They have come for you, Stuart. Better on your way quickly. But one more word before we part.'

Without warning Orkney's fist pounded against Stuart's teeth. He fell backwards on to the cobbles. The marching feet were nearer now ...

'My lord!'

Gregory dragged him into the shadow of a close. After a minute silence returned.

'Have they gone?'

'Yes my lord, all of them.'

'My lord Orkney likes cats,' said Stuart, gingerly touching his torn cheek.

'He talks to them, my lord, and they talk to him,' said Gregory.

'What do you know about cats, Donald?'

Stuart thought he saw the Highlander's eyes light up.

'Cats, my lord! A chancy tribe. A cousin of mine knows all about them. Duncan, he's called.'

'Duncan,' said Stuart. 'Goodnight, Donald.'

He rubbed his head where it had struck the ground as he trotted across the cobbles of the main street towards the gap in the city wall and the open country that lay beyond it.

Madeleine and Jamie rode through the night and at first light pulled up at a change house to rest their horses and themselves. After a sleep they went on at an easier pace and as Jamie thought in a slightly altered direction. Gradually they approached the barrier of mountains which during the journey had been a constant presence to the north.

Most of the time Madeleine rode in advance as a young nobleman should. Wearing a doublet of the Bannerman livery, Jamie was convincing as her groom.

He had named a place to her when they set out, a place which his father had spoken of long ago, a lake with an island in it. She had looked surprised but, yes, they could pass that way. It would add some distance to the journey—fifty or sixty miles—but on the other hand pursuit would be less likely to follow them.

All that morning they rode, saying little to one another. Stuart watched the sky above this strange country he had come to. Hanging what seemed only a few hundred feet above the horizon was a deep purple cloud, dramatic against a bank of distant brilliant pink. The woods—for by this time they had ridden out of the shaven farm lands and were moving through shaggier country —confronted one another like armies in pictures of war. One was dense, black, threatening, the other clad all in silver, carrying orange banners.

The light lent the scene an emotional intensity, a power to probe and unsettle the mind. The low, purple cloud passed over them, subduing the landscape. Then suddenly everything was brilliant once more. The sunlight lay pale on the fields while the trees displayed the jewellery of their branches against a cushion of blue cloud.

Madeleine told him that before the light faded they would find a valley which would lead them to their halt for the night—'The place you wish to see.'

The sunlight had left the low country by the time they reached a place where he saw a level grey light low down. Water?

For hours they had been riding towards the setting sun on a drove road that had dwindled into a bridle-path. A moment came when she dropped the reins on her horse's neck. 'Find your own way, friend. I can help you no more.'

Stuart had the impression that the brute saw a track where he could not. 'We shall soon be there,' Madeleine told him.

Houses were few and looked uninviting. The country grew wilder and the hills were nearer and steeper. The muir was alive with game. He remembered his father: 'Wonderful shooting country, my boy. Nothing like it south of Lapland.'

And then, quite suddenly, 'There!' she pointed. Through a screen of trees he saw the lake and the island. For him at least, this was the end of the journey.

There would be time—but no more—to row across. If they could find stabling for horses—and a boat that he could hire. There was no reason in the world why he should not postpone the crossing until morning light. But the long ride, which had made him saddlesore, had also provoked him to an irritable impatience.

Madeleine found a stable behind one of the row of white-washed cottages near the water's edge which marked the end of the road. They hurried down to an old wooden jetty by the lakeside.

A boat? Of course there would be a boat, said the wild-eyed woman who had given them stabling for the horses. She gave them a worried gaze—a young lord who spoke with a woman's voice, and a groom with blond wavy hair. Did they want to go fishing? It would be a fine night for the fish.

He told her that he would like to visit the island over there. She frowned at that. Could they not wait until the morning? It would be better in the morning. No? Then if they must, they must. A boat would be at the jetty.

An old boat from which the paint had long since peeled off was moored by a rusty chain to the pier. A pair of oars lay in the bottom of it.

The lake was a sheet of saffron glass taking its colour from the evening sky. Round it was a frame of reeds above which rose young birch trees, slender, silver, moving to the breaths of air, whispering to themselves. Beyond them the mountains lifted, the light still golden on them. Seen over his shoulder as he rowed was the island. Inchmahome. That had been the name his father gave it. A water bird drew a line across the surface of the lake and rose with a sudden bluster of wings.

It was a strange and secretive place, and Stuart, accustomed to a gentler and more seductive beauty, found something that clutched at his heart, as if a string there had been plucked for the first time. He rowed up to it in silence. Swinging the boat broadside on, he reached for a ring fastened to the stonework of a small landing-place. Another boat, even older and more rotten than the one they had come in, had been pulled in among the reeds nearby.

Once ashore, waist-deep in rank-smelling bracken, Stuart could make out the grey walls of the old priory just as they had been described to him, deserted and sinking back into the soft earth of the island.

The windows were without glass. Some of the carved masonry had vanished. But the roof was still whole—after how many generations? And the weeds and saplings that were growing up round the walls had not yet invaded the church.

Silence arched over them, deep, flawless, chilly as the sky above. No sign of a path among the trees. Probably nobody came there any more now that the last monk had died or wandered off. It was a desert island on which they had put their impious feet. He knew where he should seek what he had come for. His business was with the burial ground.

95

'As I remember it,' his father had said, 'it is between the monastery buildings and the water at the far end which should lie towards the east. But it will all be changed now. Fifty years will have done something to the place—and probably to my memory too, my dear.'

As well as he could recall them he repeated the words to Madeleine. She gave him a puzzled look but said nothing.

Fifty years *had* done something—their frosts had split the low retaining walls of the enclosure. They had let in the briars and the nettles like barbarian swarms. They had filled the graveyard with birch, alder and young oak. They had built mounds of earth that covered all but the heads of the stones that marked the graves.

Walking here and there in the thicket, Stuart wondered whether his errand had been futile from the beginning. And then, quite suddenly, he saw it unmistakably and just where his father had said it would be.

Above thistles and rank grey grass the ornamental scrollwork of the stone emerged. There was lettering disguised by thick patches of moss and a flaking armour of lichen. But he could see 'CA ... C ...'

He pulled out his dirk and began to scrape at the stone. In ten minutes he had uncovered the name as clearly defined as on the day the mason had finished his work: Caterina Carmichael. At some time in the past, a chisel had crudely obliterated the rest of the inscription.

He glanced up at Madeleine.

'Why?' she asked. But she was excited rather than puzzled.

He shrugged.

'My father told me it was here. It was one of the things I came to Scotland to find.'

'Who was she?'

'Among other things, my grandmother.'

Suddenly they were no longer alone.

Silent as a ghost, an old woman with a gaunt face, seamed with wrinkles like deep clefts in the shining brown leather of her cheeks, stood beside Madeleine, watching him.

Behind her appeared a second woman, smaller, bowed with age, holding her hands crossed on her stomach as old peasant women do.

The expression of the first woman was serious. And she was shaking her head. She might have been the spirit of the place, warning the intruder to go.

'Those who sleep should be left in peace,' she said.

Her voice was twice surprising, once because it was so deep for a woman and again because it was so musical for one so old.

He answered her in a voice as solemn as her own.

'I have come to disturb no one's sleep. I am looking for something.'

'But you will not have found it.'

'And how do you know what I am seeking?' he asked.

'Treasure. Treasure. Is not that what all men look for?'

'In this lost old graveyard!'

'God does not put His gold where it can be found with the least trouble. And others have sought before you. Do you know who is buried here—or was?'

Stuart said nothing.

'She was a queen. That is what they say. A queen. But you know, sir, what nonsense people will believe. And why she was buried here, you may ask? If I knew, I would tell you. But it was all long ago, hundreds of years, maybe, before my time. I hear only the stories people tell, daft old women like me, making up fairy-tales to please the neighbours.'

'A queen,' he said. 'The Queen of Elfland?'

The old woman shook her head. Stuart's gaze moved from one woman to the other, looking for a clue. But the second woman said nothing and gave no sign.

'Who kens? Who kens? When I was a girl there came men to this kirkyard at the hinder end of harvest. They came riding to the town and rowing over. They dug up the queen in her coffin and carried her off.'

'Where to, good woman?'

She shook her head.

'Who kens? Who kens? ... Other folk have a different story. There was a treasure buried with her, they say. And they came to take it away. You can believe what you like, sir. I was a lassie then and can tell you only what I heard. But men came. That

I'll swear. The light was much as it is now and there were not so many leaves on the birks.'

'And the lake was as still as a mirror?'

'The lake is aye as still as a mirror,' she said.

'I came from far to find my grandmother's grave and here it is.'

The old woman's expression changed. Anxiety, grief, desolation came crowding into her face.

'But she was a queen, sir.' Her lips trembled.

James Stuart rose and dusted his knees. 'In that case, good wife,' he said. 'What am I? A king?'

He clapped on his hat at an angle and laughed softly across the foundered headstones.

She shook her head and would say no more. Standing behind, the second woman tapped her forehead twice.

'A king,' said Madeleine, looking at him curiously.

Across the border

He woke from confused and anxious dreams when the first sunlight streamed in at the stable door. He had just said, 'The Queen of Elfland'. Why, he did not know and, in fact, within a few seconds all recollection of the phrase—that he had uttered it; that he had heard it; what it had meant—was wiped utterly from his mind.

He was shivering with cold and his joints ached. Yet he had slept well enough on the straw. He rose and shook himself like a dog and plunged his head into a bucket of water. He waited for the morning air to dry him. After that he saddled the horses and led them to the cottage where Madeleine had spent the night in bed, comfortably, as a young nobleman should.

In the sparkling light of early morning, with sleep and waking still confused in her eyes, and innocence and mischief together on her lips, he found her more enticing than ever. He was ready, for a moment, to believe about her what he knew could not be true.

'Did they think you were a man, wearing those stockings?' he asked her.

She shrugged. 'Did they think you were a horse sleeping in that stable?'

'How long will it take for the news that we have come here to reach our sovereign Lord the King?'

'Longer than it will take me to become Countess of Cluny,' she told him.

They ate—trout fresh from the lake, and oatcakes warm from the griddle, then they mounted and rode on. Still the mystery lingered in his mind: who had dug up his grandmother's grave and why?

After an hour or so Madeleine found a stony track which twisted uphill through the trees of an unkempt forest. So far as he could judge from the way the shadows fell, they were heading northwards.

He had the impression that Madeleine was not so sure of the route as she had been the day before. Every now and then, she seemed to pause irresolutely and look about as if she were searching for some clue, perhaps for a sign of earlier travellers. Once she pulled round her horse's head when the path swooped sharply down through dwarf oaks and young bracken curling in shapes like strange musical instruments. There was a sound of rushing water far below. She shook her head as she passed him, returning.

'That must be wrong,' she said.

A little later, they came out on an open space where bushes with small glistening leaves filled the spaces between grey rocks. The sky above them was a shining buoyant blue. Somewhere in it a lark burst into song. Over the crests of the trees ahead he caught a glimpse of a line of mountains far away. She drew rein and dismounted. It was safer to lead the horses over this ground.

'I have not seen the country from this side before,' she said. 'And we must take the right glen if we can find it. Otherwise ...'

'Otherwise ... ?'

'Up till now we have been riding away from danger. Now we are riding into it.'

'But a different sort of danger,' he said. It was half a question.

'When the risk is that you may have your throat cut, is it different? Ahead of us on the way to Cluny's house, there are families, clans, whole tribes, who think they have a better right to the Bannerman lands than we have. Impudence! But who is to say they are wrong!' She laughed.

His arm swept the landscape in a wide gesture.

'I should think there is enough land for everybody.'

'How little you know of my people, Jamie!'

'My people too, remember.'

'You have been in this country only a few days. How can I think of you as one of us?'

'You stood with me last night in the graveyard. You know who was buried there. Does that not make me one of you?'

'I do not know what it makes you. But I know what the old woman said. A queen,' she said.

'She is mad.' He tapped his forehead.

'No,' she said. 'She may be touched, as they say. But mad she is not.'

For a moment they stood gazing into one another's eyes, saying nothing. Stuart thought that she looked very beautiful with the throat of her hunting shirt open and the thread of pale gold showing from which hung the hidden locket.

One day, he would ... one day, soon ...

Her green eyes with their brown flecks roamed over his face. Then she turned abruptly towards the hills ahead.

'I think that one.'

She pointed to a wavering line in the hills which slanted downwards from the skyline. It seemed to be made by light falling on the crests of trees. It could mark a wooded ridge beyond which there might be a glen.

'It will be an hour or more before we reach it and, if we are mistaken, half the day has been wasted. Come!'

The horses picked their way delicately over the broken ground. Jamie's shied once. When he looked down he saw, grey and glistening, a coil of young adders.

After a little, the surface grew smoother. They mounted again and followed a cart-track downhill, through small clearings where hay had been cut. From one field to another a clumsy bird, black and dun-grey, flapped before them as if to bring warning of their coming. At last they pulled up on a platform of ground where the trees parted and a great expanse of country was laid open to their eyes.

Beyond a narrow, sunlit valley running east and west, the mountains rose, green-clad on their lower slopes, tawny and russet on their upper. Stuart thought he could hear a stream chattering excitedly somewhere below as it tumbled downhill through a rocky cleft hidden by rushes and alder.

'Somewhere below,' she told him, 'is a ford which we must find and cross. This is a dividing line.'

'Between what and what?'

'Between Us and Them. Beyond the river, the people are of a different kind. A strange lot. You can't always be sure what they are thinking. We shall need a bit of luck.'

She touched her horse with the spur and in a moment they were moving at an ungainly trot towards more level ground which stretched between them and the river. Following a track, they reached the ford at a canter and splashed over wide, flat stones to the further bank. It was high and steep but she put her horse at it with spur and whip.

It was clear that at this point in the journey she feared they might be observed. They rode at a fast canter up the wooded shoulder of a mountain to the west of their course in a series of ascending escarpments, each armoured in rock, each crowned by a platform of heather, regular, bold and purposeful, as if a military engineer had designed the complex.

Madeleine waved her whip at it and called out a name, but the wind carried the sound away. After that they plunged into a rocky gorge where trees grew close together and the horses picked their way carefully. A stream ran fast below them, with a bridle path on the far side of it.

Madeleine kept to the pathless bank they were on, heading for the narrow throat of the pass. The music of falling water filled their ears until they emerged on a loch, a narrow sheet of lilac-coloured water, stretching out towards the north and pinned between noble hills.

The easier route would lie to the east where there was an expanse of flat ground before the hills began. Madeleine chose the western shore, which looked steep and dangerous. Stuart was not surprised. He was beginning to understand her method.

Half-way along the loch, she pulled up suddenly. 'Listen!'

At first, he could hear nothing but the bees in the heather.

'Yes, yes,' she said, frowning impatiently. 'Now you can hear it, surely.'

The air was motionless and very clear. After a moment, he thought he could detect some faint disturbance in the sounds which, together, made up the huge soundlessness of the hills; it seemed to be coming from the loch itself.

'Look!' On the far bank, maybe half a mile away, there was a company of men in clothes of black or dark green marching south.

'The water carries the sound,' she said. 'They have seen us.'

The marchers on the other shore had halted. They stood in a motionless dark line, looking across the loch.

'They can't reach us unless they swim,' Jamie pointed out.

'No. But having seen us here, they will carry the news farther south, and there will be no lack of people who are interested to hear it. We could have had better luck, Jamie.'

He looked at the men in the dark cloth. Two of them were mounted, the rest on foot. All were armed. 'Who are they, Madeleine?'

'Who is to tell! Murrays perhaps. Grahams. Erskines. Livingstones. Or dependants of the Campbells. Who is to say? We shall be wise to hurry and wiser still if we change our route.'

She shook the reins on her horse's neck and cantered ahead. Jamie took a last look at the ominous row of dark figures watching from across the water.

Bedraggled but not at all ridiculous. Like a line of scarecrows, but they might scare more than crows. He could not see the expressions on their faces but their gestures were stabbing, ferocious.

Madeleine was right. They had passed over a Border into danger of a different kind. He kicked his horse into a canter and followed Madeleine. A mile or so farther on, she bore off to the left, turning her back on the loch and climbing a glen which after a time narrowed into a pass. Now the water flowed in a different direction. The glen broadened as the land fell away. He could see a stretch of water ahead.

Here had once flourished a forest of noble, widely spaced trees of great stature, pine and oak for the most part. But that must have been centuries ago. Few were left. Huge grey stumps stood here and there covered by blackberry bushes. A secondary growth of gnarled roots and twisted stems had sprouted and then had been arrested.

Madeleine pointed to a cottage on the hillside which she judged belonged to a shepherd. She would go there and get some food. He should not come until she had made sure that the inhabitants were friendly. In his Bannerman livery, he would betray who they were.

'Besides, Jamie, you don't look like a groom.'

'Thank you. It's too damned hot to wear this jacket anyway.'

He slipped it off and hung it over his saddlebow.

'Now I am your equal.'

'Don't speak until I address you. They will not be able to resist gossiping about your accent.'

As they approached the cottage, a blonde young woman appeared, looked at them shyly and vanished. Then a man came out, with a couple of noisy black and white dogs at his heels. Madeleine rode forward and spoke. After a few words she turned and nodded to Jamie.

'They are friends, servants of a man who is married to one of my cousins. I'll talk to him in his own language.'

They ate—sharp-tasting white cheese and oat biscuits. Jamie gave the blonde girl a friendly smile. With a glance of pure alarm she fled from the house. After that he listened, uncomprehending, to the ebb and flow of talk, musical and meaningless to him, between Madeleine and the man. Hens wandered in and out at the cottage door. Stuart fed them with crumbs from his biscuit. When the time came to leave, they were not allowed to pay for the food. He guessed that it would have been bad manners to insist.

While they rode slowly downhill through the ruined forest towards the distant water, Madeleine told him what the shepherd had said.

'There is trouble among the clans in these glens. Farms have been raided, cattle carried off, some killing. It is thought that the government are going to send men from Perth to bring order. It does not make it easier for us to break through to the North, Jamie, with the country roused and every house barred and bolted against strangers.'

'We were lucky that he did not shoot us at sight.'

'For days he has not seen a living soul from outside. He wanted to talk and to listen. You can guess how it is. One gets lonely. Now he says we are to turn westwards at the loch end and look for a very tall man with a ginger beard, cut square. He will be riding a light chestnut with a star on its forehead. We can trust him to tell us the best way to take.'

She gave her horse a touch of the spur. In half an hour they rounded a rocky bluff which jutted out on to the shore of the loch. Madeleine pulled up sharply and reached for the small pistol she kept at her saddle bow. A hundred yards ahead of them was a group of a dozen or so men.

Round leather targes, studded with brass, were slipped down from shoulders to forearms. Swords glinted. With extraordinary speed, men ran up the hillside above the water. In less than a minute they were scrambling over the crags above Madeleine and Stuart. One was aiming a musket. Then a man on a chestnut horse appeared, riding forward.

When Madeleine saw him, she thrust her pistol back in its holster.

'That's he! Look at the beard,' she said.

'Who?'

'Forsyth.'

'Forsyth?'

'The man I was told to look for.'

'He is called Forsyth?'

'Didn't I tell you?'

They sat on big stones at the water's edge and passed round a flask of spirits Forsyth had produced from his saddle-bag. All round lay his men, chattering softly in their language, their targes shouldered, their swords put away. Two of them stood sentry, inconspicuously placed, but watchful.

Stuart had mentioned Quentin Forsyth, who turned out to be some sort of distant cousin to this man. When he told how his comrade of the galley had been killed, Forsyth heard the account with grave composure. He picked up a fallen branch and began whittling it with a knife he carried at his belt.

'I always kent that my cousin would finish in a fight,' he said. 'He was that kind. But I am glad you and he got free of those damned fetters before the end. I can see him now making the file and keeping it hidden under his bench. Quentin was always a crafty bugger.' He chuckled. 'Wait till I tell my aunt the tale! She'll be proud of the boy. You say he got one of those Spanish gaolers?'

'A minute before the shot killed him. The file went into the man's belly.'

'Good lad! Have another dram, Mr. Stuart. Now, about your business—what brings you two here?'

He listened while Madeleine spoke. He said nothing. Sometimes

105

he frowned, sometimes tugged at his beard. At the end, he made a sound which was half-way between a laugh and a groan.

'A fine pair you are!' he said, lifting the flask to his lips and, while he tilted it, looking at them with round, glistening eyes.

'A hundred miles from Cluny's place, a hundred miles of the wildest country in Scotland, teeming with every kind of life—the wolves won't be the worst! And behind you the hue and cry rising! Don't think you're far ahead of it. News travels fast in these parts, especially when it's news of rewards, plunder—'

'Plunder?' exclaimed Madeleine.

He nodded emphatically.

'Plunder. There are men hereabouts who would slit your ladyship's throat for the saddlery on that horse of yours. And you are carrying jewels, too, or I'm wrong. What's more, you are the most kenspeckle brace of riders in the Highlands. At ten miles' range they will recognise you. Now—must you go to Cluny's?'

He paused for a minute in his task of turning the branch into a short-pointed stick.

Madeleine nodded.

'So be it!' he went on, whittling once more. 'You'll want to know what road to take. If times were not as they are, I would tell you to ride to the loch end. There—' he pointed east, 'and then turn northwards into that glen you can see. Those hills are Macgregor country, a tribe friendly to your family, my lady—and enemies to the rest of mankind, especially to our lord the King! The trouble is that the Macgregors were swept from their lands a year ago. They had the imprudence to unite Argyll, Tullibardine and the King against them. It was hard to do, but they did it, wild cattle that they are. Where they are hiding now, God knows. They are forbidden even to use their own name.'

'Like the Ruthvens,' she put in.

He looked at her sharply.

'What do you know about the Ruthvens, my lady?'

Madeleine raised her eye-brows. 'They are forbidden, too,' she said.

'Your cousin, Quentin, knew Lord Gowrie,' said Jamie.

'Not that ever I heard of,' said Forsyth.

'How do you know that, Jamie?' asked Madeleine.

'He met Gowrie one night in Paris. He told me so.'

'That sounds like the start of another story,' said Forsyth.

'A long one.'

'Just now there is something more urgent than Lord Gowrie to think about. What should you two do now? Here is my advice.

'Go on with all the speed you can muster. You have no time to lose. But the day is hot and will be hotter. Your nags are weary. Look at them. If you go along the loch side that way'—pointing to the west—'you come to a smaller loch. There is an island about the size of a sporran, with a hut on it. The hut is mine. I keep it for the fishing. I'll give you the key and you can take one of the men with you. He'll find food for you. Everything else you need is there.

'The horses? You can tether them at the lochside, although I'm thinking that horses will not be much use for the journey you are going to make. Goats, wild cats—yes; horses—no.'

His ginger beard wagged in amusement.

'Wild cats?' said Stuart, looking up.

'Wild cats. You can find plenty of them on your journey. But if you take my advice, Stuart, you'll keep out of their way.'

'They might be on our side, Forsyth.'

Forsyth made a derisive sound.

'Wild cats fight on one side only, Stuart. Their own. As for horses, it would be best to leave them with Seamus there—' pointing to a young man with raven black hair and deep-set, wild eyes. 'He will go with you if you like. Now! As to the path you should take—when you strike into the glen, follow the road which goes like this. Come and see.' He went down to the water's edge, where there was a crescent of fine white sand on which he began to draw with the stick he had made. 'There is the loch and the hut ...'

He was still talking when someone gave a long whistle. Forsyth and the others looked up. One of the look-out men was waving his hand above his head. Then he made signals with both arms. Forsyth acknowledged them by raising his arm once. The sentry came running towards them.

'A party is coming this way,' said Forsyth, speaking rapidly.

'Horse and foot. More of them than we are. Who they may be, he does not know. But we can take no risks. Take my counsel. Mount and ride. Here is the key to the hut. Give it to Seamus when you have finished. He will go with you on foot. He can run as fast as you will ride. Seamus!'

He kissed Madeleine's hand. 'The Lord Gowrie story must keep for another day,' he said.

He spoke in Gaelic to Seamus. Then he gave his red beard a pull and turned towards his horse. His men were scrambling up the rocky hillside. They were moving fast. Stuart held Madeleine's stirrup while she mounted.

When he looked back three minutes later, Forsyth's party had vanished among the birks and rowans above the loch.

The white hind

Forsyth had not given them a fair picture of the hut on the island. When they reached it they found two thatched, stone-built cottages built at an angle to one another, with a sprinkling of low trees about them. In one of the cottages lived a woman who looked after the place. The other cottage was to be Madeleine's.

Seamus left for the shore as soon as he had rowed them over, refusing Madeleine's invitation to stay. By Forsyth's orders he had been told to see to the horses which would spend the night tethered in a grove of young trees on the shore.

As the afternoon wore on, the heat became oppressive. Cloud-heads of the faintest, most dazzling pink showed for a little above the mountains to the north and died of exhaustion. Jamie tore off his shirt and hose and plunged into the loch. When he came out, Madeleine was sitting beside his clothes.

'What is the water like?' she asked.

'Wonderful, and devilish cold,' he told her.

'Men feel the cold more easily than we do.'

'Try it, then,' he said.

He saw her for a second, poised, slim and small and pale by the water's edge. Then she flashed downwards and he heard the soft explosion as she dived. She was a far stronger swimmer than he. This, he recognised, was a manly sport that had been neglected at M. de Pluvinel's Academy.

When her body was dry and her hair was still glistening as it clung to her head, she put on her shirt and lay beside him under the trees. He turned towards her.

'No,' she whispered. 'No, Jamie. Now we must sleep.'

'Sleep comes later,' he said ...

When the heat began to wear off, he brought a trestle table out and set it up between the cottage and the loch. The housekeeper had roasted a haunch of venison and had opened a bottle of red wine. She served it bashfully and spoke hardly a word.

'She is not sure yet whether you are a man or a girl,' Jamie told Madeleine. 'Who is to blame her? You have the clothes of one and the shape of the other. There should be a law against that.'

'There is. I'm certain that there is.'

'And the penalty? Do you know what it is?'

Frowning, she put his hand from her waist.

'No,' she said, laughing softly.

'Witch,' he said, fingering the gold locket on her breast. 'Let me open it.'

She shook her head.

'In this locket you have hidden the secret of your witchcraft,' he said. 'I see mysterious letters cut into the gold. What are they —Greek? No. Not Greek.'

'Hebrew, I believe.'

'The language they spoke in Eden! So it must have come from Jerusalem. All the way. And inside there is a magic charm— words of power written on vellum. You speak them and a djinn appears, ready to do your will. No wonder the King is afraid of you, Madeleine ... Won't you let me open it?'

She shook her head.

'The King will not be so gentle as I am,' he pointed out.

'What he wants is not hidden here.' She touched the locket. 'It's here, here!' She struck her breast with her fist. Her voice changed. 'Or he thinks it is. And one way or another, he means to stifle it where it hides.'

'What is it, Madeleine? What is the secret? You can tell me. He is going to kill me anyway, remember.'

'Why is he going to kill you, Jamie?' she said in a voice like a little girl's.

'Because he thinks I know it already.'

'Do you? ... Perhaps you do ...' She laughed suddenly. 'And what if neither of us knows? What if there is no secret? Except a secret that walks like a ghost through the imagination of a king?'

After a silence, he spoke in a quiet voice.

'What do you think, Madeleine?'

'We shall exchange our secrets—'

'I have no secrets.'

'—When we arrive at Cluny—*if* we arrive at Cluny,' she said. 'I warn you, the most dangerous part of the journey is still to come. Do you see that cleft in the mountain where snow is still lying in the crevices? How high do you think it is? Three thousand feet at least. A good climb. We must cross that pass in the morning. Beyond, there is the river that Forsyth spoke of. And after that—'

'A hundred miles of tribes that hate you and will cut my heart out if they catch me. You told me that.'

'If we start early, we have a chance—a fair chance—that the alarm will not have been raised from Edinburgh.'

'When we arrive at Cluny—you were about to say something.'

'Was I now, Jamie?'

He leant forward.

'You were going to promise you would tell me the secret then. Weren't you now?'

She rose and ran her fingers through her hair.

'First we must reach there,' she said.

'Come, let us walk round the island ...' There seemed to be laughter in her voice.

Next morning, they woke early. Birdsong. It was hot, hotter than the day before. They had not the heart to leave. So there, on the island, they lost a day.

After a few miles they left the horses with Seamus. He warned them, 'The news of you has reached this country from the south. It was wrong of you to stay where you did. Now I shall not answer for your lives. The people are awake. But go with God.'

Jamie answered, 'The Devil looks after his own.' But he realised that it was not a moment for light talk.

Seamus frowned and said, 'Look after the lady. Bad men are about.'

Jamie was about to give the Highlander money when Madeleine stopped him. 'You are dealing with a gentleman,' she said hurriedly. 'That is not to say he will not steal your purse if he gets the chance.'

'Thank you,' said Jamie. 'Dealing with gentlemen is apt to be a ticklish business.'

After two hours of climbing, they reached a point where the land began to fall away towards the north. All that time they had seen no living soul nor any animals except a small herd of red deer on the mountainside a few hundred feet above them. Until then the sky had been clear and the air oppressive. There was not a breath of wind.

Now, it seemed, a change was coming, one of those drastic transformations in the weather which at those altitudes can come about in a few minutes. From the glances that Madeleine threw towards the skyline on either side, it was obvious that she expected something to happen. By this time, he realised that she was an experienced mountain girl, sure-footed and tireless amongst those sage-green slopes with their outcroppings of orange-coloured rock.

Now that they had passed the crest, before them stretched a tumbled wilderness of stones and heather and rough grass. It was all in rich browns and purples, accented by the silver strokes of birch trees. The light was falling in a steep slant like rain before a moderate wind. Madeleine looked up, scanning the sky.

'Jamie,' she said. 'They are coming after us. Listen.'

She pointed to the east to a crest of jagged rock that ran parallel to the track they were following. He listened but could hear nothing.

'They are not far,' she said. 'And they are coming this way. They have brought dogs with them. Let's hope they do not have friends who will bar our way out of these hills.'

'Damned unlikely,' he said. He thought it the most likely thing in the world.

One magnificent dark cloud soared behind the hills and rode across the sun. The air seemed heavily charged with moisture, clammy on the skin.

They plunged into the dusk of a glen, hardly more than a crack in the surface of the moorland. No one was in sight although Stuart saw signs of habitation around them: two rough fences of undressed tree-trunks running parallel to one another on either side of the glen. He pointed to them and made a gesture with his hands to show that he did not understand the purpose of the structure.

She did not answer and he decided that the barriers were probably used in connection with the driving of cattle. This was all the more likely because the fences seemed to draw more closely together as they came to the lower part of the glen.

By this time Madeleine was showing increasing signs of nervousness. She stopped once or twice, listened, and ran her eye over the ring of hill-crests that surrounded them. It was as if she was hearing noises and trying to locate them.

Stuart could neither hear nor see anything, apart from a herd of red deer which appeared from a corrie where they had been hidden. The deer kept on the move, walking daintily as they approached. This was strange, certainly, although he would not have thought about it had it not been for Madeleine's increasing nervousness.

His ears picked up the sound of dogs baying, somewhere over the hill-crest out of sight. Madeleine signalled to him to get down, to vanish.

They crouched side by side in a dark brown pit where someone, long before, had cut peats. They waited, eyes straining, nerves tingling.

Stuart was the first to see anything. His hand gripped Madeleine's forearm.

'Look!'

On the skyline, half-an-hour's march behind them, a line of heads had appeared. Five of them, scattered on a line some hundreds of yards across. Men with round targes at their shoulders and claymores already drawn in their hands. One of them shouldered an arquebus.

The dogs were nearer now; from the sounds they made, they were hunting animals of some size. The deer kept on the move diagonally across the glen. Soon they would pass between Madeleine and Jamie and the men on the distant crest, who were still coming forward, methodically, unhurried.

The men seemed to be combing the mountain area on some prearranged plan. No doubt there were other searchers. And no doubt the dogs were guiding them.

Jamie looked questioningly at Madeleine but she was not ready to move. It was just as well, he thought, for his bad ankle was beginning to ache. It was amazing that it had stood up to the rough journey as it had. But, very soon, it would be hurting abominably.

From their moss-hag she watched the movements behind them, the deer, the men. Stuart thought he understood. She was waiting until the deer, trotting across the glen in some numbers, would come between them and the pursuers. The animals might hide them from view for a little. The scent might be confused.

Madeleine said, 'Now.'

She rose and began to walk in a light, long-legged, springy gait that was faster than a run. Stuart followed, praying that his bad leg would hold out.

'Go on,' he cried. 'Don't wait for me.'

She stopped and turned back.

'Never mind me,' he said angrily. 'I can look after myself. Damn you, Madeleine, leave me.'

But she put an arm around his waist. 'We'll both be caught,' he said. 'What will be the use of that?'

'Run as fast as you can,' she said. 'It won't be for long.'

'You're damn right,' he said. 'It won't.'

Ahead he could see the ragged crowns of pines, probably the outposts of a forest that would thicken as the ground fell away. Behind, he heard men shouting and dogs, wild with excitement. He did not look back.

The light was fading—fading although it was still before noon —fading—no, it was changing in some extraordinary way. It lived on the hills, transformed into a lucid substance in which colours showed more deeply. Beautiful, beautiful. He would remember it—if given the chance.

The warmth had not gone with the sun. The glen held it in a cup. Sweat, pouring down his brows, stung in his eyes. If he stopped running now, he would never move again, never. The pain that had been building up in his ankle would spring out on him and nail him to the ground.

The sky, now a deep, lurid blue, spread its brilliant light to the mountain summits, so that the greens and yellows and browns were each raised to an unearthly vividness. He had never seen

114

anything of the sort before. Colour had become light and light had become crystalline. It was like living in a prism. As if the earth had become part of a rainbow.

So overwhelmed was he by what he saw during those moments of time that he forgot for a few minutes he was taking part in a hunt—a hunt in which he was one of the hunted.

The red deer, close behind them now, had halted. The wooden barriers on either side of the glen had come closer together and at last he understood their purpose.

His father had once told him about a great hunt in one of the royal forests in the Highlands in the old days. The beaters had driven the deer into a cunningly devised trap—it was called a tinchel, Jamie recalled—which narrowed until a horde of terror-stricken animals—wolves, foxes and hares as well as deer —were driven on to the spears and arrows of the hunters.

'This time they may catch something worth while,' he thought grimly.

They were approaching the throat of the trap.

Madeleine stopped and, as if she had been shot, let go of his arm and fell to the ground.

'Get down, Jamie. Down.'

Ahead, where the lines of fencing had drawn together so that there was only a space of thirty yards between one side of the tinchel and the other, men were drawn up, waiting. They were well provided with firearms, swords and targes. The expression on their faces, the fierce grin, the glittering eye, was the look of hunters, the look that this race of men was born with. He could understand that savage joy, most intense when the quarry is not a beast but a man.

From behind, the beaters approached with their dogs. Between the lines of men were the deer and Madeleine and Jamie.

'We are nicely caught, my darling,' he spoke with his teeth clenched. 'It's a pity you are mixed up in this. I wish I could tell you how to escape.'

She showed him her pistol.

'At least I may take one with me.'

At first glance, the best escape lay on their left where the rough fencing ran along the border of a small wood. But the waiting line of hunters was thrown forward on that flank. Men

115

with firearms stood on the watch. At that moment he caught sight of Madeleine's face. She was gazing backwards with a look of wonder, intensified by the extraordinary light reflected in her eyes from the shining hills. As he looked the look changed to pure, wild triumph.

She clutched her head in her hands and uttered a cry that was almost a scream. He turned to look.

The deer were almost on them now and had broken into a trot which, as he watched, became a loping gallop, a movement of incredible speed and grace. They were heading for the line of men ahead as if driven on to the slaughter by some impulse they could not resist. At that moment, from the dark red mass of the oncoming animals emerged a strange creature, the sight of which made Stuart gasp.

It was a pure white hind, magically lustrous and silvery in that light. A beast of exceptional majesty and grace, outdistancing the leader of the oncoming thunderous torrent of deer. The whiteness seemed to cling like smoke to her flanks.

Now the charging herd was on them. He threw Madeleine to the ground and covered her with his body. He was aware of one animal, then another, leaping over him in the onrush.

There were shouts but, strange to say, nobody fired a shot. When Stuart at last looked, he saw that the hunters who had been waiting in the neck of the trap had broken and were in flight, almost as if that wild onset of the deer had thrown them into confusion.

Or had it been the sight of the white hind, like a visitor from some realm of magic or heraldry?

'Come on,' said Jamie. 'We'll run for it. This is our chance and I'll take it if it kills me.' He pulled her to her feet.

Together they ran forward close behind the galloping deer. Even now the hunters did not fire, as if a spell had been laid on them by the presence of the animal.

Far ahead, she was visible, the mystical light shining on her head as she led the herd downwards in the glen. Soon Stuart was stumbling, half-blinded with sweat, reeling with fatigue and the hurt of his ankle, over the roots of heather of a steep slope covered with twisted oaks.

Scrambling down, with Madeleine before him, he became aware

of new events. Some of the hunters had, it seemed, recovered from their panic. There was a sound of scuffle below him on the slope. Swords clashed.

A man rose from the undergrowth and aimed a musket at Madeleine from a distance of a few yards. He heard the crack of her pistol. The man fell. 'Good girl!' somebody shouted. A few seconds later, he decided that it was himself.

Further on, a man wearing a yellow shirt was at swordplay with one of the hunting party when a second assailant approached him with claymore raised. On an impulse, Jamie struck this second man hard on the jaw. Caught off balance on the steep ground, the swordsmen fell, cursing. Jamie hurried on.

In five minutes, all was quiet about him. Madeleine? There she was, flushed and panting. She still had that wild look in her eyes.

'Did you see her?' she cried. 'Did you see her?'

Suddenly he saw that they were not alone on the hillside.

Silently, four men had risen from the bracken. Each held a pistol, aimed at Stuart. They were as choice a quartet of ruffians as he had ever seen, and as naked. They were dressed in the mountain fashion: deerskin brogues, tied on with leather thongs criss-crossed about their calves. Above that, they were bare to mid-thigh. Then came coarse yellow shirts held at the waist by broad belts. Over that each had draped a plaid. No hat, no bonnet, on a mat of dark-red hair, streaked with a light colour by sun and weather.

He thought they might belong to one family. They had something in common, beside the general likeness of their costume.

'If it's money you're after, lads, you're unlucky,' he said.

But in that he could be wrong. The leather bag hanging inside his shirt contained the best part of a hundred crowns in gold and silver.

The four closed in on Stuart and Madeleine, grinning and apparently much pleased with themselves but keeping their pistols aimed. One of them talked rapidly in Gaelic. Another imitated a curlew's call. A voice some distance above them answered.

Suddenly a young man with a lean and wolfish look wearing a saffron shirt with a tattered plaid kilted round his waist came down the slope. A cruel scar on his face gave him a lopsided distinction which could either be charming or sinister beyond words.

After a minute, Stuart decided that on this occasion the stranger intended to be charming.

'You saved my life,' he said to Jamie, 'when you knocked that rascal down.'

'Oh, it was you, was it? You'll excuse me if I sit down and rest this foot.'

'It was quick work. Thank you. You'll be James Stuart?' he said.

'What makes you think that?'

'News flies fast. We heard yesterday. And this is—'

'Madeleine,' she said.

He bowed politely.

'I—am Alistair MacIan—or as you might say, Alexander, son of John.'

'I like to know the surname of a man I meet,' said Stuart curtly, 'before I start talking about more important matters.'

'We have no family name. That is what the law says—and we are all bound to obey the law. Put your guns away, children,' he said to his four companions.

'I had word from Edinburgh to waylay you, Mr. Stuart, so that you would not return there until you had heard our message. How the word reached me is not so important. I have relations living in that town, some of them well-informed.'

It occurred to Stuart that the rascally caddie, Donald Gregory, might be one of the relations.

'You know a gentleman in Edinburgh named Sinclair?' Alistair continued.

'What if I do?'

'The message comes from him.' The softness left his voice.

'Here is the message, just as it reached me.'

On a scrap of paper were the words: 'This lady your companion is thought to be a mortal enemy of the King—if not worse. You are a murderer. So change your name, dye your hair. And take a ship out of Scotland.'

It had no signature.

Stuart said nothing for a few seconds. He was frowning deeply.

'My name such as it is,' he said, 'is the only valuable my

118

father left me. My hair has been a long time in the family. On ships, I am apt to get into trouble with women. Explain it as you like. What would you do in my place, Alistair MacIan?' he asked.

The eyes of the Highlander glittered. It seemed that he was going to speak but his lips stayed shut.

'Thank you,' Stuart said. 'That's what I think, too. I waited nineteen years before I came to this country. The only country I ever had. I don't mean to leave it so quickly. Besides,' he added, 'I am going with this lady to Cluny.'

The Highlander looked grave.

'Dangerous,' he said. 'Dangerous. You have had one narrow escape, in the glen, up there.'

'It was not an escape, Alistair MacIan,' said Madeleine. 'It was a miracle. We were saved by the white hind.'

'The white hind!'

'She came and our enemies fled.'

Alistair's eyes opened wider.

'You have seen her? Truly seen her?'

Madeleine nodded solemnly. The five Highlanders looked at the pair with something like awe. Jamie noticed that two of them crossed themselves furtively.

'The hand of God is on you,' said Alistair, gravely.

'There might be another explanation,' she said.

He looked at her curiously. Then he turned to Stuart.

'You can't sit there long, Mr. Stuart. We must go fast, surprisingly fast,' he said. 'Those soldiers will not stay away for long. Besides some Lowland gentlemen have the foolish notion that a few poor cattle we have at the hill foot are their lawful property. The mistake is easy to make ... But we who dwell with prejudice all round us must be by-ordinary prudent. There will be a pony for you, my lady.'

'I am used to walking,' she said. 'Mr. Stuart needs the pony more than I do.'

'Very good. Let us be on our way then.'

Duchy in the clouds

Stuart found himself on a floor of grey rock at a point where the slope of a mountain was suddenly broken, making a shelf before resuming its upward climb.

Below him a glen curved towards the north-east, nakedly beautiful in its upper section and running into ragged woods of oak and birch as it fell away. It was quite empty of life. For hours now he had been watching intently and listening for any change in the breathing of the woman who slept behind him ... After the long march, sleep had overwhelmed her.

The scene had a beauty of shape and colour, of variety and emptiness, which affected him with a positively sensual longing, a desire, a lust. Lust? The word had an earthly connotation and his feelings at that moment were aesthetic and spiritual. But it fitted the exaltation the vast panorama of delicately tinted desolation aroused in him.

Here among the rocks and the heather he would carve out a kingdom—or, at least, a duchy—for himself. He wished that Madeleine were awake so that he could tell her what was in his mind. It would stretch from one purple mountain to another and he would fill it with chosen companions of both sexes, for even in his most exalted mood Jamie could not conceive of Arcadia without nymphs. Madeleine for example, would have an important place at this court. And Mary Beaton ... ? For a moment he mused on the girl with the deep blue eyes and the musical laugh ...

Realistically, he conceded that the Arcadians could scarcely live on trout, deer, grouse and water from the burns. What then? They would lay tribute on their plain-bound neighbours down below. Which would hardly be an injustice. In any case he imagined Alistair MacIan was doing much the same thing already. His would be a kingdom among the clouds, nurtured mainly on beauty, concerned mainly with philosophic discourse and refined dalliance. There had been baser political ambitions ...

After several hours, he heard a stirring behind him. Alistair appeared.

'On a very clear day, with the sun in the right place,' he said, 'you can see the Castle Rock of Edinburgh from the top of this hill. That's sixty Scots miles away.'

Sixty miles. Stuart narrowed his eyes, looking in what he supposed to be the right direction. He could see nothing but an endless tumbled sea of peaks. They might have been the mountains of the moon, so remote did they seem, although the colours were more pleasing than anything he could imagine might be found in a lunar landscape.

He heard the whispering noise of a stream down below, so small as to be invisible among the rough grass. The sound was so clear that it might have been murmuring at his feet. He was above the larks, above the hawks, above every living creature— except a solitary great bird—an eagle?—that hung motionless over the scene. He had the uncomfortable feeling the bird was watching him`... A warm purple shadow was beginning to steal across the hollow of the glen.

'They are not likely to find us here,' he said.

'Don't be too certain, James. They know that these hills are a haunt of mine. And they have their own ways of looking for what they want to find. Do you see anybody in the glen below?'

'Not a soul.'

'I have an idea the King's men are not far away.'

Madeleine stirred faintly in her sleep and uttered a little sigh. Jamie leant forward and gently tickled her cheek with a blade of grass. She woke with a start.

'Don't be alarmed,' he said. 'We are safe here. This is an independent duchy which I have established in the mountains. I have appointed Alistair as Lord Warden of the Marches.'

She sat up and shook the sleep from her head.

'I was dreaming just now of the white hind.'

'All those years I have never seen her,' Alistair complained. 'Then you come from God knows where and she shows herself.'

'The white hind is an old story in these hills, Jamie. Let me tell you the legend,' Madeleine said.

'The white hind is seen once every hundred years in the forest. It is called a forest although it has not many trees. Once there were more trees, many more. It was a forest stretching from sea to sea. That was long ago ... Always the hind appears on the eve of some great event. Usually—Scotland being what it is—she appears on the eve of a calamity. She was seen last on the day of Flodden, so they say. As long ago as that.'

'Flodden,' said Jamie lightly. 'My great-grandfather was killed at Flodden.'

'And mine,' said Madeleine.

'And mine,' said Alistair.

'A calamity!' said Jamie. 'But yesterday the white hind saved us.'

'There is another legend,' said Alistair, after a pause. 'The white hind is believed to have her favourites—people she protects.'

'All ignorance and superstition,' Madeleine said.

'Who can be sure, my lady?'

'Speaking as one who is much in need of protection,' laughed Jamie, 'I am inclined to believe that part of the superstition.'

'My children believe it,' said Alistair. 'They look on you both as favourites.'

Jamie laughed again and shook his head.

'You are a warlock, Jamie,' said Madeleine.

'The hand of God may be on you,' Alistair spoke gravely.

'And, as you know, I am a witch,' she said.

Pushing back a lock of hair from his forehead, Alistair turned away, frowning. He did not like to hear flippant talk about a serious subject.

Madeleine followed him with her eyes.

'A savage,' she whispered. 'A barbarian. And so handsome.'

Jamie looked at her in astonishment. A face twisted like that! Women had curious ideas.

Alistair was already on his way down the slope. Soon he was hidden by an angle of the rock.

Madeleine turned to Jamie.

'Many people will think like that about you, that the hand of God is on you. Others will think differently.'

'What do *you* think, Madeleine? Am I a warlock?'

She looked at him intently for a moment.

'I don't see the hand of God on you. No. What do I think? That you're a lightminded man used to getting your own way too easily. Morals you may have, but you keep them under control. Where you are bound for in this life is a question you think can be answered later on the road. Luck you have had and count on having more of. You will probably need it. The Devil's luck. But a warlock?—no, James.'

'You have been studying me carefully,' he said, astonished by the directness and energy of her attack.

She laughed.

'You are so easy to read, Jamie. If only you knew!'

'You talk about morals. What about your own?' He was angry now. 'Why are you going to Cluny to marry an old man you don't love?'

'For one thing, I shall then be able to defy the King. Oh, how I look forward to my first audience at Holyrood when I make my curtsey to the viper!'

'Yes,' he agreed. 'You'll carry that scene off well.'

'By that time, I shall be the richest woman in Scotland north of the Forth.'

He said nothing. He had no right to feel bitter.

'Land means money, power, fighting men,' she said. 'Revenge will be sweet!'

'Revenge? For what?'

'For what?' she cried. 'For the murder of the man I loved!'

'Loved?' he said.

'Yes, *loved*!' She drew her shoulders together in a gesture which he might have thought affected if he had not known her. 'In any case,' she went on, her mood changing again, 'love is a word with many shades of meaning, James. One chooses the shade that suits one's complexion. But I am telling this to you, a Frenchman!'

'*L'amour!*'

'As you speak it now, it is already different from love ... James

Stuart! You don't bear that name by chance. You have the family failings if not the family rights.'

'What do you know about my family?'

'I have only to look at you to see what tree you're a branch of. I told Rory that when I first clapped eyes on you on the Shore of Leith. A Stuart! By looks, name and nature!'

'Nature?' he asked.

'Yes. We women are your weakness and maybe your strength. Whether you mean to or not, you'll aye seek fortune by way of a skirt. It's born in you. You can't help it. But look out, Jamie! One of us may give you a heavy fall some day.'

'You, for instance?' he asked.

'No, not me.' For a moment he thought he heard a tinge of regret in her voice. It was an absurd fancy. 'I'm too kind.'

'Kind! What about the red-haired girl in Edinburgh—whipped three times round the yard and thrown naked into the street? What about her?'

She answered in a voice of childlike coolness.

'She'll come back on her knees—begging to be let in. What do you think?'

He thought she was a devil. Ill to cross. Cruel. A witch, with all the other strains of wickedness he could sense. Why did he long for her so much? ... Because her wickedness appealed to his?

Watching the play of mockery and malice on the small, pale face under the darkly gleaming curls, the frown that stayed while the smiles came and went, Jamie found her tempting beyond words.

Holding her chin between the thumb and fingers of one hand, he began with the other to caress her shoulder. His fingers touched fine metal links. The locket. Oval, slim, with its strange incisions. If he opened it—as she was daring him to do—what would he find? A lock of gleaming hair? A portrait?

He was nettled by the description of himself she had given. No doubt he should be flattered that she had spent so much time analysing his character, but the verdict was hardly pleasing. Stripped of all the trimmings, it meant he was a man who lived on women.

'You have painted the perfect picture of a scoundrel,' he said.

She laughed.

'Oh! Our feelings are hurt!'
He silenced her laughter with a rough kiss.

It was a long time, and darkness was approaching, before Alistair came into view again, climbing the mountainside with his tireless lope. Jamie could tell at once, from the exultant glint in his eyes, that the news was bad.

'Well?'

'Terrible,' said Alistair cheerfully. 'The people to the north of us here have been warned that we may be coming this way. They have put a watch on the river crossings. Not that it is much of a river: broad, but very shallow. And the two villages at each end of the big glen are on the alert. These are enemies of my people, Lord Orkney's vassals. It will be a pleasure to maltreat them.

'We shall hear more news before many hours have passed. Understand, James. This is my country. I have eyes everywhere. When other people are in darkness, we will be able to see. So stay here if you will. There is a place for you in the driest cave in Breadalbane. And the lady can sleep comfortably in an old shieling nearby. The building has the magic quality of being invisible from any place below. And one of us can be sentry at the door. It could be you, James.'

Stuart could not be sure whether, at that moment, Alistair's eye was affected by a momentary nervous twitch.

'By tomorrow, we should know more about the enemy's dispositions. I shall send a man out. Then perhaps we can plan a safe way for your journey.'

Jamie woke before the first light. Outside, a murmur of men's voices. He sat up. Alistair and one of his clansmen were talking, their heads close together. He rose and went towards them, shivering in the morning air.

'More news,' said Alistair.

'Good or bad?'

'Bad,' Alistair grinned. 'How bad I cannot tell yet. Rob here went down to an old hunting tower which rightfully belongs to our people. After a while he heard a body of horse coming on the roads. There was a moon just then, so he crept close to

125

the road where there is a spinney and he saw them pass. Forty of them. Forty! Soldiers. He could see the light on cuirasses and steel bonnets. At the head rode a tall man in a dark riding cloak. A madman.'

'You're sure?'

'What do you think! Do you know what he was doing? Talking to a cat.'

'A cat?'

'A cat, curled up on his saddle-bow. What do you make of that, man?'

'That was Lord Orkney. What the devil brings him to these parts?'

In a few sentences, he told Alistair about his dealings with Orkney and Kennedy. The Highlander gave a low whistle.

'In that case, boy, you are threatened by one of the worst men in Scotland and one of the craftiest. You have an adversary worthy of your talent.'

'What do we do?'

'First, we find out where he means to quarter his men. No doubt he will string out a cordon along the roads so that you can't break through to the north. And he will make use of the local clans in the rough country where horsemen can't go. They will sweep you into his net. But wait and see! There will be a weak link somewhere in his chain. We shall find it.'

He gave a curlew's cry. A man rose out of the darkness.

Alistair talked with him in Gaelic for some time. Somewhere in the course of their discussion, Madeleine appeared. She had pulled a plaid round her shoulders.

'What is it?' she asked, in a whisper.

'More misfortune,' he told her. 'Orkney has arrived with forty of his soldiers. He is a few miles away on the lower ground to the north.'

'So the King enlists the Devil on his side!'

'How do you know Orkney acts for the King?' asked Alistair.

'Because only the King knows that I plan to wed Cluny,' said Madeleine, smiling.

'What is certain is that he is here,' said Jamie. 'You must flee with Alistair, if he'll take you. He knows the way and the hiding places. I do not. Besides my ankle will slow me down.'

'And you will stay and be taken by Orkney?'

'You haven't much faith in me, have you! The man the white hind saved! No. I shall stay on the hills. I shall learn Gaelic and wear a saffron shirt. Alistair will find me a cave somewhere and when Orkney has gone, I shall join Alistair's band of brigands. The future is not too grim.'

'Except that you promised to go with me to Cluny and you are a man of your word, Jamie.'

'Damn it!' he cried in exasperation. 'Haven't I told you that your chance of reaching Cluny with me is *microscopic*! To stay with me is to risk capture at the hands of Orkney and torture, even death at the hands of the King. You've told me so yourself!'

'First, he must catch you!' said Alistair.

'He must do more than that,' she told him. 'He must hand me over alive. It may not be so easy.' There was something in her voice that made both men look at her sharply.

Light was washing back into the sky. The lesser stars were dying. Some colour could already be seen on the rocks.

Two clansmen were vanishing downhill into the shadows of the valley. Jamie decided that they had probably been sent by Alistair to find out where Orkney had quartered his horsemen. Soon afterwards another scout left them, climbing the shoulder of the mountain behind, going westwards. There was a deep glen on the far side into which Orkney might send one of his search parties.

The sun caught the wings of a great bird that hung almost motionless over the scene. The wings flashed gold. Jamie pointed.

'He is very patient. What is his name?'

'That's a golden eagle.'

'I wish I had brought my white falcon,' said Madeleine. 'This is the place for him!'

'Do you hawk?' asked Alistair. 'There are plenty of fine hunting birds kept in the cottages below us. You should see them. But now I'll fetch my bow and see if I can find any game for dinner.'

'Bow?' Jamie was astonished.

Alistair grinned.

'An arrow makes less noise than a shot. And noise travels far in these glens. Come on, Jamie. There is a bow for you.'

'No. I'll stay here.'

'Didn't they teach you archery when you were at school?'

'They did, but—'

'Come on. Madeleine will stay here and help with the next meal. It may be our last for some time.'

'Madeleine will put on some clothes,' she said.

Ten minutes later, when they were alone on a stretch of moorland where hares were plentiful, Alistair spoke abruptly to Jamie.

'Today I don't trust you out of my sight. You will go off on your own and God knows what will happen to you.'

Thirty yards from them a hare started, stopped, and started again. Alistair took aim but Jamie's shaft was first to fly. It struck the animal behind the ear. It lay suddenly still.

'By God,' said Alistair, admiringly. 'You didn't waste your time in Paris, after all!'

Jamie gave a sheepish smile. It was a fluke.

Fortress of an anarch

After a while, Alistair sighted a stag in a small corrie a few hundred feet above them. They made a long detour so that the wind, which was light and changeable, would not betray them. Even so an hour was spent in crawling silently from rock to rock before at last Alistair was in position to shoot. The stag ran a few paces and then crumpled.

'Now we must go back and fetch a pony to carry this one,' said Alistair.

They were now in a wilderness where there was no sign of a living creature. But Alistair set out confidently for home with nothing to indicate which was the way back to their starting point.

It was mid-afternoon when they climbed the last steep ascent and, within earshot of their eyrie, Alistair gave the curlew's cry. There was no answer. A few minutes later they were back at the entrance to the cave. No one was in sight. There was no sign that anything unusual had happened. Alistair set about skinning and cleaning the smaller beasts they had killed. Jamie stayed on watch.

After half an hour he called out, 'Somebody moving down there! Look!'

Alistair paused, knife in hand, hare's blood to the wrists.

'You're right. It is Dugald helping Fergus. The boy seems to be hurt. I'll bring the pony. But where the devil is Lady Madeleine?'

'What has happened?' Jamie was alarmed.

They scrambled downhill towards the two. Alistair dragged the pony after him. As they came nearer, the unhurt one shouted in Gaelic. Alistair replied. He turned to Jamie. 'She has gone. I don't understand it yet. Fergus is badly hurt. Look at his colour, will you! See the way he is staggering.'

When they met on a stretch of boggy ground near the hollow of the glen, Alistair and Dugald exchanged volleys of words. Then Alistair turned to Jamie.

'A damnable folly! The girl has been carried off.'

At that point the injured man swayed and fell to the ground, his face the colour of whey.

'Take his head, Dugald!'

He let go with a volley of Gaelic curses. Then he continued. 'I'll tell you as we carry him up.'

'This is what happened as far as I know. My lady and Fergus went together to a cottage along the glen in search of eggs and milk. They found nothing there. Fergus was for turning back. But the girl would not. And she prevailed.'

'I am not surprised,' said Jamie.

'There is another cottage a mile or two further off. They were told that there might be food in it. What they were not told was that the people who lived there were servants of Lord Tullibardine. When they reached it, Fergus sensed danger.

'I think that someone there, the man of the place maybe, sent word to a patrol of Orkney's lurking nearby. Meanwhile he kept Madeleine busy with talk about a kestrel he had, a hunting bird of the best quality which he meant for his master. She must at all costs be taken to see it in the outhouse where he kept it. So she went. And that wasted more time. All this while Fergus was on guard.

'But in the end he could do nothing. He saw mounted men coming. But they had arrived before he could warn Madeleine. He used the claymore. Dugald found it close to where he was lying. But a crack on the head with the butt of an arquebus did his business.'

'And Madeleine—what about her?'

'Vanished. Carried off. Kidnapped. How do I know what happened to her!'

'Good God! She's in Orkney's hands!'

A wave of black hatred swept over him, mingled with another emotion which he could not identify. Jealousy? Distrust of

Madeleine? Fury with himself for having failed in his mission?

By the time they reached the camping place, the other scouts were already there. They all had the same story to tell. Orkney's outposts had melted away. Alistair explained it to Jamie while they both sat on the rocks outside the cave.

'They have gone further north, along a difficult mountain track through devilish country. You may think, James, that it is hard living round here. Let me tell you, this is paradise compared with what lies further on.'

'Whither do you think he is heading?'

Alistair shook his head morosely.

'To read Orkney's mind a man would have to be the Devil himself. I'll send a man on his heels, one of the best trackers in the Highlands. He'll leave us a sign at each fork of the road which way to follow. Not that Orkney has much choice of roads before him. To the west is Campbell country, while if he goes too far in that direction'—throwing an arm out to the east—'he will come into Atholl lands.'

'And Atholl is an enemy of his, do you say?'

The Highlander gave a derisive laugh.

'Everybody is an enemy of his although some are too frightened to show it. When Atholl hears, as he is sure to do, that Orkney has a prisoner worth a good ransom, he will be all the more eager to waylay his troop. So Orkney will waste no time admiring the scenery. At this moment if I'm not mistaken his riders will be urging their horses on the road to the north—and a damned rough road it is, infested with MacDiarmids, Macphersons and God only knows whom else.'

'But where will he be going, do you think?'

'At a guess—only a guess—' He spread his hands expressively and hesitated a moment before speaking.

'Home,' he said at last.

'Home?'

'Just that. Lord Orkney has a stronghold lying in a river valley between terrible high mountains. It will be two—close on three days' march from here although if we were eagles, Jamie, we might reach the place in an hour or so. I think he'll go there.'

James rose and began walking to and fro, his hands clasped behind his back.

'Can you lend me a man to take a letter to Edinburgh—fast?'

'I can lend you the man who brought me the message from Sinclair two days ago.'

'Good. Now, if you please, let me have paper, a horn of ink, a pen and sealing wax. I will write to Sinclair asking for his help.'

'At your grace's pleasure,' said Alistair, with an ironical bow. He brought the writing materials from the cottage. 'And now you'll excuse me,' he said. 'The gentleman who'll be doing your business in Edinburgh is making ready for the journey now. He'll be on hand in a little.'

'I'll be ready,' said Jamie. 'What is the name of this place of Orkney's?'

'Castle Roy. Tell them it's where the Nethy runs into the Spey. That's a hell of a long way from Edinburgh, boy. And now,' he continued, 'I have private matters to attend to.'

'Meaning?'

'It will be necessary to burn down the cottage of that man who betrayed us to Orkney. The law is the law, Jamie. Also to carry off his beasts, if he has been stupid enough to leave any at the steading. But I don't suppose he has.'

'What about Fergus?'

'The boy will be ready to move when we are.'

'After that crack?'

'He has the skull of an ox and the brains of one.'

Jamie shrugged and went back to his writing. His spelling of this language was shaky but he thought that Sinclair would understand the simple message he was sending.

The scent of the pines was everywhere as Jamie worked his way cautiously forward over the bone-dry carpet of needles. For three days they had travelled northwards, picking their way carefully through lonely glens and across desolate moorland. His leg healed well, despite the rough going. The mountains grew wilder, the glens emptier as they went. Now, suddenly, they had come to a country of forests and a wide river valley. He and

Alistair were scouting ahead of the others. They were near the end of their journey.

The trees, which were tall and of great age, clutched the ground with roots like the claws of heraldic birds of prey. At last, from the sudden increase of light ahead of him, he judged that he had come to the summit of the crag he had been climbing for half an hour. He lifted his head, swept the vista with a swift, circular gaze. Then he turned and gave an onward jerk of the chin which Alistair, crawling at some yards' distance behind him, saw and obeyed.

'That's it,' whispered the Highlander a minute later. 'That's surely it. God, man, that will be a hard nut to crack!'

On the far side of an urgent stream a golden castle rose before them in the early morning sunshine. Built on a rocky outcrop above a noisy water, it seemed to have grown out of the primal substance of the land, made from the same stone, hewn in heavy blocks and closely morticed together, covered with the same lichens as the crag on which it stood. It was as if it had stood there above the stream from the dawn of time.

Yet it was a work of thought and cunning. A presiding intelligence had ordered it. Craftsmen had made it. It had consequence and style, asserting affluence and power as emphatically as a fist.

Looking down at it through the branches of the seedling pines in front of him, Jamie saw a curtain wall, on an irregular five-sided plan topped by a corbelled walk. He counted five towers of different sizes and shapes joined to one another by the wall. All of the towers but one were capped by steep roofs of heavy yellowship slates. The fifth tower, the tallest of the five, was round and surmounted by a platform, from which rose a flag-staff bearing a gold and scarlet standard of intricate heraldic design.

Inside the walls were buildings in a more sophisticated style. Delicately moulded stonework appeared round their windows, which were protected by heavy cages of ironwork. There would, he judged, be room in that fortified enclosure for a few score people.

Jamie recalled something his father had told him about the way the aristocracy lived in this country, the style, the pride, the insolence—'Like little kings, my boy, each answerable to God alone for what goes on in his lands, and heaven help the man who thinks of interfering! A cruel, tyrannous crew. But what a life!'

Here on a bluff above the tawny river, stood a building which was unmistakably the fortress of an anarch, the palace of a little king.

Suddenly Jamie put his head down. On the walk above the curtain wall of the castle a figure had appeared. A man with an arquebus on his shoulder. A sentry going his round.

After counting fifty, Jamie looked up again. The man had passed on.

Alistair tugged at his elbow and nodded towards the right. Then he began to crawl backwards. Thirty yards away there was a spot where the outcrop of rock they had reached approached nearer to the castle. From there, they would get a better survey from a different angle.

They had a sidelong view of the main entrance to the castle —the drawbridge which was up, the portcullis which was down, the stone gallery above it from which an assault party could be met with a hail of missiles. Jamie could see only one man on guard. There were undoubtedly more of them not far away, under cover, ready to be summoned.

The two lay quietly there for some time watching Lord Orkney's stronghold, listening to the sounds from across the stream. It was extraordinary to Jamie how sharp his vision was in that clear upland air, and how easily he heard, for instance, a horse stamping with its hoof on a stable floor, the whistling of the sentry on his beat, and somewhere, hens.

Rescuing Madeleine from such a fortress would not be easy.

They crawled back to the rest of their party and made a bivouac a mile away, in deep woods. There they could easily avoid Orkney's patrols, who would be scouring the countryside for them.

For two days he and Alistair took turns watching the castle and trying to discover some means of piercing its defences ...

One morning while they lay side by side on the crag above the river, Jamie heard a thin, squealing sound like a wheel that needed oiling. The drawbridge was coming down. It all happened very quickly. The bridge was not even allowed to touch the ground before it was lifted upwards again. In those few seconds a figure ran across and leapt gracefully from it. A dark-haired young woman wearing a dress of faded scarlet.

'She could tell us something about what goes on inside,' said Alistair under his breath.

'That's what I was thinking myself,' said Jamie.

'The trouble is, man, that she won't talk.'

'What makes you so sure of that?'

'Because Orkney would cut out her tongue!' said Alistair.

They watched the young woman as she ran lightly down to the water's edge and began to cross by a line of flat stones which just reached the surface of the stream. In a few moments she had reached the river bank immediately below the rocks where the two young men lay.

Jamie began to push himself backwards on the ground.

'Where the devil are you off to?' Alistair's voice rose in alarm.

'To see whether she will talk or not,' Jamie answered with a grin.

'You damned fool!' said Alistair. 'I'll bet she doesn't.'

'We'll see. Be with you later on, Alistair MacIan.'

Rising to his feet, he slipped noiselessly through the trees. Sooner or later, her path would cross his. By that time he might have a story to tell that would hold her attention.

Moving through a grove of young birches, he could still see no sign of his quarry. Then somewhere close by there was a cracking of branches. Someone was walking in the wood. He moved cautiously towards the sound and two minutes later emerged on a path which ran diagonally across his. He sat down and took off his left boot. When he caught sight of a red skirt out of the corner of one eye, he uttered a groan or two. Then he fell over as if pain had overcome him and lay still.

When he opened his eyes again, she was standing beside him, silent, wide-eyed, suspicious but not alarmed, ready to run.

The look of extreme agony which he had assumed died on his face, to be replaced by a slow smile. The young woman in the red skirt was comely—she was more, she was damnably attractive. Better still, the suspicion in her face faded slowly, replaced by a dreamy, reflective gaze in which there lurked, not too far away, the ghost of a smile.

She was a thought too broad in the cheeks for beauty and was stained a gypsy brown by the wind and the sun. Her hair, glowing with reddish tints where it was exposed to the light, had not seen a comb for weeks. Her legs had large splashes of darker colour—mud? He thought so and was surprised that he did not find it disagreeable. They were shapely legs, slender-boned and not over-covered with flesh. He thought that her eyes were black but they were so large and luminous he could not be sure.

She spoke first—a question in Gaelic. When he shook his head, she said in English, 'Are you hurt, man?'

He pointed to his ankle and began to unwind the dirty bandage round it. She came a step nearer.

'It looks worse than it is,' he said, and was gratified by a little intake of breath with which she greeted the livid scar that the galley-chain had left. 'Don't look at it if it upsets you.'

'How did you come by it?'

'This is a cruel world. I'll say no more. What is your name, beautiful?'

'Margaret.'

'A cruel world, Margaret. Men suffer for their crimes and sometimes for their beliefs.'

'And which of them do you suffer for, sir?'

'Which do you think? Tell me. Speak frankly. Do I seem to you the criminal kind, Margaret?'

Her eyes did not leave his. She frowned, then her smile widened.

'Yes,' she said, 'you do. There are crimes I would not put past you.'

'Such as?'

'I can think of one or two.'

'If it's a crime to find you a good-looking girl, then I'm the blackest criminal in Scotland.'

'Don't talk such nonsense!'

'It isn't nonsense and it isn't a crime, either, Maggie. Can I call you Maggie?'

'Others call me Meg.'

'Then I'll call you Maggie and you will call me Jamie.'

'If you don't mind, I'll call you James. I once knew a laddie called Jamie. I didn't like him.'

'Then James it shall be.'

'Why have you come to this part, James?'

'I am looking for cousins of mine who may live hereabouts. Maybe I'll find them in that castle and maybe I won't. But this is a family secret I'm telling you. You'll keep it, won't you?'

'If you want me to. But what about your ankle, James?' She got down on her knees to see it.

'Much better.'

'It looks bad.'

'Then don't look at it.' He took her chin in his hand. 'Forget it and look into my eyes. So! By God, your eyes, Maggie!'

'What of them, James?'

'Don't move. Keep your hand there—so. Please. I could have sworn they were black, but—'

'What are they?'

'Deep, dark blue. Marvellous!'

'Blue?'

'Did nobody tell you? Then my day is not wasted. I have proclaimed an important truth.'

She looked at him doubtfully. He could see that in a moment she would tell him not to be daft. There was only one way of preventing that. He found to his pleasure that Maggie responded to his kiss with enthusiasm. In fact, it was he who drew back first.

She looked at him severely.

'It's sinful to kiss anybody like that,' she said.

'Then I've been committing sins all my life without knowing it. But show me a virtuous way. I'm willing to learn.'

She shook her head.

'No. Let me go, James. No more nonsense. I have to fetch milk from the dairy for the lady we have in the castle.'

'Oh, there's a lady in the castle is there. Young?'

'Young.'

'Beautiful?'

'Aye. Bonny.'

'Why does she want to drink milk? To put on weight?'

'Drink!' she said, with a toss of her head. 'She doesn't drink it. No. Her ladyship washes in it. Did you ever hear! They say it's good for the skin, though.'

'Washes in it! What is so delicate a lady doing in these parts?'

'You may ask! She's here because she must be.'

'Ah! She is married to the man who lives in the castle?'

'Married? Not she! She is there because Lord Orkney keeps her prisoner there. In the lady's rooms of the palace which belongs by rights to Lady Orkney, poor woman. There with a sentry on guard at the door to see she does not get out. No one can see her, no one but me. I take her food—'

'And milk.'

She nodded.

'And I do her laundry.'

'And this poor girl is moping in her cell?'

'Moping! You wouldn't say that if you saw her! She has told Orkney she'll live to see him hanged. He would like them to marry, although he has a wife already. But the lady won't.'

'Maybe he'll kill her.'

Maggie shook her head.

'Orkney has a cat,' she said. 'A witch cat. He does what the cat tells him to do. And the cat will not let him lay a finger on the lady.'

'You mean, the lady and the cat are—?'

Maggie nodded vehemently.

'Yes. Both of them witches. Cat and lady alike. And the lady is a queen among the witches. That's my belief.'

She looked with wide, dark eyes into his frowning gaze.

'Now it's time for me to go—' she said.

'One more kiss.'

'Your kisses take too long.'

'Then you shall say, Stop, when you are ready.'

'If only I could, James! If only I—'

It turned out that she could not.

The first law of war

The firelight shuddered on the faces of the young men who sat on the rocks under the tall trees. When James Stuart brought his narrative to an end, a sigh ran round the circle.

He said, 'So, as I tell you, there is a way of sending messages into the castle. And more than a message maybe.'

'If only we can find someone who will open the way to us,' Alistair pointed out.

'If only we can find a judy who will open—'

Somebody laughed.

'What's important now,' said Stuart, 'is that tomorrow I will see the lassie again when she goes to fetch the milk. By that time, Madeleine will have had my message—'

'If the lassie is true to you!' said Alistair gloomily. 'Women are the devil.'

'She talked,' Jamie pointed out. 'You didn't think she would. But she did.'

'Women are the devil,' Alistair repeated.

'True enough. But I'm on the Devil's side, remember. I've sent word to Madeleine by the girl. I've told her that the King of Elfland is knocking at the door. She'll know what that means.'

'And then? What happens?'

'Then—how do I know? But Madeleine is not the girl to let others do all the work.'

He looked round at the ring of faces shining in the flame-light. They were thoughtful and excited. Somebody said a few words in Gaelic. Somebody else laughed. Alistair frowned. Jamie looked a question at him.

139

'Ian was forgetting himself for a moment,' said Alistair gently. 'He said that somebody was a wild cat. Now, who would that be, do you think?'

'Do wild cats wash in milk?' asked Jamie.

'They drink blood,' said Alistair.

'H'sh.'

A finger was raised. Silence. Then, small but clear the cry of a curlew rose from below through the trees.

A Highlander rose to his feet, holding out before the fire a plaid sodden in water from the river. Soundless and swift as startled animals, the others moved into the postures from which they could be on their feet in an instant.

The curlew's cry again.

'Douse!' said Alistair.

The plaid fell on the fire. Jamie blinked in the sudden darkness, and choked back the irritation of the wood smoke.

Alistair laid a hand on his arm.

'Don't move,' he ordered. 'My children will tell us what it is.'

Jamie thought he could hear in the distance horses' hoofs on a hard soil. So far as he could judge, the sound came from a level below them.

'That will be people coming from the south,' Alistair said softly. 'Two horsemen, maybe three. They will be friends of Orkney's riding to the castle.'

'Or they will be friends of mine coming from Edinburgh,' said Jamie.

Alistair made a sound of disapproval with his tongue.

'In that case, the gentlemen are taking risks. Yes, dear God! Think if they slipped past our outposts and fell into Orkney's hands! What a misfortune!'

He continued in Gaelic, speaking urgently into the darkness. Jamie was aware, from slight noises among the trees, that the Highlanders had stolen away in the direction of the riders.

'I have told my people to be careful not to harm the strangers when they accost them.'

'If it is the man I expect,' said Jamie, 'they had better be careful for themselves. He has had some experience of sallies at night. I expect he will first try to find the Castle.'

'We shall try to save your friend the trouble of going so far.

If only he behaves with prudence!'

'And if only he is my friend.'

'Listen, man! Do you hear that?'

The sound of horses' hoofs could be heard no longer.

'Now we shall soon know,' said Alistair. 'One way or the other. Let us hope that nobody jumps to conclusions. Dark or no dark, Dugald is a dead shot with that gun of his.'

'Do I hear voices?'

'Yes. There is a parley. Do your friends speak the language?'

'God knows.'

'It would help. There would be less danger of a misunderstanding.'

They listened in silence for a minute or two. Then Alistair's hand fell on Jamie's wrist.

'They are coming, whoever they are,' he said. 'I shall go forward now. You stay here, James. Be ready to whip the blanket off the fire when you hear us give the cry.'

The signal came five minutes later. Jamie pulled the scorched blanket aside and kicked the fire into life. A flame shot up, making wild shadows of the trees. He heard someone come towards him over the pine needles with a heavy tread. He put a hand to his sword, then let it fall.

'Captain Sinclair!'

Ruddier in the face, blonder in the beard, huger in the body than before, with his vast knuckles on his hips and a broad grin on his lips—there stood the captain in the service of His Royal Majesty the King of the Swedes, Goths, Vandals, etc.

'At your service!' He swept off his hat with a creditable flourish.

'The devil!' said Jamie. 'It's you. But where's your army?'

'I might ask, where's your war? But all in good time, Stuart. My army—since you have the bad taste to mention it—is not yet in a battleworthy state. In fact, I was forced to return one recruit to the gaol from which he had escaped—if escaped is the word. So I came here without the main body, by forced marches. But not alone. Look!'

Sinclair gestured behind him with his hat. Stuart saw, coming into the firelight, a sordid, villainous and familiar figure.

'Gregory!'

141

The caddie smirked and cringed.

'You know my cousin, I believe,' said Alistair, coming out of the darkness.

'Cousin! By God. I knew there was somebody you reminded me of,' said Jamie.

'No doubt a calamity as a human being,' said Captain Sinclair, 'but as a guide and interpreter in these parts, Gregory is a man beyond price—I brought him along and three men like him.'

'Have a dram, Captain.'

'Your health, Alistair MacIan!' He threw his head back and gasped. 'By God, this is the real water of life! Aquavitty as it should be! Now about this war of yours—'

'Sit down and we'll talk,' said Alistair.

'Who begins?' said Sinclair.

'I always begin,' said Jamie.

At the end of Stuart's narrative, Sinclair cleared his throat. 'Bathing in milk,' he said. 'They used to accuse the King's mother of the habit. I always supposed it was an invention of her enemies, poor soul.' He paused, considering, then went on abruptly.

'The important thing is that now we have a friend in the enemy camp. The story with Maggie reminds me of that red-haired lassie in the Edinburgh tavern. She has an unnatural liking for you, Stuart. God kens why. I used every kind of argument on her but nothing would cure the woman.'

'The plain innocence of my mind,' said Jamie. 'Pass me the flask, Captain.'

'So in the morning you'll meet the wench again and, with luck, we'll ken better then what we should do. There's one strategic problem, though, that plagues my mind.'

'What's that?'

Sinclair leant forward so that his face hung above the fire, enormous and crimson.

'It's this, gentlemen. Orkney may decide to leave the castle and take the girl with him to Kirkwall in Orkney. He has a stronghold there that would be ten times harder to take than this one.'

'It would be like him, the cunning knave,' said Jamie.

'First he must get to Kirkwall,' Alistair pointed out.

'That would not be so hard. A day's march to the north are the harbours on the Moray Firth. From one of them he can take a ship and if the wind is right be in Kirkwall a day after or thereabouts. Kirkwall, his own town, which he would like to make the capital of an earldom under Denmark or Scotland or better still under neither! That's the story they tell of him in Edinburgh. Believe it if you like.'

'So?' Stuart asked.

'We must be sure his lordship stays where he is until we are ready to open the cage door and let the bird go free. How to do it? There are ways ...

'The King wants both Jamie Stuart and the Bannerman girl. He will be willing to give Orkney a good price for them. Whether he pays it when the time comes—that is another matter. We can leave it to those two rogues to settle between them. But Orkney's position in this business is not just the same as His Majesty's. He wants the girl for himself, if he can have her! If he can't then he'll hand her over to the King. But the Bannermans and their relations are not the forgiving kind! So Orkney may hover a blink. But Jamie Stuart—that's a different matter. He has no friends in high places. Nobody kens the lad but ourselves who are here. There's something else, too.

'Lord Orkney's pride has been hurt. Madeleine spurned him, yet rode off with Jamie. So Orkney wants to string the boy up.'

'Or starve him to death in a dungeon,' said Stuart grimly.

Sinclair nodded vigorously.

'Very likely. So what should we do? This I say. Write a letter to Orkney proposing to the noble earl to hand Jamie over to him at a price. What about that? We'll leave the letter with the porter at the castle gate. Then see what happens.

'Orkney will answer. That's sure. And we will talk and talk about the price he is to pay—talk until we are ready to break into his house. And while this is going on, Orkney will hold the girl where she is.'

'Orkney will do something else,' said Alistair, after a pause. 'One day he will find our camp. Then he'll come down on us with ten men for every one of ours.'

Sinclair glanced at him impatiently.

'We'll give him other things to think about. Oh, we'll keep

143

my lord's mind fully occupied, believe me.'

'One thing more,' said Alistair. 'How do we deliver the letter?'

'I'll take it to the castle,' said Gregory.

'No,' said Alistair thoughtfully. 'I have a better notion.'

He rose and walked to a tree nearby against which his bow was leaning. He picked it up and bent it. Then he fitted an arrow aimed and let go. The arrow struck a tree trunk not a foot from Jamie's head. And hung there quivering.

'You could have killed me,' said Jamie, indignantly.

'When I kill you, James,' he said, cheerfully, 'you won't know it.'

'Damn you, Alistair MacIan.'

'It was in my mind that I might shoot the letter into the castle with this,' he said, pulling his arrow out of the tree-trunk.

'But first the letter must be written,' said Sinclair. 'Paper! Paper, pen and ink! Who among us can write a fair hand?'

'M. de Pluvinel thought that mine was most gentlemanlike,' said Jamie.

Sinclair made sounds of contempt.

'You'll write like a Frenchman and spell like one. Orkney might miss the point. Alistair MacIan—you?'

Alistair frowned and shook his head.

'I have no practice in the Sassenach.'

'I'll do it myself,' said Sinclair. 'I'll see if I can draw the fox.'

'Donald,' said Jamie to the caddie. 'A word in your ear.' They rose and moved out of the circle of light.

'My Lord Orkney is a man who likes cats. Remember? The time has come when we may be able to please his lordship's fancy.'

'Indeed, my lord, indeed. We are in the cat country now, you might say. There should be no difficulty. I'll ask some questions among my friends.'

Gregory moved off towards one of the Highlanders. In a few seconds they were whispering together.

Sinclair was reading aloud to the company.

'Most noble earl and my very good friend ... How is that for a start?'

A murmur of approval rose.

* * *

Jamie woke at daybreak and sat up abruptly. He must not be late at the rendezvous with Maggie. As he slipped away as quietly as possible, he met the caddie returning from some private errand.

'My lord, I have been talking to friends.'

'Go ahead, Donald. What sort of friends?'

Gregory made a gesture of apology.

'Distant relatives,' he said, 'on my mother's side. Good people, but poor, my lord, very poor.'

'It happens, Donald, in the best of families. What can we do for your friends?'

'I am just coming to that, sir. They think they can have the commodity that interests you, probably by nightfall. They know where one of the kind has its hunting range and they have set a trap. Of course, it may be expensive ... a man's time, and the problem of carriage ...'

Jamie felt for his purse.

'Oh, there is no hurry, sir ... When you are dealing with gentlepeople ... But you don't have a drop of the stuff, by any chance? This morning air is terrible for the throat.'

'Alistair MacIan has the flask. He is sleeping on it, if I know him.'

Jamie went on his way.

'Maggie!'

He called to the girl from his hiding place among the trees and she put her milk pail down. For a minute he looked round cautiously and listened. Then he went forward towards her. She looked at him accusingly.

'They're black, not blue,' she said.

It was a second or two before he remembered, and his face relaxed.

'Who says they're black?'

'Very dark brown then.'

'What you need is a better looking-glass, girl. I never saw bluer eyes in my life. They are more blue every time I look at them.'

'You imagine things, James. My father was a Spaniard, they say.'

'Your father was a Spaniard! *My* mother was French. My grandmother was Scots. My great-grandmother was English.'

'English?'

'That's what they say. My great-great-grandmother—let's sit down here. On this beautiful cushion of dead leaves.'

'No, I must not be late. They'll begin to think—'

'Let them think, girl. Just for a minute or two. Just long enough to exhaust them.'

'Well ...'

After a little, he went on.

'Did you give her the message? What did she say?'

'That if you are the King of Elfland you'll find your own way to reach her.'

'And that was all?'

'Then this morning she told me milk was good for other things besides washing—she has a bonny skin, has she no'—'

'Beautiful. Anything else?'

'She gave me this. I'm to give it to you.'

It was a blank sheet of paper.

'It's one of her jokes,' he said, putting the paper in his doublet.

'A funny kind of joke.'

'A witch's kind of joke.'

'She is a witch who does not make jokes,' said Maggie, with strong conviction. 'But who are you to her? Are you betrothed?'

'Maggie, just for a moment suppose I am the King of Elfland, and suppose I want to get inside the castle. How would you advise me to go about it?'

She thought for a moment.

'There is a way through the old conduit—but you are not to give me money, James!'

'I want you to buy something for me. You said the conduit?'

'But it's sealed now, more or less.'

'What do I do then?'

'You could try the wee door beside the main gate when the porter is not in the gate house and the drawbridge is still down.'

'You mean that the porter is not there all the time?'

'I suppose he has to have a drink sometimes like other people.'

'Of course, of course. About when would that be, Maggie? And, don't forget, you are going to tell me about the conduit.'

When he left her, he made her promise to buy a ribbon for her hair. If she wanted to please him, it would be red. Scarlet rather than crimson.

He promised to bring her a mirror which would faithfully report on the colour of her eyes. Then he made his way back to the camping place.

He held the sheet of blank paper next to the heat of the cooking-fire. As he had expected, the words Madeleine had written in milk were soon visible on it.

The message was brief: 'At sunset, new warders come on duty. They are used to drinking whisky—too much whisky for their wits. They have not found my pistol.

'There is a rumour here that your friends are going to sell you. I cannot believe it.

'The cat man was about to take me away somewhere, but suddenly I hear no more of that.

'Do not wait too long.—M.'

Below, in a hurried scrawl, 'You can trust Maggie. God knows why.'

While he was still thinking about the message, Alistair appeared. Jamie handed him the piece of paper.

'Do you think of doing it tonight?' asked the Highlander, handing it back.

Stuart shrugged.

'Let us wait and see what reply his lordship sends to Sinclair's letter. Is there nothing yet?'

'Not a word,' said Alistair. 'But I should not expect him to answer yet.'

The letter which he had fastened to an arrow and fired by bow into the castle had included instructions as to how it should be answered: By a note placed under a stone on the summit of a naked rock above the stream, where a man coming towards it could be watched for the last hundred yards of his approach.

Alistair went on, in his soft way, 'If I am to guess what's in his mind, he will wait until nightfall—'

'When the guards are changed?'

Alistair nodded.

'Then he will carry the girl off secretly. The fox will guess that we are preparing some trouble for him here.'

'He will be right,' said Stuart cheerfully. 'Have you any word of what the Captain has been doing all this while?'

That morning Sinclair and Gregory had set off by horse on a wide sweep through the country for the purpose of falling on outlying farms worked by tenants of Lord Orkney. Two of the Highlanders, men experienced in the work, had gone with them on foot. Kindled thatch, blazing stack-yards, stampeding cattle would be the first outward signs of the raid.

'So far, nothing,' said Alistair. 'But don't be impatient. This is what would be best for us: that Orkney has time to send men out to deal with the Captain but not the time to get them back again. When our moment comes, his garrison will be depleted.

'Come, James, and see the whole theatre of war spread out before you like a banquet. I have found a place where you can see it all as well as the angels can.'

Half an hour later, Stuart paused, his heart pounding, on the brow of a steep bank surmounted by the red columns of a tall row of pines. He had been climbing behind the Highlander, who seemed to have no regard for the force of gravity. For him there were no slopes, either steep or easy.

Alistair gestured with his arm, embracing a vast and splendid landscape.

Jamie was glad that, for a moment, he need not say anything. Wiping the perspiration from his brow, he took in gradually the details of the scene.

Running across it like a silver ribbon was the river, a broad, stony, barbarous water, now pinned between headlands of rock that were crowded with dark trees, then gushing out between green slopes. Behind, there were high banks of gravel left by the spring floods. And farther off rose shining hill country leading up to the frail blue of the distant mountains. On the far rim of his vision, he thought he could see a pale yellowish streak of light which might be the sea. The sky was clear, apart from a delicate frill of pink clouds on the horizon.

In the middle of the scene was the castle, master of all this expanse. Its site had been chosen, its walls and towers laid out by someone who knew his job. And now they were proposing to assault it with—good God!—not even ten men.

148

'What the devil are you laughing at?' Alistair asked irritably.

'At the impudence of some people I know. They have the notion of taking Lord Orkney's castle.' He was still shaking with laughter.

'And what's wrong with that?'

'Nothing. Nothing at all, Alistair MacIan. Only that once again impudence is going to be proved the first of the laws of war. What's that?'

The Highlander had drawn his breath in sharply.

'Look, man. Look there.'

In the middle distance some miles beyond the castle, a thin, dark line wavered into the faultless sky. He thought he could make out a succession of bursts of orange flame below it. He looked at the Highlander.

'Sinclair!' said Alistair in his gentlest voice. 'He is going to give Lord Orkney something to occupy his mind. His lordship's tenants will come asking that these cruel raiders be punished. Poor men, it is not their fault that their stooks are being burned down and their cattle are probably being driven off! Look, another one is going up!'

Another thread, more delicate than the first, crawled hesitantly into the sky.

'He will have arranged with Donald that they work together,' Alistair explained. 'You would not think it of the man, but Donald has a long experience of this kind of warfare.'

Jamie could well imagine that Gregory was no apprentice hand in the business.

'It would not surprise me at all,' said Alistair, 'if we were to see a third fire very soon. I cannot believe these two of mine have failed in their duty.'

'They haven't,' said Stuart, pointing to a fresh column of smoke not far from the others.

Alistair exclaimed in Gaelic. 'Good boys!' he said. 'Now it is time for us to go back. We have seen all we need to.'

'I am not so sure about that, Alistair,' said Jamie. 'What do you think of that?'

A few miles to the south where they were standing, a dozen horsemen were riding towards them along the cattle track running parallel to the river.

'We have visitors,' said Alistair in a minute. 'More visitors.'

'Just so. They may be innocent wayfarers like ourselves. But I have an instinct that this is not a day for innocence. Besides, unless I am deceived, they are carrying lances. But your eyes are better than mine. Tell me what you make of them.'

Alistair gazed in silence for a minute.

'Armed men,' he said at last. 'With lances, certainly. And steel caps on their heads. Not any of our people.'

'You mean, they are Lowlanders?'

'I think they come from further south than that, Jamie.'

'English?'

'No, there are bad people living in the hill country between us and the English.'

'Look again. Tell me more.'

'One man is riding a few horse lengths ahead of the others. He is short and broad. I would suppose him older than either of us. A gentleman, I should say.'

'Alistair, let us go and meet those riders.'

'Meet them? They will ride us down like bucks.'

'It is a risk. But we will take it. I have an idea that man and I have met before.'

'And he is a friend?'

'That remains to be seen, Alistair. Come on.'

Stuart began to slither down the slope they had mounted before.

Half an hour later, on the summit of a dry pebble bank above the river, they lay watching the horsemen approach.

'It isn't the first time they have been on a foray like this,' said Alistair. 'Look at them. You can tell they are old hands at the business. Rough. Brutal.'

He shook his head disapprovingly. Jamie grinned.

Now they could hear the gentle splashing of water as the horses advanced in single file through a burn which ran into the river. It was followed by a light clatter of hooves as the troop came to a stretch of pebble beach at a point where the main stream turned. By this time, it was possible to make out features under the steel rims of the skullcaps.

Suddenly Jamie rose and went forward to the leading horseman. 'Sir John!' he shouted.

Bannerman pulled up, scowling. Behind him two horsemen aimed handguns at Jamie.

'You're the young devil that's caused all the trouble,' said Sir John. 'What have you done with that niece of mine? Bringing me to this Godforsaken place, and these gentlemen with me!'

'I want you badly, that's certain. And these gentlemen, too!'

Sir John snorted and jerked his thumb at the riders who were crowding up behind him, as wary a group of cavaliers as ever Jamie had set eyes on.

'Let me tell you who they are before you say you want them. Put away your guns, boys.' He pointed at one man after another. 'Tam Dalgleish—he with the snub nose—Jock o' the Side, the biggest thief in Liddesdale. Archie Fire the Braes. Red Roly Forester—English, but we'll forget that. And— But the rest can wait. You have a hiding-place hereabouts? Take me to it. Lead on, Stuart, and tell me as we go how you've come to be in such a scrape.'

He who hesitates ...

The council of war did not meet until Sinclair and his marauders had returned in the late afternoon, hot with riding and exultant with the easy success of their expedition. Patrols of mounted men had been seen to leave the castle to hunt down the raiders who had done Orkney's tenants so much damage.

By that time, a message had arrived from the castle:

'To whomsoever you may be. Bring James Stuart to the draw-bridge an hour after darkness falls. You'll be paid the blood money at that moment.'

'He must think we are children,' said Sinclair, indignantly.

'But what do we do?' Alistair's brow was knitted in thought.

'What do we do! Nothing could be easier. Send him a message agreeing to what he says. Tell him we cannot do what he wishes until two hours after sunset. Then we shall send a trumpeter to the gates. That is what we should say. Long before then, the business will be finished, although not at all as his lordship would like.'

'So we will try it tonight, as the last light is fading. Agreed?' Jamie looked sharply round the ring of faces, the Bordermen serious, the Highlanders excited. Sir John had brought formidable reinforcements to the affair, eight mosstroopers and himself, to add to the nine men already assembled.

With companions like these, James decided, even this crazy enterprise may have a chance! The twenty-foot wall; the sentinels; the numerical odds of three to one against them—all these became less important than they had been.

'Tonight will be as good a time as any,' said Sir John Bannerman, after inspecting Orkney's castle.

'Orkney should pay masons to see to that stonework of his. I have seen stronger walls at Carlisle.'

'The question is,' said Sinclair. 'Who will lead the storming party?'

'It is a matter of seniority,' said Sinclair.

'The hell it is!' said Jamie.

Alistair interrupted, 'Draw lots for it. That is the best way.'

Jamie shook his head vigorously.

'To the devil with that,' he said. 'I shall be the storming party.'

Sinclair snorted. 'That would be a foolish thing to do, since you are the one among us that Orkney wants. I won't let you spoil a good plan with your vanity.'

Alistair murmured agreement.

'Vanity be damned,' said Jamie. 'I said I would escort Madeleine to Cluny and escort her I shall. So—'

'That is fair enough,' said Sir John. 'She was taken while in Stuart's keeping. If she had come with me she would have been in safer country.'

'There are robbers everywhere,' said Alistair, flushing.

'There will be something for everyone to do,' said James quickly. 'Alistair—you, for instance. You know that sentry who makes his round on top of the wall?'

'I've seen him.'

'He's your meat, boy.'

'What do I do? Strangle him with my bare hands? If you like! But how. am I to climb up there?'

'The way into the castle is through the conduit that used to lead the waste water from the kitchen. It hasn't been used for a hundred years. It stands just eight feet above the ground under the wall. I've measured it with my eyes. What is more, I can tell you that the stones put in to seal the conduit are without mortar. How do I know? My black-haired girl tells me so. She is deep in the plot, deeper than she knows.'

'How did you buy her, James?'

'Buy? How do you think? With the silver of money and the gold of love. And something else as well. Between Maggie and me there is a complete understanding. She has a natural talent for the game. I see a great future for Maggie as leader of a robber band.'

'Go on, man,' said Sinclair to Jamie. 'Spin the plot—'

'This is what I have in mind. I shall enter by the postern door when Maggie gives me the signal that the porter has gone to fetch his drink. When I am safely inside, I shall make my way to the old conduit and prise out the loose stones so that other men, Sinclair, Alistair and as many as can manage may get in.

'Standing underneath the gap I have made, you, Captain Sinclair, will lift Gregory and the rest so they can scramble in and join me. As soon as they are safely in, they will lower a rope and pull you in too—if you think you can do it.'

'Do it!' said Sinclair testily. 'Do you imagine, young pup, that this is the first fortress I have stormed?'

'What about me?' asked Alistair. 'What am I doing all this while?'

'You are the key to the whole affair,' said Jamie.

'You flattering French devil,' Alistair grinned. 'Go on—you spoke about the sentry.'

'Listen, friend,' said Jamie, leaning forward. As he spoke Alistair reached for his bow. He was laughing.

After Jamie had finished, and all the questions had been asked and answered, Jamie saw Donald make a covert sign to him to come over.

'It has arrived, my lord,' said the caddie in a low voice. 'I have it close by, in a strong basket that two men can carry between them.'

'Is it a good one?'

'Good one! It's like a devil straight from hell. With eyes wild enough to shrivel the marrow in your bones. And teeth! Like sabres ... it hasn't eaten for two days.'

'Excellent. Keep it near by and keep it hungry. Later on, we'll find some way of feeding it.

Gregory grinned like a demon. 'As you will, my lord.'

A cloud on the horizon had changed from gold to pink.

In a few minutes it would be time for Jamie to make his way to the postern. In the meantime, he and Alistair were lying flat on a rocky height with the river between them and the castle, surveying the scene.

'Now, what will those buildings be on the far side of the close?' Alistair asked.

He pointed to a structure laid out in a half square with a more domestic look than the rest.

'That's what they call the palace. That's where Orkney keeps the girl under lock and key.'

'Her prison, you might say.'

'That's what he thinks, Alistair. I'm not so sure myself. The lock is open and she has the key in her purse.'

Alistair made a thoughtful sound.

'Do you see—look, there—the parapet walk seems to join the Palace by what looks like a bridge, at that far corner.'

'It looks like it, as you say. In a time of trouble they can send up more troops from the palace to man the wall.'

After a minute of silence, Alistair spoke again.

'You trust that girl, Maggie, don't you?'

'I trust nobody, Alistair, especially when she has black eyes and is persuaded that they are blue.'

They fell silent.

Both men lowered their heads as a sentinel approached on the walk above the battlements. They waited. By this time, they knew how long it would take for him to pass.

They lifted their heads, almost together.

'It will be a hell of a fine shot, Alistair.'

'Yes, James. Quite a good shot, although I have done better in my time. From that place under the oak tree—just there—it is near seventy yards. He will come forward. Someone will give a whistle. It could be myself. Then, God willing, he will step up on to the parapet at the angle of the tower. That will double the size of the target.'

'It will be a hell of a shot, Alistair. He must be hit and he must not utter a cry!'

The Highlander gave one of his warped smiles.

'The moment has come for you, Jamie, to slip away about your business. I give this sun seven minutes before it says goodnight.'

'I give it ten,' said Jamie.

'Optimist.' Alistair pulled an arrow delicately from his quiver and, examining it carefully, began to turn it over between his fingers.

Stuart pushed himself backwards on his stomach to the point where he would be in the shadow of the trees. Then he moved faster, in the stooping bent-knees gait he had learnt in the last few days.

By the time he came down the slope at the water's edge, the light was lifting out of the valley, like a bird with golden plumage and silent flight. He slid without a splash into the river at a point where he could not be seen from the castle. He waded across and shook himself when he arrived on the other side. Near him, behind a juniper bush, Sinclair was lying still.

'Jesus, it's cold,' said Jamie.

'You should have tried crossing those Dutch canals, boy.'

Jamie said something rude in French. Sinclair tut-tutted.

'Do you know that you have forded the best salmon river in Scotland? Or don't you care?'

'You talk too much, Captain Sinclair.'

'Don't lose your nerve, Mr. Stuart.'

'Careful, or a stone may strike you by mistake.'

He reached the causeway leading up to the castle gate at the moment when the full gold of the sunset fell on it. It was hard to believe that this was a good moment for him to move, that the eyes of a sentry on the wall above the gatehouse would be likely to be blinded.

But he could see nobody there. And he could see the white cloth Maggie had promised to show if the coast was clear. He hoped she could be trusted. The postern was open.

He went forward quickly.

When he reached the conduit, it was steep and dark and smelled as a drain might be expected to smell. But he found that only a single course of rubble had been used to fill the gap in the castle wall. He could see square holes in the wall where there had once been a grating. Of that nothing remained.

With an iron bar which he had picked up on his way through the cellars, Jamie set to work loosening the stones from their mortar. As each came free, he pulled it inwards and put it down at one side. In a few minutes, he had made an opening three feet or so across. Putting his head out, he could see Sinclair already in place below at the foot of the wall.

Suddenly Jamie's elbow dislodged a loose stone. It fell outwards, struck the ground at the foot of the wall, and rolled down the slope towards the river. Without question, the sound could be heard on the parapet walk above. If by ill-chance, the sentry was passing at that moment, the game would be up.

Peering out anxiously, Jamie saw a figure appear on the other side of the river. The man stepped forward suddenly out of the shadow of the trees, bent a bow and took aim. A faint twang of bowstring—a pause—and Alistair threw up his arm in a triumphant signal. The sentry was dispatched!

Immediately below, Sinclair was planting himself firmly with his back to the wall, his hands clasped to take the foot of the first man to scale the wall. In a few seconds, Stuart was pulling Donald Gregory into the castle. God, how the man smelt of whisky! A second man came quickly after him. Also a Highlander—then two of the Bordermen who had arrived with Sir John.

'Now for the Captain,' said Stuart. 'Where's the rope?'

'We must take out a few more stones first or his worship will be stuck half-way in,' said the caddie.

Sinclair was pulled in, panting and scratched by the stones. He muttered a few curses in some Low-German dialect.

'You all but killed me with that stone you let loose. God only knows why the sentry did not hear the noise you made.'

Donald spoke up.

'He heard and looked down. At that moment my cousin gave a cry. The sentry looked up and Alistair's arrow hit him in the throat.'

'Did he, by God!'

'A wonderful shot! But where is Alistair?' asked Jamie.

'Below, below, unless I am much mistaken. Yes, he is there.'

'Drop the rope to him, man, and pull him in. We have no time to lose. Captain, you will make sure of the gatehouse. Up there—' he pointed. '—you come to the cellars and kitchens. The gatehouse is to the left. Take Donald and one more with you. Alistair will come with me. Forward!'

With luck, they could count on having a minute or two. The accident to the sentry, coughing his lungs out on the walk twenty feet above, had still not been noticed. No trumpet calling the garrison to arms. No bell ringing the alarm. The luck of the Devil and unlikely to last for long!

A noise behind him told him that Alistair had arrived. Jamie began to climb the conduit, using hands and feet, Sinclair close behind him.

'Why do you swear in Dutch?' he asked.

'I don't swear at all.'

'What were you saying just now?'

'That in operations of this kind, surprise is the key to everything. I remember well—'

'Less noise in front,' Alistair whispered.

Sinclair stopped. 'Who are you talking to, you Highland robber?' he asked, 'To a man who has—'

'Shut up, both of you,' said Jamie.

They reached a heavy wooden door set in a rough stone arch; Jamie took the lead.

Now he was in a wide stone passage leading into a scullery where a morose man stood at the large basin washing plates. He looked up, startled, and opened his mouth wide. One of Alistair's men ran forward quickly and put a knife to his throat. He muttered some persuasive words in Gaelic. The scullion's eyes widened; his cheeks whitened. If he had thought of making a sound, he changed his mind.

Jamie looked round the corner of a door-way at the castle close. Even in that sour after-light of evening, it had beauty: an enclosure of ochre-yellow walls on which there were patches of grey lichen and at one point a silvery stone sundial. The slates on the roof of the palace building had the same silver sheen. Here and there, there were fat velvety cushions of grass-green moss. A flight of shallow stone steps led to an arched doorway over which was a carved lintel. That was where he must go.

'Remember,' he said in an urgent whisper. 'No shooting unless they shoot first. We don't want to warn them that we're here.'

Behind him as he ran were Alistair and a clansman with one of the Tweeddale men whom Sir John had brought with him. Sinclair made his way towards the vault which housed the machinery for moving portcullis and drawbridge.

Jamie mounted the three steps leading to the door of the palace.

Inside, no guards were visible. So far luck was with him. He turned to the left in the flagged passage.

If Maggie's description was correct, it would be the second door along. He pushed it open. Two guards were seated at a trestle table on which jugs and cups were set. Beside them was a young woman—Madeleine!

One guard looked up with wild unfocused eyes. It was Kennedy. The other jumped to his feet and reached for the dirk at his hip. Jamie was about to run him through when there was a loud explosion and the room was filled with acrid smoke. The guard uttered a cry and fell forward on the table, holding a hand to his elbow.

Madeleine stepped past him. Her little pistol was smoking.

'Quick, girl! Out of here!' said Jamie.

She ran towards the door. At that instant, Kennedy recognised Stuart. With an enraged yell, he got up and pulled his sword from the scabbard. But it was no moment for pretty sword-play. Alistair rushed into the room followed by his clansman. They threw themselves on Kennedy and brought him to the ground.

Stuart followed Madeleine out of the room at a run. But by this time the run of luck was ended. Orkney's garrison was awake.

From all round came the creak of seats being pushed back; the clash of weapons as men fastened belts and put hands to their blades.

At that moment an elegant black cat appeared soundlessly and stood in the passage between Jamie and the door which opened on the close. Jamie recognised it and on an impulse stooped to lift it.

'Don't touch it, man,' someone cried behind him in a Highland voice.

As Jamie turned, the cat lunged at him viciously with claws outspread.

Alistair, having slammed the cell door on Kennedy, went past him at a rush followed by the other Highlander and the Border man. The cat stood furiously before Stuart in the passage, yellow-eyed, arched, and malevolent, mewing insistently and loudly enough to be heard all over the yard. The other three men clattered out into the open air.

Jamie might have gone with them but for a voice, something

between a howl and a screech, full of anguish, barely human yet strangely familiar. The voice came from further along the passage. 'Mawksie, Mawksie, what are they doing to you, my darling.'

Lord Orkney appeared, tall, gaunt, his long, coarse eyebrows drawn together, his face livid and convulsed with emotion, something between a mad wizard and a pirate chief. Behind him was a group of scowling faces belonging to armed men wearing his livery. More of them were tumbling down the stairs one after the other from the rooms above.

'Go on, girl!' Jamie shouted. Instead, Madeleine reached one hand out to him.

It was the briefest pause. It was too much. In that fraction of a second, a heavy body hurled itself between Madeleine and the doorway. Kennedy! The clang of heavy steel resounded in the passage.

A hinged grille made of criss-cross rods of iron laboriously hammered together by a smith—had slammed into position across the exit, driven by Kennedy's foot. Stuart pushed Madeleine roughly aside so that he could get to grips with the man.

He heard someone command, 'Take him alive, the bastard,' and felt a sudden intolerable pain in his head.

He fell forward, senseless.

'It's a savage world'

Far away, a man was talking. What he was saying Stuart did not understand. In any case it was no concern of his. None at all, as the supercilious smile which now formed on his lips showed clearly enough. Yet—and this was puzzling—the man's voice was familiar.

'The girl has a pistol. Take it from her.'

The sounds were well-defined. What a pity they made no sense. If he were patient, the time might come when they did. He would be patient. It was easy ...

Another voice. One he did not recognise. And again making no sense.

Stuart decided to learn the words by heart so that, later on, he would piece their message together.

'They have gone, my lord. Aye. All of them. Vanished.'

'Do you take me for an idiot, man.' It was the shrill voice again. 'They are about somewhere. Lurking outside the gate, I expect.'

'We can't go out to look, my lord. Someone has damaged the portcullis machine. With a hammer, my lord.'

'Push it up with your hands, fool. Use the few brains God gave you.'

Stuart smiled to himself. He would like to tell them how wrong they were. He thought they ought to know the Captain. How had he forgotten the Captain?

'He's coming to, my lord.'

'Pull him to his feet and let me look at the smaik.'

Someone was treating him badly. Someone was causing a

terrible pain in his head. He shut his eyes firmly.

But the other world which he had enjoyed so much, where there was no understanding, and no pain, had gone.

He opened his eyes. Slowly, but not slowly enough, a wasted, threatening face appeared close to his own. The face of a man he had seen before. The Earl of Orkney. The man who loved ... who loved? ...

'Don't shake him. Don't jolt him. Treat him as if he were made of glass. I want his head to clear, quickly. I want him to talk.'

They were in a small vaulted room, he and Orkney, a room with a stone floor and a stone roof.

Orkney went on, 'Just tie his wrists behind his back, Jock, and sit him down on that stool with his back to the table so that he doesn't fall. And see that his hands are tied properly. If he can get them free, it will be a piece of lead for you in the nape of the neck.

'The girl. You've taken her pistol. Does she have a knife? Make sure. Ah, I thought so. Hidden in the place you would expect. Look at her. She isn't the kind to blush.

'Now stand back all of you. Out of hearing. I am going to talk to these two.'

Boots scraped on the flagstones as men drew back.

'Jock, you stay. And you, Kennedy.'

Orkney sat down on the only chair in the room, a drawn sword in one hand, a pistol in the other. The black cat sat on the arm of the chair, composed and aristocratic. Jamie found that if he shut one eye he could keep Orkney in focus.

'James Stuart,' he heard. 'One of the Name. Cousin!'

Jamie said nothing. But he was beginning to understand things better by this time.

Orkney went on, 'You frightened little Mawksie. That was careless of you. Really careless. You are lucky to be alive after a mistake like that. Or are you? Lucky, I mean? It all depends.'

Jamie looked back at him, blinking at first and then more steadily. He said nothing.

Orkney was worth more than a glance. He sat in his chair, his black coat pulled about him, looking like a gaunt, unclean bird. A bird who lived on carrion. A bird that had been turned into dark stone. He looked, Jamie thought, like something imagined by an architect of cathedrals. An architect who worshipped the Devil.

He was still smiling quietly at this fancy when the high-pitched voice intruded again.

'It depends, cousin James,' the voice was saying. 'And mainly on yourself. You don't want to talk, do you? Not yet awhile. But soon. Sooner than you think. Yes. You're a sensible man at bottom. You know that it will be better to talk. It will save us time and trouble.

'Do you know, you interest me, James. Damn me if I know why, but you do. There are things about you I'd like to know.'

Orkney turned his head slightly and spoke to someone, a servant perhaps.

'Jock, rake out the fire in the chimney. See that it is burning clearly.'

Then he looked again at Jamie.

'Call it family interest if you like. One Stuart bastard interested in another. I'd like to know some things about you. For instance, why have you come to Scotland, with that Paris accent?

'Just what made you travel to the land of your ancestors? Was it plain curiosity—a longing to see the country? I don't think so.

'There's something else, too. The King seems to be very anxious about you, James. Just why should that be, do you think? It looks as if King James knew more about you than I do. And as if what he knows makes him want to put you somewhere safe, a place where he will be sure that you are quiet. Now why is it that the King wants to be rid of you, James?'

Orkney leant forward in his chair, his yellow eyes glittering.

'You don't want to talk, do you. But I'm in no hurry. I can wait. I have all night and all tomorrow and all the next day, too. And long before then you will have remembered everything that now you have forgotten and you will have told me all that I want to know. You will be eager to talk. Jock, how is the fire burning?'

'Well, my lord. Well and clear.'

'And hot?'

'Unco' hot, my lord.'

'Kennedy, come here.'

The gallowglass came forward, glowering. His eyes shone for

an instant as he glanced at Jamie. Then he turned to Orkney and awaited his orders.

'You see that bracket above the fire where the chain and the hook are hanging?'

'I do that.'

'If a rope was looped over that hook and a man were tied with the rope so that he hung over the fire, what would happen, do you think?'

Kennedy's brow was wrinkled in perplexity. He stared stupidly at his master and said nothing. Orkney made an impatient noise with his tongue.

'You must be as stupid as you look, Kennedy. What would happen, you fool?'

'The man would be burnt.'

'To ashes, Kennedy. To ashes. If we left him there,' said Orkney. 'Now here is the man who nailed you to a door in Edinburgh with your own dagger. What would you like to do with him?'

Kennedy's teeth flashed.

'Kill him, my lord, kill him.'

Orkney sneered. 'Show some imagination, man. Some spark of fancy. Kill him? Of course you'd like to kill him. But I am going to show you how to do the job in a clever way. See that rope beside the fire? Yes? Now tie Mr. Stuart with it. And while you are busy with that, I will go on talking to my cousin.

'Jamie, you may wonder what is going to happen to the girl. What do you expect?'

Stuart said nothing. He was thinking now. The time might come when he would want to talk. But not yet.

'Either she becomes the Countess of Orkney or she will be sent to Edinburgh,' said Orkney. 'If for some foolish reason she will not be a Countess, married to one of the first nobles in Christendom, then she will be handed over to the officers of justice who have their own ways of proving what she is. You know what that is as well as I do. She is a witch, Stuart. A witch.

'Look at her, man. Have you any doubts? The girl has sold her soul to the Devil. His Majesty knows it and His Majesty is an expert in these matters. So what will happen? She will be sentenced to the only punishment prescribed by law for those who have renounced allegiance to God and given themselves up to Satan and his ministers.

'She will be consumed by fire, burnt at the stake on the Castle Hill of Edinburgh, as her sisters in perdition were before her. A terrible fate for a lassie, Stuart. Terrible. But better to burn the body and save the soul, eh!

'Maybe you don't think so. And maybe you'll think so even less in a little when that fire is licking about your toes. Don't worry, though. I won't let you die. Not this time. But you won't walk so well after it.

'You have the rope ready, Kennedy? Well, pull off his boots. Pull off Mr. Stuart's boots, man, so that we can warm his toes.'

The room was silent for a moment. The men gathered at the door leant forward, watching eagerly. They were still. The soft noises of the fire glowing on the hearth seemed suddenly louder.

Somewhere behind them, Jamie thought he could detect another sound, fainter and hardly to be identified.

Kennedy knelt before him and grasped his left boot by heel and toe. And with all the force of his right leg Jamie drove the other boot full into the gallowglass's face.

Kennedy howled like a wounded animal. A stream of blood poured from his mouth. He held his hands to his face. At that moment, Orkney's pistol flamed. Jamie felt a sudden sting in his shoulder.

Madeleine leapt forward soundlessly, snatched the drawn sword from the earl's left hand and held it to his breast.

Orkney's men rushed forward, snarling.

'Move, one of you!' she shouted, 'and this goes through your lord's black heart.'

For an instant they hesitated.

'Dinna heed the bitch,' Orkney screamed hoarsely. 'Use your brains ... Don't you ken I wear a mail shirt under my coat.'

They resumed their advance.

Madeleine, her lips quivering, her teeth bared, drove the sword at his throat. At the last instant he twisted and escaped with a scratch under one ear. Jamie struggled wildly to free his wrists. The noises he had heard were growing louder.

Then they were drowned by the enormous clamour of a bell,

resounding from the stone walls of the vaulted chamber. The tocsin!

The castle was being attacked!

'To arms!' Shouting men crowded in the doorway, pulling out their swords as they ran. Orkney, one hand clutching his neck, wrested his sword from Madeleine's grasp.

Kennedy stood motionless, staring, stupefied, at the blood on his hands. Madeleine snatched a dagger from his belt and slashed the rope binding Jamie's wrists.

'God knows what's happening,' cried Jamie, 'but this is our best chance. Come on.'

He thrust her roughly before him into the passage outside and slammed the door behind him. Outside, he slid the bolt into place.

Then he turned and saw Alistair MacIan and Captain Sinclair half-jump, half-fall and arrive, breathless, in the passage at the foot of the stair leading from the floor above. Appearing from somewhere in the darkness, the black cat spat at him.

Sinclair was about to slash at the animal when Alistair caught his arm.

'Don't touch it, man.'

'Never mind the brute now,' said Jamie.

'Is anyone in the room?'

'The earl and Kennedy locked in. Don't heed them. Both can wait. Just tell me what's happening.'

'Happening?' said Sinclair. 'Everything. They threw us out of the gatehouse. Oh, a skirmish in grand style. What they did not know was that some of us had found our way from the gatehouse up to the parapet walk. There's a turnpike stair leading up. So we worked our way along the walk and waited for the moment when Bannerman made a new attack on the postern. He is outside now with his reivers. That was when the bell rang.

'Then we ran over the bridge between the walk and the palace. Alistair knew of it. You've seen it too, have ye not? And so we are here!

'We hold Lord Orkney's palace while his soldiers, poor devils, run about in the yard looking for somebody to attack. A siege within a siege! What do you think of that?'

'I think it's all right,' said Jamie. 'All right, if we can get out.'

Sinclair frowned scornfully. 'Get out! Of course we can get

out. There's been nothing like this since the Duke of Parma first came to Flanders. Boy, we are writing a chapter in military history!'

'Military history can wait. Let us leave this place before it's too late.'

'Up to the floor above,' said Alistair. 'Over the bridge and down the wall. We need a rope!'

'In that room he kept me,' Madeleine put in.

'I'll get it,' said Alistair. He vanished and, a second later, was back with the rope. 'It looks as if it would be strong enough to take our weight.'

Sinclair looked at it doubtfully.

'Maybe, but is it long enough?'

'I think not,' said Alistair, 'we must drop the last few feet and hope that we land the right way up.'

'And hope that Bannerman keeps them busy at the gate. Come on, boys,' Jamie shouted from the stair, already half-way up.

'We let Bannerman know what we had in mind to do,' said Sinclair. 'One of Alistair's boys took him the message.'

'My uncle will keep them busy at the gate,' said Madeleine, who was first to reach the upper floor. She brandished a sword and looked more beautiful than ever.

'It's dark outside: not pitch black yet, but soon it will be. We must hope for the best,' said Sinclair.

'I'll go down first,' said Alistair. 'I can see better in the dark than most folk. I'll catch Madeleine as she comes down.'

Taking Madeleine by the hand, Jamie went quickly into the open air.

Out on the parapet walk above the wall the night wind was blowing freshly. Sounds of a scuffle came from below. The land lay in darkness all round except on a high peak in the distance. There a faint last beam of sun died away.

'I've found a stanchion let into the wall,' said Alistair. 'For a flagstaff most like. It will do well enough for the rope.'

Alistair went down first. After all, the rope was long enough. Agile as a cat, Madeleine followed. Jamie was about to go next when he heard a voice from below.

'My lord! Mr. Stuart.'

Donald Gregory.

Peering down, Jamie thought he could make out a knot of dark figures at the foot of the wall.

'How the devil did you get there?'

'That commodity you spoke of. It's here. It would be a shame to take it away!'

Now Jamie could distinguish something like a small square hamper dangling from a pole which two men were carrying on their shoulders.

'By God and it would!' he cried. 'If it's the last thing I do I'll take it to his lordship. Fasten it to the rope and I'll pull it up.'

'Watch out for its claws, my lord.'

'What the hell have you there?' Sinclair demanded, at his side.

Jamie pulled up from below a strong basket from within which came a terrifying assortment of noises, scrambling, scratching, thumps and subdued shrieks.

'Lord Orkney is a man who loves cats,' said Jamie.

Sinclair's eyes glowed.

'You devil, Stuart,' he said, in a voice full of awe. 'You devil!'

'Captain, help me to deliver my gift to his lordship,' Jamie interrupted.

'By God and I will.'

'Mind he doesn't get your fingers.'

Sinclair slid back the bolt on the door leading into Orkney's chamber. Jamie with his foot pushed the basket into the chamber. Then he pulled open the lid and jumped back. He was just in time. Sinclair slammed the bolt home again.

'Jesus, did you see—?'

'Come on, Captain!'

Only one man got in the way of their escape. Sinclair's pistol took him hard on the head.

Jamie and Sinclair dropped to the foot of the wall and ran, while desperate screams emerged from the little room in which Orkney and Kennedy were locked with the most famished, vicious wild cat in all the Highlands.

Sinclair grabbed his arm.

'Did you see? You said Lord Orkney loves cats!'

He was shaking with laughter.

'It's a savage world!'

Jamie strode ahead where he could see Madeleine waiting.

Part III

The twin of the brooch

The two had ridden far if not fast—far and dangerously, with the light changing from the strange, luminous, after-glow of the northern evening, in which colours became darker yet more intense, to pitch-black night.

Not once but a dozen times, Jamie had lowered his head smartly to his horse's mane in time to escape a blow from a tree-branch. Several times the horse, which could see better than he, pulled up suddenly. Jamie abandoned to the horse the task of path-finding, content that its gait should be balanced and that he should be balanced in the saddle. It would be enough if he kept Madeleine in sight ahead of him ...

Before he left, Sir John had spoken to him alone, standing with half-a-dozen horses about him, 'You go on with her, Stuart. She wants you to take her to Cluny. Go, and God be with you! On the journey you are taking, you want no company. Whether you reach Cluny is another matter. Whether that is where she wants to go, I know not. Maybe you do.'

'Does *she*?' asked Stuart.

Sir John raised his bushy black eyebrows, shrugged his broad shoulders, and dismissed the question.

'I have picked the best horse for her,' he said, 'one she has ridden before. For you I have found a sturdy brute that should stand up to the kind of country that lies ahead of you. A hard-mouthed jade. Don't think you are going to play any fancy tricks with her.'

By this time, noises in the distance had made it clear that Lord Orkney's men were riding across the drawbridge. The pursuit was going to begin. Sir John lifted an ear to the sounds.

'They had better be careful,' he said. 'In this light, they might ride into trouble.'

As the woods were sown with men who could shoot by one method or another, it did not seem unlikely.

By this time, Jamie could see Madeleine had mounted and was riding away. He swung into the saddle. 'Goodbye, Sir John. Thanks for the nag.'

'Make good use of it, boy,' said Sir John grimly. 'You've let this girl come into danger once. Now see that you keep her out of it.'

In the gloom, he spotted his companions of the siege.

'Goodbye, Alistair! you're a devil of a fighter. We shall meet again.'

'Goodbye, Jamie. A great fight!' Sinclair's voice boomed through the darkness. 'Remember boy, I'll be leaving within the week.'

'To Cluny!' said Jamie. 'And then we'll see, Captain!'

Just at that moment Jamie saw a girl coming towards them through the trees.

'Maggie!' he cried. 'Come here, my blue-eyed beauty!'

Leaning from the saddle, he caught her round the shoulders and kissed her full on the mouth.

'Sir John! This is the girl who let us into the castle. See that she does not pay for it. But for her, Madeleine would burn on the Castle Hill at Edinburgh.'

Sir John frowned dubiously at the girl.

'And don't think you'll have trouble looking after her,' Jamie went on. 'Maggie can look after herself, given a chance. Fare you well, Sir John.'

A trumpet sounded somewhere. A derisive call, shrill with insult.

Sir John grunted, 'That will be Jock o' the Side bidding Orkney good-night.'

Stuart put spurs to his horse. It started angrily forward, throwing its head up and tugging at the reins ...

And so he and Madeleine had ridden for an hour or more without exchanging a word. Then suddenly Madeleine pulled her horse up to a walk.

They had broken out of the forest land. Before them the land fell away, steeply at first and then more gently. Below there opened out a wide expanse of country threaded in long zig-zag stretches by a river, not so wide as that on which Orkney's castle stood, but nevertheless of a respectable size.

Jamie looked up; saw pale stars he knew. He was gazing towards the north. And from a damp tang in the air he knew that the sea might not be far away.

'Beautiful,' he said. 'Beautiful.'

But it was not the word he wanted. This dark plain, sloping north towards the sea, demanded a description that would convey some appeal to more than the senses. Wonderful? Mystical? He did not know.

'Beautiful?' Madeleine said. 'More than that. All that we can see to the west of the river will be mine the day I marry Cluny. Everything between here and the Pole.'

'Lord Orkney owns some islands,' he said sourly. 'Over there.' He waved a hand towards the North Star.

'They are far away. Mere specks of rock in the sea. And he will not keep them for long.'

He said nothing. She was probably right. Sooner or later, Lord Orkney would come tumbling down.

'Jamie,' she said suddenly, laying her hand on his arm. He could feel her excitement.

'Yes?'

'No. Something I was going to say—but it would have been stupid.'

He thought he knew.

'You need not go to Cluny,' he told her. 'Not yet awhile.'

'And what of the marriage feast?'

'The bridegroom and you can eat it cold.'

Cold. Cold as the Arctic floes. Cold as the heart of an unloving wife.

'The family,' she said. 'Rory ... My brother ... He will be waiting for me there.'

'When you arrive, he will not have waited too long.'

'What do you know of Rory?'

'I know this marriage will be his doing.'

'He is my brother.'

'Yes,' he said. 'Your brother. Your loving brother.'

173

'Where shall we go, Jamie?'

'You know the way,' he told her.

'What makes you think so?'

'Lead on, you beautiful devil,' he said savagely.

Her grip tightened on his wrist for an instant. Then she let him go. Her horse kicked up stones on the path as she turned its head to the east and touched it with her heel.

She spoke over her shoulder.

'Look at the sky ahead. It will be daylight within the hour. Will it keep you from sleeping, Jamie?'

'First let us find a bed.'

Now her horse's pace was faster. He could hear her laugh as she was swallowed up by the darkness.

Daylight had arrived by the time she pulled her horse up in the cobbled barmkin of a little tower coated with roughcast in the local fashion and washed in a girlish shade of pink. It stood at the tail of an oak wood on a long stretch of moorland sloping down from the north.

Madeleine turned and eyed him mischievously.

'Where are we?' he asked.

'You said, "Find a bed". Here it is.'

A window above them was opened. A woman looked out and uttered a shrill cry.

'This is my house, Jamie,' said Madeleine, 'the only house I own in all the world. I promise you the beds are soft enough.'

A door opened noisily. The woman he had already seen at the window above appeared and clattered down the steps to kiss Madeleine's hand. 'My lady! My lady!'

A few minutes later, they were inside the house. 'What do you think of my hermitage?' she asked.

'Where you come to escape from the world, to weave your spells, to brew your magic potions?'

'No. Just to hunt with my Greenland falcon.'

'Ah. Where is it now, that beautiful white bird?'

'Not far away, James.'

Her room was panelled in Danzig pine. It looked warm. The bed would be comfortable.

'You promised that before we came to Cluny you would tell me why the King wants to have you killed.'

'It will keep till morning.'

'This *is* morning, Madeleine.'

'We have had a long day. First, we must sleep.'

She kissed him and, untying the scarf that bound his head, ran her fingers through his curls.

'Jason,' she said, 'and the Golden Fleece.'

'Medea,' he replied. 'This boy's doublet—it suits you.'

'Then why do you take it off, Jamie?'

'Because you are tired and that bed looks as if it wished to be slept in.'

'There is another bed next door,' she whispered.

'The good guest makes as little trouble in a house as possible. I was taught that at school.'

'You were well brought up, James.' She bit him on the cheek-bone, kissed him on the lips and slid into bed, shivering slightly.

He could feel the pull of her arms round him drawing him closer. He laughed in the darkness.

'Why?' she asked. 'Why do you laugh.'

'I remember the first time in Edinburgh. When you sent me to take a bath. I stank, you said. I must be much fouler now.'

'And I am much more sleepy. Come!' she said, softly.

He woke up once. She slept at his side still, a lovely idol of ivory and gold, stolen from a pagan temple, with the gold locket round her neck. He swore that when she woke, he would open the locket and she would not resist.

When next he woke, thin yellow blades of sunlight from cracks in the wooden shutters were slicing the darkness of the room. Madeleine was not there. The house was full of delicious cooking smells.

He had dreamt a great deal and now the smarting had gone from the near-miss of Orkney's pistol shot. He touched the spot cautiously. The bruises were still tender but would not trouble him for long.

He thought she had told him a great many half-truths. But then, she was under no obligation to tell him anything at all.

175

And probably they had seemed true enough when she spoke them.

The little bedroom was full of her belongings. Her perfume, her books. Did she read Latin and Italian? Probably. But Greek? Surely not.

A few pictures which must have been taken from some church at the time when the churches were being (as they said) 'purified'.

In a perfumed wardrobe, woman's clothes, among them a court dress encrusted with pearls which must have been worn in Holyroodhouse and was splendid enough for the Louvre.

On a table, standing against one of the walls, was a crystal ball like the one he had seen in her chamber in Edinburgh. Beside it was a small silver casket ornamented with a delicate design in high relief. He had seen work of that kind in France.

She had skewered a half-sheet of paper to the pillow with a jewelled pin. He read:

'Jason! Before the Golden Fleece is won, you have more tasks to perform. I have looked into my crystal ball and that is what it tells me.

'I have gone hunting on the hills. But you looked so innocent lying there I had not the heart to wake you.

'I do not love you, Jamie. Does that matter, since you do not love me? Medea.'

Whistling thoughtfully, Jamie rose and pushed open the shutters. Sunshine on the fields. He began to dress. Someone had put a jug of water outside the door. It was still hot. He shaved and combed his hair. In the mirror he inspected himself dispassionately: a wicked glint in those cold blue eyes, a cruel twist to these predatory lips ...

He put down on the table the jewel-headed pin that Madeleine had used to fasten her note to the pillow. Surely it belonged in the silver casket from which in all likelihood she had taken it when she got up. He prised up the lid, which opened easily enough.

Then with the casket still open, he stood quite motionless for a moment or two. The jewelled pin was in his hand but he was not looking at the pin. Something which he had glimpsed in the casket interested him more.

A slight noise outside the door brought him out of his musings.

He dropped the pin into the casket and pulled down the lid quietly. Madeleine came in, her cheeks flushed with walking in the morning air.

'Hungry?'

'Hungry as your white falcon!'

'He is not hungry any longer.'

They ate. She chattered excitedly. He asked her how Lord Orkney had behaved during her captivity in the castle. She shrugged her shoulders and smiled.

'He was charming!'

Jamie asked no more questions. Finally, when they had finished he said, 'Now is the time for us to talk about serious matters, Madeleine, you and I.'

'Oh?'

'Yes. Usually I begin the debate, but this time I give way to you. After all, you are in your own home. So—'

'Debate?' she tilted her head to one side and pondered the word.

'Discussion—or perhaps confession.'

She seemed to push the notion away. 'No. Not yet, Jamie, please.' She put out her hand. But he nodded insistently.

'Yes. Now. Look. Watch carefully,' he said.

He untied the neck-tape of his shirt and pulled up a small leather bag. The fine cord of plaited leather on which it hung ran through rings and held the bag shut. He opened it and took something out. Then he held out his hand. Something glittered on his palm.

'Look, Madeleine.'

Her eyes widened suddenly.

'You have taken it from the casket,' she accused him.

'Look in the casket.'

But already she had leapt from the room. In a moment she was back, holding in her hand the twin of the diamond and emerald brooch which lay in his and had, not many days before, fastened his plume to his hat.

'Explain,' she said.

'Explain? That requires two people who will talk. Who begins, Madeleine?'

'Where do I begin?' she appealed to him.

'With Lord Gowrie,' he said. 'He seems to be the common thread in our two stories.'

She wrung her hands. For a minute she did not speak. Through the open window of the room sounds came in from outside—farm sounds, forest sounds, birds, water running over a dam.

'Gowrie ... John, Earl of Gowrie.' As she spoke, her voice became quiet. 'If you had seen him—but you have seen the painting, haven't you? Such beauty, don't you think? To make the heart turn over in the breast. Of either a man or a woman—it made no difference. Beauty such as you read about in the old stories. Magic! A girl had one idea only. To hope that he would ask her—so that she could say, "yes".'

She paused, then went on.

'In the end, he was angry with me. That was after he had been in Italy. Four years! Only a letter or two in all that time!'

'He was jealous?'

He thought she nodded.

'About the man who sent you the Greenland falcon?' he asked.

She seemed to shake her head. But she said, rather too quickly, 'Yes. Yes, of course.'

'And the brooch,' he said. 'Was it Gowrie who gave it to you?'

'Gowrie was given it by an old man he met in France, a Scot, an exile, a Catholic, who served in the King of Spain's army. When the old man heard that Gowrie was going to Scotland, he gave him the brooch. He said that it had a sister—'

'And here is the sister.'

Jamie put the two pieces of jewellery side by side on the table.

'Do you see!' she cried. 'That fits into that—so! Together, they make a clasp for a cloak.'

'A woman's cloak,' said Jamie.

'A great lady's! Diamonds! Emeralds! Now, tell me how you came to have the other half of the clasp.'

'Simple,' he said. 'My father left it to me in his will. He told me he thought it had belonged to his mother. He did not seem to be sure—or to care much, for that matter. But he said that if ever I went to Scotland I might find out more about it. Myself, I did not think it in the least likely that I would even go to Scotland. I left the brooch in a jewellers' in Amsterdam and forgot it. And then ... one day—'

'One day, what, James?'

'I've told you I became a galley slave? Next to me was this Scotsman, Quentin Forsyth. From Quentin I heard about my Lord Gowrie. And that made me swear that if ever I got off that damned galley I would visit the land of my fathers. But what chance had I?

'The best I could hope for was that one day, in the Mediterranean, we would fall in with an Algerine corsair and be captured. Sometimes these Moslems are willing to let a Christian go free so long as he isn't a Spaniard or a Catholic. As it turned out, I was lucky. Luckier than poor Quentin.'

'What had John Gowrie said to him?' she asked.

'That if Henry Stuart was still alive, he had something to tell him. Something important. Concerning the family. You can imagine I wanted to stay alive long enough to meet Gowrie! Henry Stuart was my father. What concerned him might concern me. Besides, those words 'the family'. You know which family he meant. But my father was a bastard. Bastards don't have a family. They begin afresh—something new. Like Adam. So—here I am, Madeleine!'

'And that's all?'

'That's all. The rest is only guesswork—vague hints dropped by Gowrie when they were drinking together in Paris and talk was wild. Quentin heard something and imagined more.'

'What did he hear, Jamie?'

He shook his head.

'That's enough from me! Now it's your turn to talk, Madeleine. What did Lord Gowrie tell you?'

She hesitated for a moment.

'He told me so many things! And some of them were madder than others ... The time I remember best is when we were up in his hunting place in the hills at Trochrie. It is a place rather like this, a little hunting tower. That night, he had taken a lot to drink, although God knows his tongue was wild enough at any time! And it made him talk more carelessly.

'During dinner—there were seven or eight of us there, lairds and their women—the talk turned on the man you know of, the man who is the head of your family, Jamie. And John said, suddenly, in a voice we could all hear "Him the King! He has no more right to the crown than I have."

'You can imagine a silence fell at that. And then, all of us began talking at once and laughing as if it had been a joke. But it wasn't a joke. John sat for a few minutes saying nothing, his head hunched between his shoulders, frowning, his lips moving. I thought we were going to have a new scene. Then suddenly he reached for the wine, filled his glass and emptied it at one gulp. For the rest of the meal, he sat silent. His thoughts were black and far away.

'When the others finally went to bed, I was left with Gowrie. "Why did you say that?" I asked him. "You may have thought it something to laugh about but one of those fools at your dinner may repeat it." "To the Devil with them!" he said. "You know the King distrusts you already," I told him. "Why do you talk treason. He can hang you for this." He sneered at that. "Treason is talked at every table in Scotland. Why not at this one? And since when has the truth been treason?" "The truth!" I said. At that he rose. "Yes, the truth. Wait! I'll show you something." He went out of the room then, none too steady on his feet. He came back and held out his hand. *That* was in it!'

She pointed to the diamond and emerald brooch.

'"Look," he said. "Bonny, isn't it. Find the other half, Madeleine, and you'll have proof that James the Sixth is no more rightful King of Scots than I am!"'

For a moment, neither of them spoke, looking at the pattern made on the table by the flashing coloured stones.

Jamie broke the silence.

'Here they are, the two sisters. But where is the proof?'

'There is no proof so far,' she said.

She was right. All he had heard so far was the story of an indiscreet outburst by a drunken young nobleman, and an offensive remark about a monarch who was not the most respected member of his line.

Treason? The idea would be ridiculous. Even to a king as thin-skinned as James the Sixth, even if Gowrie's father and grandfather had, in their time, been guilty of treason ... As for the two jewelled brooches which had turned out to be the halves of a jewelled clasp, what did they add up to? A pretty little fairytale.

'How much did Gowrie say he paid for the brooch?' Jamie asked.

'He didn't say and I didn't ask. This old officer in the Spanish army—'

'Down on his luck?'

'I expect so.'

Somehow the idea of a penniless old soldier peddling pieces of jewellery with some romantic story attached to them was not so far-fetched.

He grinned at her.

'Anyway, the stones are real enough. I had them valued,' he said. 'All we need now is the proof. Did Gowrie tell you anything about that?'

'Yes. He said that when the two pieces were put together, then the proof could be found.'

'Did he say how?'

'Yes, he said that when the two halves of the clasp were assembled, they were to be taken to a sword-slipper's booth in Edinburgh, kept by a man who had the King's crown over his door.'

'By God! I know the shop! And then?'

'What do you think? When the clasp is shown, the sword-slipper will be bound to furnish the proof that the King is not the King.'

'A likely story!' he said.

'No, Jamie, not a likely story at all, but the story as John Gowrie told it to me.'

'And he believed it—as he would believe anything that might harm the King.'

'But something more—' She rose from the table.

'What?'

'The King believes it,' she said. 'At least he thinks well enough of it to hunt you over the Highlands and to seek to have me burnt as a witch. Don't you see! Somehow, from an agent in Paris, perhaps, he knows why you have come to Scotland. And he knows I have Gowrie's secret. It was for this he had the Earl of Gowrie and his brother, Alec, murdered in Perth. This is the truth about the famous tumult in Perth in which the King was attacked and Gowrie was killed—a mystery nobody in Scotland can solve!'

Her cheeks were flushed and her eyes flashing.

'So what do we do, Madeleine?' he asked.

'Do? You can leave the country at once, by the first ship you can find. Most people would tell you that was wisest. From here to Aberdeen is not so far and just at this moment His Majesty's friends are looking for you in a different quarter, more to the north, towards Lord Cluny's lands.'

'And you?'

'Me? I am going to be married to one of the richest nobles in the land.'

'I said I would take you to Cluny. To Cluny we are going. After that, I shall visit that sword-slipper in his booth in Edinburgh and he will tell me the truth about King James.'

'That you can't do,' she cried, the suggestion of a scornful smile on her lips.

'Why not?'

'Because—' she picked up one part of the clasp from the table—'he will tell you nothing unless you bring him both halves of the jewel!'

'By God!' he said, 'Sometimes I should like to slit your throat, Madeleine. And sometimes I shouldn't! ... So we'll ride to the wedding and perhaps I'll give you my half of the clasp as a wedding present.'

'I have a better plan,' she said. 'We will go to Edinburgh and visit the sword-slipper's booth together.'

'Wonderful!' he scoffed. 'You are burnt as a witch and I am hanged for treason! Thank you!'

'And the question that brought you to Scotland is answered, one way or the other.'

He frowned at her.

'God! You hate him, don't you. The King, I mean.'

'He murdered the man I loved.'

'The man whose picture you keep in that locket you wear round your neck. The beautiful Earl of Gowrie.'

She looked down suddenly.

'It's a pity,' he said, 'we cannot go to Edinburgh.'

'But we can, we can!'

He shook his head.

'We've escaped once, Madeleine. We had some luck. We cannot expect to be as lucky next time.'

'It is not a question of luck, James. What is needed is cunning. Intelligence! Here, in this room, are the two best brains in Scotland. Together, we shall find the way into Edinburgh and the way out again.'

'You are the most arrogant, the most impossible, the most beautiful—'

She took his hand in one of hers. With her other hand she rumpled his hair.

'What nonsense you talk! Come! I will show you the loveliest falcon in the world. And while we admire it, we shall plan our journey to Edinburgh.'

But the journey was not to begin for a few days. The weather was warm. The ground alive with game. Day after day, the pair roamed the woods and the wild hills above the house. Madeleine launched her great white predator at the hares.

They made love and swam in the icy lochans of the region fringed with spongy moss. They came to a quiet flowing stream with a shallow bed haunted by wading birds with long orange beaks and a strident cry. Oyster-catchers, she told him. They returned in the evening to the little tower. There they ate ravenously, waited on by a taciturn old woman who had known Madeleine as a child.

'She is suspicious of you, Jamie. She thinks you mean to marry me. Nothing I can say will persuade her to think differently.'

'If I were the marrying kind I would certainly want to marry you.'

'If I were not marrying Lord Cluny I might consider you.'

'You told her about Cluny?'

'Yes, I told her. She laughed.'

Madeleine sent one of the stable hands to the Bannerman house in Edinburgh. On the fourth day, they returned from hunting to find Rory awaiting them, coldly angry. After brother and sister had spoken briefly together, Madeleine came to James: 'The hunt has died down, Jamie. Someone has spread the word that you have fled to France although others have seen you on the way to Ireland to fight for Tyrone.'

'I might do worse.'

'Tomorrow we shall leave for Edinburgh. You will be a Frenchman, a servant of the French ambassador.'

'And you? What will you be, Madeleine?'

She laughed.

'I shall be interesting and mysterious and all the town will talk about us.'

'What of Rory?'

'He will find his own way to Edinburgh.'

At that moment Rory Bannerman came into the room.

'I will talk to Mr. Stuart for a moment, alone,' he said.

Madeleine shrugged.

'If you wish, Rory.'

When his sister had left the room, Bannerman opened his attack without preliminaries.

'You were going to escort my sister to Lord Cluny's house. Instead, you are now planning to return to Edinburgh where she will be in deadly peril. What explanation do you have?'

'Have you ever tried to make your sister do something she doesn't want to do?'

There was a second or two of silence. 'I suppose you want to marry her, Stuart. Why not? She is a beautiful girl with a fortune and you are—what you are. Let me warn you then. I'd have you killed if there was no other way to prevent it.'

A smooth, polished, poisonous little snake, Jamie thought; he just might do it.

'I don't mean to marry her,' he said, 'but I won't promise not to. God knows, she is lovely enough and money is always useful. Did she tell you why we are going back to the town? She has some wild story. A brooch of Lord Gowrie's. How wild a story we'll soon know. Will you come with us to Edinburgh? Since you don't trust me.'

'No, I don't. But I have business. I cannot ride with you.'

'A pity. But it is hard to be in two places at once.'

'I shall see you in Edinburgh, Stuart.'

With a nod, he left and, a few minutes later, Jamie heard him riding off.

Daniel in the lion's den

They arrived in Edinburgh two days later just before nightfall. They found the gates still open. Madeleine, wearing a mask which nobody had the bad manners to remove, remained in the saddle. Jamie dismounted and spoke in a mixture of French and Scots to the porter, brandishing an elaborate document Madeleine had concocted. He had a message for the French ambassador, he said. Covered by diplomatic privilege.

'And the lady?'

Jamie went near enough to the porter to whisper: the lady was a special friend of the ambassador's. He gave a Gallic wink.

'Is she covered by diplomatic privilege, too?' asked the porter.

'Emphatically,' said Jamie.

After that there was no trouble.

He remounted and together they rode into the town.

Then after a few hundred yards, they separated. Madeleine took the horses by a circuitous route to the stables behind Bannerman's Lodging. Jamie waited until it was dark, then made his way on foot to the court that housed Monypenny's Tavern.

He opened the door and peeped cautiously inside. Then he whistled with astonishment.

'Maggie!' he cried. 'What the devil are you doing here, light of my life?'

He strode forward and took her in his arms. She struggled free.

'You must not do that, James,' she said. 'What will the customers think?'

'You serve the drink here? By God, that's good news. There used to be a red-haired woman—'

Maggie tossed her head indignantly.

'She was nothing better than a whore, James.'

'Dear, dear!'

'In the end she took up with a sea-captain and went off with him.'

'Serve her right! Now bring me a jug of wine to drink to our happy reunion. But first, give me a kiss, and to hell with the customers.'

Two minutes later, he sat with the red wine before him, on a bench which commanded a good view of the door.

'Now, Maggie, tell me all about your adventures on the way to Edinburgh. All that you can tell without making me blush.'

'*You* blush! May I see that day! Do you remember a little Highland rogue named Gregory? Well, he said he would find a place for me in Edinburgh.'

'I know what kind of place!'

'He came on an old lady—a pious old body, who wanted to visit her sister in the town, if you please, and must have someone to go with her on the way. So I became the waiting woman and Gregory was the groom. God, was I glad when that journey was over! The old lady has the same weakness as Gregory.'

'The bottle?'

She nodded gravely.

'When she wasn't praying, she was boozing. They had nights together, those two, drinking dram for dram. I don't think one of them drew a sober breath all that way. For all that, she was a good old girl.'

'They often are. Where is Gregory now?'

'If you ask me, he's sleeping it off,' Maggie shrugged. 'But he found me this job when that whore bolted with the sailor. I'm grateful to Gregory for that.'

'I'd like fine to see the little smaik again—' he said. 'If you can get word to him.'

'I'll see what I can do.'

Jamie cocked an eye at the window. Outside, the dark had closed in. The closes and wynds of the town would be in deep shadow. In a little while, it would be safe for him to venture out. There was one visit he wished to pay. He would finish his wine and go out quietly.

But before he had finished the jug, the door leading into the close was thrown open. With a thump of heavy boots and a jingle of spurs, a huge bulk loomed redly in the candlelight.

'Captain!' cried Jamie.

'By God,' said Sinclair, holding out a hand as broad as a spade. 'It's you, is it? James Stuart, the man who will pass into the history of war if I have time to write the story.'

He threw one leg over a stool and collapsed on it with a crash.

'The storming of Castle Roy. Maybe the stratagem was mine. But I am a modest man. Truth compels me to say that Ensign Stuart— Here's the wine. Do you see this girl?'

He slapped Maggie's solid flesh.

'I brought her here to save her from a life of shame. That was what Gregory had in mind for her, the little Highland tod! God, it's good to see you, Stuart! What will we do this time? Seize Edinburgh Castle? Just give me ten minutes to prepare a plan.'

He threw back his head and poured half a jug of wine down his throat.

'How is you expeditionary force, Captain?'

Sinclair frowned and lowered his voice.

'Half of them were cowardly dogs who made off while their commander—' he smote his chest— 'was in the Highlands helping you to beat the Earl of Orkney. The other half are still eating the King of Sweden's rations. But tomorrow or maybe the next day, they'll be sailing across the North Sea to war and glory.'

He frowned.

'The movement of troops by sea is a complicated business. But just leave it to me! All will go smoothly. And while we are talking about it—'

Sinclair put his elbows on the table and brought his big scarred face close to Jamie's.

'You'd better come too, ensign. For two reasons. Last night, Orkney came into the town, secretly. He has not been seen yet. But, so they tell me, his face is still bandaged, poor gentleman. And he has a terrible dislike of cats. He has brought a score of his assassins with him. And whose throat do you think they mean to slit?'

'But I'm not here,' Stuart objected.

'No. You are in Ireland fighting for Tyrone, up to your knees in the bogs. Everybody kens that and most people believe it. But not Orkney! And he has sent a man to Ulster just to make sure. You'll find Russia a safer place than this for you, boy.'

'My ankle's troubling me,' said Stuart, excusing himself.

'Yes. I saw how much it bothered you in the North Country! Now, listen to a second argument for foreign travel. Do you remember that cateran who calls himself Alistair MacIan? A young man with a twisted face? He is coming with me to Moscow with some of those nameless ruffians he calls his children. I've given him the temporary rank of Lieutenant. I'll do the same for you, James, if you come.'

'Where is Alistair?'

'Where is he? Somewhere in the town. Please God not drinking too much and please God not fighting. He will make a good comrade for you on the field of battle.'

Jamie was pleased that Alistair was at hand at a time when Orkney's bravos would be ranging through the town.

'I'll like to see him again, here, this minute.'

'So would the Law,' said Sinclair. 'They have a list of complaints against him as long as your arm and every one of them a hanging matter. Alistair is lying low. Gregory can take you to him though, if for once Gregory is sober.'

'Yes. But who'll take me to Gregory?'

Captain Sinclair made a scornful noise with his lips and went to the door. Opening it, he called in a voice like resounding brass:

'Donald! Donald, you drunken rogue!'

After a few seconds of silence, Jamie thought he heard a voice, thin and wavering, coming from somewhere in the muddle of alleys that led out of the close. A moment later, a squalid, familiar figure appeared in the darkness and stood swaying before them.

'My lord!'

'You've been drinking.'

'Me! Drinking! How can you think it, sir?'

'Are you sober enough to lead me to Alistair MacIan?' asked Jamie.

'Alistair MacIan. Nothing easier.'

After diving down several flights of stairs and plunging through countless tunnels running beneath the buildings, Gregory pulled up in a tiny unlit court which seemed to be a dead end. He gave the curlew's call. In a minute it was answered.

'Wait, my lord,' said Gregory.

A door creaked. A faint glimmer of light showed in the dark of an archway. And then, suddenly, coming forward into the court, hand outstretched, Alistair MacIan, looking unusually sinister in the darkness.

'By God, it's you, Jamie. Daniel in the lion's den!'

'Two Daniels in the lion's den—if you can call him a lion!'

Both burst into peals of laughter.

'Come in and have a dram. Time you met the gentry.'

Alistair led the way into a scene of gloom and misery such as Jamie had not set eyes on since he left his bench in the Spanish galley. Doss-house, den of thieves, lazaret, shebeen—it might have been any one of them and it was probably all. Beggars, pickpockets, plague-ridden or drunk, the inmates lay crowded on the floor.

When his eyes grew accustomed to the murk, Jamie decided this must be one of the haunts of the confraternity of Edinburgh caddies. Alistair spoke a few sentences in Gaelic and then, turning to Jamie, held out a horn flask.

'I'd introduce you to the company,' said Alistair, 'but there is a prejudice here against naming names.'

'Why don't you come with me. I'll find a better place for you.'

'Oh, it's not much worse than a cave on the mountains. But thank you for your kindness.'

'I want to talk to you, Alistair, before you go off to the wars. First let me ask you this: how fond are you of King James?'

Alistair turned his head sharply and spat.

'Treason, treason!' said Jamie, with a grin. 'In that case, can you be at Monypenny's in the morning tomorrow?'

'I can that! Oh, I smell infamies and bloody deeds!'

'Lucky for you that you're going to the wars,' said Jamie. 'Tomorrow then. At Monypenny's.'

In the close, he began to tell Gregory where he wanted to go.

'Just what I thought, my lord,' the caddie interrupted with a chuckle. 'We'll be there before you have made up your mind what to say to the lassie.'

'Lead on!'

Somewhere during the next ten minutes, Stuart heard singing in an alley parallel to the one they were using. He thought he had heard the tune before—and the voice, a resonant baritone.

'Sweet violets.
Sweeter than the roses are,
Covered all over—'

'Fletcher!' he cried, and headed towards the sound. Gregory gave a warning shout.

'For God's sake, it's the English actors! Don't go near them, sir. We have troubles enough as it is.'

'What are they doing here all this while?'

'Some play they are going to give. Don't ask me more. Not everybody in this town likes actors.'

'I see nothing wrong with them, Gregory, apart from the fact that Fletcher is a manifest English spy.'

'Just so. If you don't object, my lord, we'll hold on our way.'

And so a few minutes later, Jamie climbed a dark stair and knocked at the door.

'I've come back for my shirt,' he said when it opened.

'Mr. Stuart!'

'Jamie,' he reminded her.

'Jamie. I've been hearing about you.'

'And all of it to my credit, I'm sure.'

'Some of it. Come in, though. *Entrez Monseigneur.*'

'*Mademoiselle est trop gentille.*'

In the candlelight within the door, she looked at him critically.

'Thinner,' she said. 'Bonier. Rougher.'

'And wiser,' he said. 'As for you, Mary, I have bad news. You have not changed in the least. You are still the most beautiful girl in the world.'

'Liar,' she said. 'You know it isn't true and I know you don't think it is.'

'I did not say you are the *only* beautiful girl in the world.'

She tossed her head.

'You had better not. Come and meet my mother, Jamie.'

'Where is your brother Alan?'

'Somewhere in the town. Mother,' she called, 'here's Mr. Stuart, come for his shirt.'

'Mary, make ready your brother's bed for Mr. Stuart.'

'Yes, mother.' With a smile to Jamie, she left the room.

'Mrs. Beaton, how do you know I wish a lodging for the night?'

She smiled.

'There's a terrible shortage of beds in this town. I mean in decent houses, and I have a notion you might be glad of a good rest tonight, after all you've been through.'

'But your son, Mrs. Beaton? Won't he want his bed?'

'Alan! He's away somewhere on business and God only kens when he'll be back.'

'One thing I must tell you,' said Stuart earnestly. 'I'm a wanted man.'

'You are and no mistake. Placards all over the town warning folks about you. What you've done! There must be a wild streak in you, Mr. Stuart.'

'Don't believe all you read, madam,' he said.

'All I trust is my nose, Mr. Stuart. There's a whiff of gunpowder about you. Now where did you get that, do you think?'

Mary appeared in the doorway.

'Mr. Stuart has been shooting in the hills, Mother.'

'Indeed, indeed, girl! That's a chancy sport. Well, your bed will be ready for you now. If you hear a sound in the night, pay no heed. It will only be Alan, my son, back from his business, God help us!'

'And your shirt will be ready for you in the morning, James.'

James slept early and woke late. While he was shaving, there came a knock at the door.

'Come in!'

'Good morning, James. Your shirt, my lord.'

The rent had been mended so skilfully that it could scarcely be detected. On the breast, embroidered in a fine linen thread, was his monogram with a small crown above it.

'How did you know?' he asked, grinning.

'I can always tell a king.' She smiled mischievously.

'Even the King of Elfland, travelling incognito? Tell nobody else. That is our royal command.'

'No sir.'

'While I finish shaving, let me tell you of the terrible dangers I've been running.'

'Please, Jamie, no. Tell me instead about the women you've met.'

'Women. No. That wouldn't be interesting. There is nothing so tiresome for a girl as hearing about other girls. If there had been any! Let me tell you instead about the kingdom I have founded. Up in the mountains, stretching over miles and miles of the most beautiful country in the world.'

She drank in his descriptions of life in that marvellous land, the hunting, feasting, dancing, singing.

'It sounds wonderful,' she sighed.

'Only one thing is lacking, Mary.'

'What is that?'

'There is a terrible shortage of girls,' he said sadly.

'No girls at all, Jamie?'

'No— Well, almost none.'

'Almost none? That means one.'

He turned quickly, frowning. He had pulled on the shirt and stood there, his hands on his hips.

'Don't you think I look very handsome in this?'

She shook her head.

'No. Not handsome. But every inch a king.'

'Would you like to be a duchess, Mary? I could arrange it.'

She made a small grimace and for a moment there was silence. Her face became serious.

'Oh, Jamie, if only I could become a bad woman!'

'What then?'

'I'd write you a letter.'

'But you may stay as you are—as good as gold, and I'll never have my letter. Why wait?'

'Because you are a man who needs a bad woman,' she said firmly.

'How unfair!' he cried, taking a step towards her.

'But true!' She held out her hand to keep him off.

'But you promise to write when the time comes?'

'Yes, I promise.'

'Don't leave it too late,' he told her. 'When you feel you are going to become bad, when you have the first premonition of wickedness, write at once. I want to be there when it happens.'

They laughed.

'Now come and say good morning to my mother.'

The Stuart legacy

The double door that led into the courtyard of Bannerman's Lodging was shut.

Jamie and Alistair were waiting for Madeleine to come out, when her elegant brother, Rory, appeared. All three men wore heavy cloaks to prevent recognition.

'Let me introduce Alistair MacIan, with a family name we won't use—Rory Bannerman.'

The two young men—one tattered, the other sleek, both dangerous—eyed one another without enthusiasm and nodded curtly.

'You are coming with us to the sword-slipper's shop?' asked Jamie.

Rory nodded.

'Madeleine has asked me and I must say yes. We Bannermans can deny nothing to one another.'

A half-smile lingered on his lips.

Just at that moment a scream came from inside the house. Madeleine appeared like a fury, with flushed cheeks and blazing eyes, a horse whip in her hand. She was flogging a red-haired girl who ran across the yard, half-naked, weeping and trying with her arms to ward off the blows that fell on her back. Reaching the big door which led to the street, she opened it and ran out. Madeleine slammed it behind her.

'Good riddance!' she cried. 'That's the little bitch Effie who betrayed me. I found the impudent slut skulking in the kitchen, eating my food.'

'So long as she doesn't betray you again!' said her brother.

Madeleine frowned and shrugged.

'Now I'll fetch my cloak and mask and we can go,' she said.

The sign above the door said, under a gilded crown, 'Damasker, sword-slipper and cutler to H.M. the King'.

'This is the place,' said Jamie. He pushed the door open and listened to the tinkle of the bell.

Madeleine entered. Rory Bannerman went in before Jamie and Alistair.

'Do you remember me, gaffer?' Stuart asked the sword-slipper, throwing off his cloak.

The old man who had sharpened Jamie's sword all those days ago peered at the quartet who had entered his workshop and put down the dagger he had been hammering on a small anvil.

'Aye, sir,' he said. 'I remember you fine. You had a sword that came from the old King's armoury. You have it still? That's good. A fine piece! Whiles I've wondered how it came into your hands, if you'll forgive me for saying so.'

'Some day I'll tell you.' He pulled the sword out and laid it on the workshop bench. 'But today this lady and I have come on other business.'

'Ma'am, a chair for you.' The old man came forward in a fluster. 'My manners! What will you think! But you talked about business, sir?'

'Just that. We will now show you, with these gentlemen as our witnesses, two halves of a brooch, clasp, or buckle in diamonds and emeralds. If it's the right clasp, you will know what to do. Do you know what I'm talking about, gaffer?'

The old man looked anxiously up at Stuart for a minute before he answered.

'I might do that, sir,' he said, nervously.

'And you have a sure way of recognising the jewel if you see it?'

'I have. A drawing of it in colour, made in my father's time.'

Stuart and Madeleine put down on the work bench the two halves of the jewelled clasp. The sword-slipper looked at them, his eyes widening. Then he went to the shelves where he kept a row of tall ledgers bound in calf. After a minute or two he drew out of one of them a sheet on which there was a drawing in water colour.

'That's it,' he said. 'That is certainly it. Good God!'

'Yes, that is it,' said Jamie. 'Look, Madeleine.'

She nodded. Her eyes were glistening with excitement.

'Then you have a bargain to keep, Master sword-slipper,' said James. 'Damn me if I know what the bargain is, or why, but your duty is to keep it.'

'My father told me that one day you would come,' the old man stammered. ' "Sandy," he said to me, "see you look well to it for I've given my word to the King"—not this king, sir, his grandfather. And now you've come ... I must ask you to wait. I'll not be more than a minute.'

He went to the back of the workshop where it was dark. There was a squeaking noise as if a wooden panel was being pushed to one side, then a soft jingle of keys. He came back with a piece of yellow parchment, a few inches long, folded three times and sealed. With a bow, he handed it to Madeleine, who passed it to Jamie.

Jamie held it up to the light. The seal was in green wax. The impression on it was beautifully sharp but of a coat of arms he did not recognise.

'No money?' he said.

'It may be better than money, Jamie,' said Madeleine.

'You'll sign for it, sir, if you please,' said the sword-slipper.

'You should sign,' Madeleine agreed.

He hesitated for a moment.

'Sign, man,' said Alistair impatiently.

'Sign for what?'

'Sign for a sealed packet given you by an honest man in the discharge of his duty,' said Rory Bannerman.

'Give me a pen, Mr. sword-slipper.'

He signed and handed the missive to Madeleine. She broke the seal and unfolded the paper.

'Read it out, Madeleine,' he said.

'No,' said Rory. 'Not here. This document may be dangerous to us all. Let us take it to the Lodging where we can read it in secret.'

'Just one thing, sir,' said the sword-slipper to Jamie as they turned to go. 'One day you'll tell me how you came to have that sword.'

'I shall do so. Be sure of that. One day.'

Rory finished reading. He put the parchment on the table and smoothed it out with his small brown hands.

In the quiet, dark room two candles burned in silver holders on the table, making black shadows dance on the panelled walls. Although it was only afternoon, the shutters were drawn and heavy curtains had been pulled across them. Nobody passing in the street outside could have guessed that in the town house of the Bannermans a private conference was being held.

'What it means,' he said, looking at Jamie, 'is plain enough. It means that James the Fifth, King of Scots, was married by the rites of the Catholic Church to the lady Catherine Carmichael in the twelfth month of the year of Our Lord 1536.'

Stuart gave a whistle.

'Then it means that my father was mistaken,' he said. 'All his life he believed he was a royal bastard. He was proud of it. But, according to this brief,' tapping the paper on the table, 'he was born in holy wedlock by a bare month. Not much, I grant you, but enough for the law ...'

'But why all these complications?' asked Rory. 'The brooch in two different pieces, given to two different people, neither of whom knows the secret?'

'Yes, why?' said Alistair.

'I can tell you half the story,' said Stuart, 'as my father told it to me long ago. When my grandfather, the fifth James, married, he did it in secret, in a little abbey on an island—'

'Inchmahome,' Madeleine broke in. 'The island we visited?'

James nodded.

'My grandmother was near her time then, and she died a few days after my father was born. She had one half of the jewel, a fastening for a belt that my grandfather had bought for her. This she left to the nurse to give to my father when he grew up. That was all my father knew about it. I know nothing about the other half.'

'About that I can tell something,' said Madeleine.

'Whether it is true or not I can't tell but it is the story as Lord Gowrie told it to me before we—before he died. James the Fifth on his deathbed gave that half of the clasp to a man he trusted—the old Scots officer who in the end sold it to Gowrie to keep himself from starving.'

'What I still don't understand is this,' said Jamie. 'All these precautions to keep the marriage—if it was a marriage—secret. The gravestone defaced. The coffin dug up. And the jewel in two halves, the sealed paper in the sword-slipper's keeping—which made no sense at all unless the marriage was one day going to be unearthed. Explain all that, if you please.'

Rory struck the table with the flat of his hand.

'By God,' he cried, 'I think I have guessed the secret. For high reasons of state, your grandfather, King James V, wished to make a marriage with a French princess. Why? Because a French alliance was his best hope—the only hope he saw—of saving Scotland from King Henry VIII of England. So every trace of the marriage to your grandmother had to be blotted out. Years pass—how many? Six? King James on his deathbed hears that his French Queen has given birth to a baby girl—a princess—a queen to follow him and rule Scotland in those dangerous years! What a disaster it must have seemed! Then he remembered that he had a son after all. A lawful son, unacknowledged. And so he gave one half of the jewel to his friend, the soldier, who was in the Palace at the time. He told him where he was to look for the rest of the jewel and what he should do then.'

'And the sword-slipper?' Stuart asked. 'Why was he chosen to keep the brief?'

'Because,' said Rory, 'in a world where he trusted few men, your grandfather trusted the sword-slipper, the father of the man you have met. As boys they had gone hunting together. That's a story well enough known in this town.'

But Stuart was not finished.

'My grandfather must have wished his friend to re-unite the jewel and demand the marriage document. Why was that not done?'

Alistair shrugged and shook his head.

'Who kens, Jamie, who kens! French power in Scotland hung on the baby Queen, did it not? If a boy were to come forward with a better claim to the throne, where would the French ascendancy be? An English army would swarm over the Border to support the boy claimant's cause. Civil war, divided families, a divided land! That would have befallen us, boy, as night follows day.'

He paused, searching the faces of the trio who sat round the table with him.

'Religion. The girl would be reared as a Catholic in France. Your father was being brought up by kin of his mother's who were Protestants.'

'And the king's friend, the man he trusted, was a Catholic who went to fight for the King of Spain,' said Jamie.

Rory nodded.

'Another thing,' he said, 'we now know the truth about the murders in Perth. Someone told the King that Gowrie had brought back from abroad evidence that would blow him off his throne.'

'Who told?'

'Ah!' said Rory. 'That is of less importance.'

Madeleine broke the silence that had fallen: 'When do I call Your Majesty by his proper title?'

She was on her knees, eyes sparkling with mischief. She kissed Jamie's hand.

'By God,' he said, 'this is the only good reason I can see for doing something I am not going to do.'

'You *are* going to do it, Jamie,' she cried. 'You *are* going to have your rights.'

She was lovelier at that moment than he had ever seen her. The candlelight sparkled in her eyes—and on the golden locket hanging from her neck.

'I was not in this country more than half an hour,' he said, 'when someone told me that in Scotland possession is *ten*-tenths of the law. Tell me. Who possesses the crown?'

'A usurper. He has no right to be what he pretends to be. And you have the proof of it.' She pointed at the table. 'There!'

Jamie took the parchment from the table and folded it so that the broken green seal was showing.

'There is another matter,' said Rory. 'This King is awaiting news from the south.'

'He can hardly hide his impatience!' she said contemptuously.

'Even Queen Elizabeth must die one day,' said Rory. 'Who will follow her?'

'A man who has stolen one crown and will use it to steal another!'

'Madeleine, what would you? He has made himself safe on this throne by thirty years of cunning and chicanery. What could drive him from it now? That piece of parchment in James Stuart's hand?' He made a gesture of dismissal. 'First, it must be attested, accepted by the Council, confirmed by Parliament—'

'The Parliament that hanged the Earl of Gowrie for treason a month after he was murdered!' she broke in angrily.

'Exactly! Could Parliament be persuaded to dethrone him?' Rory went on. 'Not without war in the land, a war which the present King would win.'

Alistair nodded gloomily.

'Yes. Every hungry hawk of a lord in Scotland thinks there will be rich pickings for him in London. He will fight for his chance of plunder.'

'My brother is one of them,' said Madeleine, looking sourly at Rory.

'No bad thing,' said Rory, 'if the old quarrel with England died.'

'But,' said Madeleine, 'all that could come about, too, under *this* James Stuart.' She pointed at Jamie. 'He can be King of both kingdoms.'

Her brother shook his head.

'No, Madeleine. King James has something this James Stuart does not have—a double right to the English throne through Mary Stuart, his mother, and again through Darnley, his father.'

'If he is Darnley's son!' she said coolly, rising from the table.

'*He is Darnley's son!* Whatever be the truth about his right to the crown of Scotland, King James is the lawful heir of Elizabeth. So ...'

Madeleine's words came in a passionate torrent.

'Jamie, you must not! You, a born king's son, with the air and presence of a king—a king of Scots!—you must not give way. To steal is base. To yield to robbery is worse. When fraud is compounded with weakness the wrong is doubled and the scorn multiplied.

'He says the lords of Scotland, if they do not rise against you, will not rise for you. But I swear that three earls, seven lords, and ten clans will take the field for you. I shall name them. And that is only a beginning! We shall call a Convention to look at that parchment. You will be there. Do you think they will put the crow above the eagle?'

She pointed to her brother. 'He says that you have no claim on the throne of England. So be it! You will all the more surely be King of Scots. Let the English have the crow. Let us keep the King.'

She bent towards him, searching his face. After a moment of utter stillness, Stuart shook his head slowly.

'No,' he said. 'No.'

He put a hand on her shoulder.

'It is no use,' he said gently. 'No use, Madeleine. We come with our scrap of parchment, which they will think we have forged. We break in on the last act of the play—the stage is set, the lines are rehearsed—the hero is about to have his moment of triumph. We interrupt—and nobody, actors, stage hands or audience, can spare us patience. We come too late.'

'A few years ago, when nobody in Scotland thought about the English succession,' said Alistair, shaking his head, 'it might have been possible. But now—too late, too late.'

Stuart went over to the table, the parchment in his hand. He held it close to the flame of the candle while they watched.

'King for an hour,' he said.

Suddenly, Madeleine snatched the document from Stuart's fingers.

'You may need that yet, Jamie,' said Alistair.

'I need it now,' said Madeleine.

Hush!' Rory stood up, raising a finger.

They heard a staccato of thuds as if on the cobbles outside, then a sound of someone running quickly and noisily up the stairs outside the room. Gregory burst into the room, white-faced.

'Master! Armed men have broken into the close.'

'I ought to have strangled that girl,' said Madeleine.

Stuart ran to the window, threw back the curtain and opened the shutters a crack. With a silken murmur his sword slid from the scabbard.

'Orkney's men,' he said.

'Out! Through the stables and into the lane!' cried Madeleine. 'They will not have a guard there. I have a place to hide. While you are gone, I shall have a horse made ready for the road. When it is dark you can come back to the stables. You will find the horse there.'

'Night's candles are burnt out'

Jamie moved quietly out into the darkening street. The level sunshine painted some walls gold, leaving others a deep blue. Gregory followed him, near enough to keep him in sight, far enough away not to annoy him. Alistair and Rory had disappeared in the opposite direction.

In the street there was a sound of music, a drum and fifes, growing louder. People were coming to their doors. Windows were thrown open. A crowd was gathering and seemed to be moving with the music.

Moments later, a burly man with a crimson face and bold black eyes—Lawrence Fletcher—appeared leading his troupe through the streets.

As they came abreast of him, the crowd of loafers thickened. James shouldered his way into the densest part of it and was carried along. In a building at the end of a close the English actors were going to give a performance. It seemed the play told the melancholy story of two unfortunate lovers in a town in Italy. Jamie pressed forward to a door which, to judge by a notice fastened to the wall beside it, led into the theatre. It said 'Romeo and Juliet'. Jamie recalled the lines of verse he had read to Peregrine Wroxall many weeks before. Money was asked at the door. Jamie paid and went in. He judged that the space in which he found himself had been a tennis court. It took a minute for his eyes to accustom themselves to the light which came from two flares at the end of the room.

The hall was filling up with people, some sitting on benches, more standing. No one had noticed Jamie's arrival.

He found a place where he could lean against the back wall

of the place. At least nobody could take him from behind. Among the spectators, he thought he could detect one or two men wearing Orkney's livery. The place was probably not so safe as he had supposed. But for the moment, he was fully occupied in making sense of what was going on at the other end of the hall, on the platform.

The play had begun. Strangely clad personages shouted and gesticulated.

And there was Peregrine Wroxall, got up as a girl, and—good God!—with his face well whitened and his belly well laced in, Lawrence Fletcher!

Jamie gathered that Fletcher was playing the part of Romeo and that Romeo was intended to be the youth with whom the girl, Juliet, was madly in love. The whole business was a bit distasteful—a coarse, red-faced man of forty-five and a pinched boy with crimped yellow hair, apeing the passion of love in public. And yet—Jamie thought, and yet ...

He stayed and listened. He did not even notice the man in Orkney's livery who came into the room and started when he saw Jamie. Seconds later the man went out again quickly and silently.

Jamie stayed. Before long it seemed to him that the fat ex-soldier and the skinny Cockney boy up there on the flimsy platform had been touched by some magic wand. The moonlight bathed the walls of an Italian city. Language more beautiful than language had any right to be had created its own world, delusive, sad, adorable. And Jamie, who should have gone, who had the most imperative of reasons to flee, stayed, tears running down his cheeks. He looked round. The man standing next to him was weeping too. He stayed on and on, listening spellbound, forgetful of his need to go.

> Night's candles are burnt out, and jocund day
> Stands tiptoe on the misty mountain tops.
> I must begone and live, or stay and die ...

Hearing those lines, Jamie shuddered involuntarily.

'By God!' he thought, 'my position to a T.'

The tears were still drying on his cheeks when he left, making his way out as unobtrusively as possible. As he was leaving, he paused to ask a man who looked as if he might have something to do with the play, 'Who wrote it?'

'Dunno,' said the man.

'Marlowe,' said another man nearby.

'Malro?'

The man nodded. Jamie thanked him and went out.

He emerged from an alley into a small courtyard and halted. Coming towards him were Kennedy and two of his comrades, swords drawn.

Jamie took a step back so that he stood at the point where the alley ran into the courtyard. There, at least, he would be covered on either flank. He drew his sword. Kennedy approached him, sneering.

'He's going to fight.'

Jamie nodded to the other two.

'Are you his seconds? I warn you, he has lost one sword to me already.'

'His *seconds*!' Kennedy grinned. 'This is not an affair of honour, young pup. You are going to lose your life. Just look on us as three executioners.'

'One at a time or all together?'

'What do you think? A little time for play first. You are going to be hurt before you die, Stuart. Sandy, you take him in the right.'

They came forward, more cautiously than he had expected.

'Mixed up in a duel, Jamie?' Captain Sinclair, immense and rubicund, appeared in the courtyard behind the trio of bravos.

'A kind of duel, Captain.'

'Oh ho! That sort of duel is it!'

With great deliberation, Sinclair pulled a heavy pistol from his belt. He touched the brim of his hat.

'Mr. Kennedy, you have some business with my young friend? So. You other two gentlemen, it seems, were about to take part in the discussion. Let me advise against it. Most imprudent. Move forward one inch and I shall be obliged to blow off the top of Mr. Kennedy's head. It will be a pleasure.'

He detected a slight movement among them. 'And do not reach for firearms if you have any about you. I have a suspicious nature.'

'Get out of our way, soldier,' growled Kennedy. 'There are enough of us in this town to chop you into food for the crows.'

'Then we must go to business quickly,' said Sinclair briskly. 'Up with your hands all of you! Behind your heads. So! Search them for pistols, Jamie, while I keep his lordship under the threat of my artillery.'

Jamie went forward, punched here and patted there, none too gently. A pistol clattered on the cobbles.

'That's all,' he reported.

'Good boy,' Sinclair went on smoothly. 'Now gentlemen, you have the choice. Stuart and Kennedy meet with swords, according to the laws of chivalry. I will be the judge. Or if that proposal does not please you, it can be you three against us two. Three to two! Tempting. I give you until I count ten to make your decision. One—two—three—four.'

'Let it be Kennedy against Stuart,' said one of the two men beside Kennedy.

'Single combat!' said the other.

Kennedy turned on them.

'Cowardly dogs!'

'It's your quarrel, billy, not ours,' shrugged one of his comrades.

'You swore you'd carve him up for breakfast,' sneered the other.

'Very prudent,' said Sinclair. 'In my time, I was the most terrible duellist in the Low Countries. Wherever I go, I am followed by the memory of twenty-four corpses. Now, Jamie, make ready!'

Stuart threw off his doublet and pulled his shirt over his head. He had learned that mind and limbs worked in closer unison without the encumbrance of clothes. He recalled the words of his fencing master at the Academy, a broken-down captain with a Gascon accent as strong as the garlic he chewed.

'James, James, you are thinking with your head! It is the blade of the sword that must think.'

After months of practice, Jamie found that, naked to the waist, he achieved a new speed and elegance of stroke. Now he would put them to good use again.

Kennedy kept his shirt on and wound his sash more tightly round his waist. He was a practised fighting animal with the little eyes and the strength of a bull.

It would be hard to wear him down, Jamie reflected, but he would probably try to end the business in one mad onset, arm straight, blade level and aimed at the heart. There was no more dangerous antagonist for the trained swordsman.

A score or so of onlookers had gathered in the little court. A rough-looking crowd of the kind attracted anywhere by the prospect of a fight—and the hope that soon there would be a corpse worth stripping.

Sinclair replaced his pistol in his sash and drew his rapier.

'Measure the weapons,' he called out. 'You—' pointing to one of Orkney's men—'bring Kennedy's sword to me. James, give me yours.' The two blades were put one beside the other, point to hilt. 'Kennedy's is longer by three inches. Do you want to change, Jamie?'

Stuart shook his head.

'It has fought well for me before,' he said. 'This is no moment to be ungrateful!'

'Very well. Ready?'

The two combatants nodded.

Sinclair held his rapier out between them breast high. They came to the salute.

'Commend your souls to God, gentlemen,' cried Sinclair, 'according to your faith, if any. And now—to business.'

His weapon caught the light as it rose in a slow arc, leaving the two fighters face to face.

Jamie made a few wary passes. He was watching Kennedy's eyes for the first clue to his intentions. When a man is going to attack there is a sudden glint of light in his eyes. Only the most practised swordsmen can avoid it.

For a second, he thought Kennedy was going to come for him straight on. Instead, there was an instant of hesitation. Something about the way Stuart handled his sword made the gallowglass pause. They exchanged a slow series of passes, Kennedy taking the measure of Stuart and Stuart waiting for the attack which he thought must come soon.

Kennedy increased the speed and power of his sword-strokes. In a moment, thought Jamie, he will rush me, or he is not the man I take him for.

206

His eyes did not leave Kennedy's, watching for the signal. But it did not come. Instead, Kennedy's gaze seemed to fall asleep, while his sword-play became more elaborate and at the same time lackadaisical.

He was beginning to succumb to the lazy rhythm of the combat when, suddenly, an instant of alarm woke in him. He had seen Kennedy imperceptibly change the balance of his body, from the heel to the ball of the foot. Without more warning, Kennedy sprang, headlong, reckless, yet covering his advance with a flurry of savage thrusts.

The court rang with the shrill music of steel on steel. Stuart gave ground, parrying the thrusts, first easily, then daringly, at last in desperation. Taking a thrust at the shoulder on his blade near the hilt, he bounded back and barely escaped a second low thrust at the leg. At that moment he passed over to the attack and struck deep into Kennedy's body.

'That got him,' Jamie thought, 'an inch into his liver or I am no student of anatomy!' But no! Kennedy had sprung back, flushed in the cheeks but full of life. There was an instant when Jamie raised his point an inch above the exchange of strokes. His steel seemed to have met something harder than flesh, bone, or the leather of a belt.

But this was no moment to wonder. Having the shorter and stronger sword, being the more agile of the two, Jamie loosed on Kennedy a volley of strokes, fierce but perfectly controlled, leading up to a corkscrew twist of the wrist which flicked Kennedy's sword from his grasp. It fell to the stones.

Jamie's blade paused an inch from his adversary's chest.

Sinclair's voice rang out. 'Halt!' He strode forward, his rapier between the duellists. 'Do you want to go on?' he asked Kennedy.

There was a moment of silence. Jamie rubbed his hand on the cloth of his breeches. His body was shining with sweat.

Kennedy growled and nodded.

'Pick up your sword, then, and come to the on-guard.'

He leant over to Jamie and muttered, 'Watch your back, boy. One of these rogues has worked round behind you. He is hiding a dagger.' He lifted his rapier.

'Fall to again, gentlemen,' he cried.

207

Jamie changed his tactics. He was almost sure that Kennedy was wearing a secret corselet below his shirt. He thrust his point at the other man's throat and face—a dangerous style, since in doing so, Jamie was forced to leave his own body more open to attack.

The light was fading from the sky. Soon there would be no more to fight by than reflections from the yellow flares outside the tennis court.

He would have to rely on neater footwork and more dashing movements of the body. If time were on his side, his swordsmanship should prevail. But the longer they fought the greater the chance that more of Orkney's men would arrive. Or perhaps the Watch! The duel must end quickly.

Jamie pressed his attack. He thought he had touched his enemy in the shoulder. The face opposite him grimaced.

Then suddenly Sinclair's rapier was levelled between them.

'Halt, gentlemen, halt!' the captain shouted. 'Newcomers have arrived! Gentlemen wearing my Lord Orkney's livery. It may happen that some of you have a notion to take a hand in our pastime here. Before you do so, please look around you.'

Out of the corner of an eye, Jamie saw Alistair MacIan and two of his ragged clansmen standing on the outer edge of the yard. They had wrapped their plaids around their left arms and were leaning nonchalantly on their broadswords.

'We are here,' said Alistair, 'to see fair play.'

'You can see what I mean, gentlemen,' said Sinclair. 'Form your own conclusions. And, once more, on guard!'

He raised his rapier aloft. Jamie plunged forward to the assault. After a rapid succession of strokes he stepped inside Kennedy's guard and grasped the blade of his sword with his hand. Then he held his own weapon an inch from his adversary's throat.

'Drop that sword,' he said grimly, 'let me hear it on the cobbles!'

There was a noise of metal striking stone.

'Agree that you're beaten?' said Sinclair to Kennedy. 'As a gentleman you will no doubt wish the quarrel to be composed.'

'The devil I will!' Kennedy stooped suddenly to pick up the sword hilt. Jamie stamped his foot on it.

'Look out!' cried Sinclair. 'He has a dagger.'

At that moment, men in Orkney's uniform rushed forward to their comrades' aid.

One of the Highlanders shouted, and suddenly Jamie found clansmen on either side of him. Broadswords were swinging and steel clashing on steel.

Like a war god from a pagan myth, Sinclair advanced, using his rapier as a flail. Men who had been listening to the play in the tennis court poured into the close, attracted by the sounds of battle. After a minute it was over.

Orkney's men made off into the darkness of an alley. Kennedy was among them, a red stain at the right shoulder spreading over his shirt.

'Good,' said Sinclair to Stuart. 'He has gone to visit the surgeon. You have the makings of a fighter, James. But you aimed too high.'

'The bastard had a corselet under his shirt.'

'Ah! He means to have your life one way or the other. He'd like best to cut your throat.'

'So what am I to do?'

'Do? Become invisible! Vanish. And leave Scotland while you can.'

Stuart scowled.

'That's what you are always saying, Captain!' he said.

'Why did you not kill him?' Alistair demanded. 'One thrust would have done the job.'

'It was too hard a thrust to make.'

'Don't think he'll spare you,' Alistair muttered.

Jamie laughed as he pulled his shirt over his head and picked up his doublet from the cobbles.

'Go now to Bannerman's stables,' said Sinclair urgently. 'Go by the hidden way. You will be safe there for the moment. The search for you has moved further on. And she has a horse waiting for you.'

'Where am I to ride?' Jamie demanded. 'Oh, I know, I know! The frozen steppes—the palace of the Tsars!'

'You might do worse, boy. Listen to what I say. There will be a boat off Gullane Sands tomorrow at first dawn waiting for a signal. I'll be there. So will my expeditionary force, providing they have been able to keep out of gaol or hospital. Remember!

Gullane Sands. Fifteen miles along the coast from where we stand. Now, vanish! Become thin air! Kennedy means to kill you—without fee. The first free murder in his career.'

'And what of yourself, noble Captain?'

'I'll stay here awhile to cover the retreat. Alistair, will you stay with me?'

The Highlander swung his broadsword in assent.

From the tennis courts came a roll of applause. Fletcher had brought one of his declamations to a heroic end. And most of the audience had remained to hear it.

Stuart made off to seek the opening between the houses on the far side of the main street which would lead him to Bannerman's stables.

He knocked at the door. From the other side came a question. He answered. The door opened.

'You've been fighting,' said Madeleine, letting him in. 'Oh, don't deny it. I've been told! Are you a madman?'

'Do you think I go out looking for a fight?'

'Yes, I do,' she said, and threw her arms round him.

In the gloom of the stable he could see two horses standing saddled and bridled. A groom hovered behind them.

'I see they are ready for the journey. Let's be off, then! To Cluny!'

'No,' she said. 'Not to Cluny.'

'Not to Cluny? Not to the marriage feast?'

'Come,' she said. 'We cannot talk here.'

She led the way into the house, talking as she went.

'I will not marry him, the old man, even though Rory will be angry with me. It was his notion and he would have gained something by it! The agreement was that when I married the earl, Rory would marry his daughter, a girl with a dowry worth a peerage. But I cannot do it—so Rory, my loving brother, will curse me, and cast me out of the family.'

'What will you do? Where will you go?'

'Where you go, James.'

He took a deep breath.

'But, Madeleine, you know me.'

'Worse than that, Jamie. I know myself.'

They arrived in the room where the portrait of the beautiful boy hung above the fireplace.

'I am a rogue, a wanderer, almost an outlaw,' Jamie said. 'God knows what will become of me. You excite me, but I am incapable of faithfulness.'

'What do you think I am?' she retorted with a smile. 'Let me tell you. Cruel. Treacherous. Accused of being a witch—'

'A witch is what you are!' he assured her.

'Now I love you but—'

He shook his head.

'You love a dead man. The beautiful Earl of Gowrie.'

'I love a dead man,' she said.

She was fumbling with the locket on the gold chain round her neck. She opened it. 'Look,' she said. 'That is the boy I love.'

The tiny oval portrait in the locket was as sharp as if it had been cut with a diamond in the brilliant enamel.

A beautiful youth looked out, bright-eyed, dewy-lipped, proud and sensuous. About the fair young face, the curls clustered, abundant, lustrous and—what was this?—the colour of gold!

Stuart looked up at Madeleine.

'The earl had dyed his hair?' He looked at the sumptuous dark crown of the portrait on the wall.

Madeleine shook her head slowly.

'This is not Gowrie,' she said, her voice trembling. 'It is his brother, Alec, who was killed on the same day as he was. Killed, by this King. Alec was my lover ... You see, James, you have still a great deal to learn about me.'

'So that is why Gowrie fell out with you? He had found out about you and his brother.'

'He suspected. There are a hundred ways a man can tell, a hundred hints, even if there are no servants to whisper. What did he expect?' she said bitterly. 'He was four years in Italy. Four years! Alec was growing up during those years to a beauty that first excited me by reminding me of Gowrie and then maddened me by being more lovely than Gowrie.

'I am as I am, Jamie. A witch? No. But a woman with the devil in her body. I seduced Alec Ruthven. Look at him. You can see that the difference between Gowrie and him is not only a matter

211

of colour. It is a question of quality, of something else. Gowrie was sensual, Alec was pure.'

'That was why you found it exciting to seduce him?'

She laughed.

'After a while he could hardly let a day pass by without making love to me. And, of course, some servants came to know.'

'And some of them talked?'

'One especially.'

'He talked to Gowrie.'

She shook her head.

'He came to me. He was chamberlain to Gowrie. His name was Henderson. He was one of those who served dinner on the night Gowrie broke out in that mad tirade against the King. He knew there was a secret. He did not know what it was. Henderson came to me.'

Madeleine broke off for a moment. She seemed to be searching for a way to continue.

'What he said was plain enough,' she said at last. 'He knew about Alec and me. He named the servants who could prove it. But he was generous! Oh, yes, he was kind! He said he would not go to Gowrie with the story and the proofs if I told him the secret about the King which Gowrie was hiding.

'I should have stabbed the villain there and then. A thousand times since, I have blamed myself that I did not. But I was not desperate enough. I thought there might be some easier way out. And I did not foresee what Henderson would do next.'

'And I suppose Henderson went to the King,' he said.

'He went to Falkland and told the King—the man who has stolen your crown, James! And the King rode over to Perth with his bravos who murdered Gowrie and Alec—the man I was to marry and the man I loved. Both of them! Betrayed by me, Jamie, betrayed by me.' She was weeping uncontrollably now.

He closed the locket and kissed her.

'It is time to go,' he said quietly. 'Where we go is another matter. Captain Sinclair has a ship that will come into sight in the morning off Gullane Sands—wherever they are.'

'I know Gullane Sands,' she said, pulling herself together. 'Gowrie had a castle nearby.'

'Good. The ship will take us to Denmark or Germany or God knows where. We will travel together, knowing that—'

She smiled at him.

'Knowing that you do not love me. And that I do not love you,' she said. 'Now let me get my jewel box. Then we shall go to the horses.'

In the stable, cloaked and masked as she had been earlier in the day, she said to the groom, 'Pringle, walk the horses into the lane, their heads towards the Park.'

'Very well, ma'am.'

'Wait for a moment, Jamie. There is a scarf I must have against the night air!'

'We must waste no time,' Jamie protested. 'If we don't hurry, we'll have the Watch nosing about. If we don't have worse.'

The groom tightened the girths and led three horses—one of them a sturdy pack animal—out of the stable. Their hoofs resounded on the causeway outside.

Jamie and Madeleine followed, moments later. The night hung over the town like a canopy of ashen light. No sun now. No moon yet, but a cool, silver radiance in which everything seemed to move, half-real, half-imagined, as if in a dream. Jamie could hear the voices of the actors on the other side of the street.

'There will be no trouble about reaching Gullane tonight,' Madeleine said. 'We shall use the King's Park, without the King's leave.'

Jamie waved an arm majestically.

'The King gives you leave,' he said.

'Your Majesty is too kind.' She curtsied.

A few yards from the stable door, the horses stood with the groom at their heads. There was no one about. He held her stirrup while she mounted. Then he swung into the saddle.

Protesting at the sudden weight, the horse lunged forward. At that moment somebody shouted behind them. 'Here he is, the bastard!'

Madeleine turned her horse's head. Jamie did the same, putting his hand to his sword. Two men had come into sight in the narrow lane behind him. One of them, he thought—in that light, he could not be certain—was Kennedy. The man raised something and aimed it. There was a spurt of flame, then a report.

213

Madeleine groaned as she swayed in the saddle, then slid to the ground.

He was in time to clasp her as she crumpled. He lifted her up and ran back towards Bannerman's Lodging. Kennedy began to pursue them, his face livid with hatred. The man at Kennedy's side fired his pistol, just missing Jamie's head. The groom, cursing and sobbing, galloped at the two assassins, who ran off into the darkness.

Jamie walked on, words echoing in his head. 'My love. My love. My love.'

Messengers of death

The surgeon came into the room where Jamie sat, his head in his hands. 'She is dying,' he said, putting a hand on Jamie's shoulder.

A little while later, Captain Sinclair came into the room.

'She was a brave girl,' he said, shaking his head.

'Too brave.'

'That butcher has vanished. He is being searched for at this moment. Gregory has every caddie in the town on the hunt. Never fear, boy! They will find him. If only the officers of the law don't find you first! Come away with me, James! Come to a a safer place.'

Stuart looked up and shrugged his shoulders. Sinclair did not insist.

Time passed. Alistair MacIan entered, looked round, said nothing and went out.

More time. Now it was Rory Bannerman, looking like a little, yellow-faced old man.

'I have hated you, Stuart,' he said in his smooth voice. 'But hatred, like love, is dead ... Madeleine loved you, God knows why.'

'No, she didn't.'

Rory frowned.

'She loved you in one of her ways,' he insisted, 'as she loved me in another. Oh, she was my sister, I know. But sisters may love—and be loved. You will never understand that, will you? I built great, foolish dreams on Madeleine. And now ... I always knew she would die a strange death. I thought it might be a worse one than this. The stake on the Castle Hill! Then you came on the stage. She said you were the man to take her to Cluny when I could not go with her. I think she sensed that you were the hand of fate. She was enough of a witch for that. I thought only that you were dangerous—and I hated you. I don't hate you now.'

He held out his hand. Jamie took it.

The surgeon came back into the room.

'Mr. Stuart? Ah, you sir. It must be you she meant although she called you'—a look of embarrassment came into the surgeon's face—'something else. The King, she said, poor lady! She wanted you to have this. They were her last words: "Give it to the King." But she meant you ... Delirium ... God help her.'

'Her last words?' said Jamie, desolately.

The surgeon nodded.

'Yes, she meant me,' said Jamie. 'Although what I will do with it—'

He did not go on. At that moment it seemed an impious act to throw the document on the fire.

A time would come when he would feel more calmly about all this, when he would think of Madeleine with a smile of regret, as one who had been destined only to graze his life briefly, then leave it again. Then he would light a candle and burn the parchment in its flame. He could see in imagination the green wax melt and fall, in flat, coloured splashes on a table. Afterwards a servant would come and with a cloth wipe away the last traces of the story, the last evidence that he might have been a king.

But all that would come later. Jamie heard someone come into the room. He looked up. Sinclair.

'Kennedy has left the town. Northwards he has not gone. Three ways he can take. East to Berwick and England. West to Stirling and so to the Highlands or the Clyde. Or South to Liddesdale. From Whitehaven or one of the ports in Galloway he could hope to reach Ireland.'

'What do you think, Captain?'

'Among the caddies the word goes that he will use the track to Berwick. They have heard something.'

'Do they think he'll make for Berwick?'

'They think it.'

'Then they know it,' said Jamie.

'It is the shortest way to England with the least chance of taking the wrong turn. You hug the coast.'

'I'll ride that way,' Jamie sprang to his feet. 'Can anyone guide me?'

Rory stepped back into the room. 'We'll go together.'

'Alistair MacIan wants to go, too,' said Sinclair. 'I'll ride with you as far as Gullane Sands. That is the rendezvous.'

'Wait for me there, Captain. At least, give me a day,' said Stuart.

'A day! Two days!' Sinclair's face shone with joy. 'I thought you would come in the end. The terrible visage of war, boy! The oblivion of danger! The beautiful odour of loot!'

Outside the room there were sounds of a crowd somewhere near, and then suddenly a trampling on the stair. Gregory appeared at the door.

'I see some ugly faces in the yard outside. Quite a rabble!'

Sinclair crammed his hat hard down on his forehead.

'Leave them to me,' he said cheerfully. 'I'm used to this kind of problem.' He glanced into the courtyard.

'The flat of the sword will be enough,' he said scornfully.

Into the leather bag on his chest, Stuart slipped the small parchment with the green seal. In the stables, he found Alistair MacIan fastening a quiver of arrows to a saddle. His bow was slung over one shoulder.

'I'm with you,' said Stuart.

They rode for hours, always eastwards, for a long time in sight of the sea, a black amorphous mass on his left hand. The two distant points of brightness would be navigation lights on the islands, Jamie thought. Above them shone a three-quarter moon. A wind blew damply off the sea.

Rory, who led the way, had paused once or twice when there was a choice of paths, but each time, after surveying the scene, he had gone ahead with confidence. Stuart had left him to his thoughts.

Alistair had not spoken since they left the town.

All this time, they had picked up no trace of the man they were hunting and had met nobody who might have seen him go by. The village streets they passed through were empty. Jamie began to wonder gloomily whether they had chosen the right route after all.

But Rory rode ahead in silence, an arquebus held across his saddle-bow. And each time Jamie looked back, Alistair gave him a crooked grin and a nod which he probably meant to be encouraging. Jamie himself could see nothing, only an empty track clearly marked out on the hard earth of the seaward plain by twenty generations of travellers.

After a time the road left the shore and rose into wild moorland with a hint of hill country beyond it. Now and again a lonely grey tower rose abruptly, with no sign of life within or around it. Ahead, the sky was growing lighter. The whole landscape had a hostile and foreboding air.

Without warning, a stormy wind, blowing furiously from the east, fell on them. The rain was cold and vicious. Jamie, his chin tucked into the collar of his doublet, squinted against the rain and lost sight of Rory. But the squall passed, as abruptly as it had come, and the slight figure hunched over his horse became visible again half a mile ahead. Jamie pressed forward.

At last, when a faint flush of colour was warming the grey of the hilltops, Rory pulled up and pointed. A small black shape far ahead was moving along the track leading downhill to the open sea. He thought that he could see a line of faint grey and lines of darker tone. Breakers on a rocky coast? It seemed likely enough.

But who was this single horseman riding ahead towards the coast? Kennedy? Jamie asked his companions the question. They pulled up alongside and nodded curtly. Rory dismounted to load his arquebus. Alistair pulled an arrow from his quiver and examined it carefully.

Jamie, almost unaware that he was doing so, urged his horse forward. In a graceful canter, he pulled ahead of the others. Soon he was on the rim of a wide, flat basin, bordering the sea. Moorland, turning into dunes with a great expanse of wet sand beyond a shallow bay, crossed by a small stream finding its way muddily to salt water.

About a mile further on, dark cliffs closed the bay.

The moon had sunk. The assembly of stars had vanished. One star remained, steadfast above the sea.

'Night's candles are burnt out.' Where the devil had he heard that? It was not a phrase that would have come unprompted.

The horseman he was following turned to look over his shoulder. It *was* Kennedy.

He gave his mount a touch of the spurs.

Kennedy put his horse into the muddy stream at a point where it seemed there was a ford. His horse went in up to the belly. Climbing out on the mud of the far bank, he plodded slowly through the soft dry sand under the dunes.

Jamie had a clear idea what he would do when he had forded the stream. Gallop on the hard, wet sand at the edge of the sea, then head Kennedy off. Force him to dismount, disarm him in a fight and, with the help of the other two, hang him on a handy tree. Only one thing worried him. The assassin carried a pistol and had probably loaded it.

He pressed his horse into a gallop. Somewhere behind him, borne faintly against the wind, came cries, whether of warning or of encouragement he could not tell.

Soon he had drawn level with Kennedy. The two men were no more than a musket-shot apart. Just at that moment Jamie's horse went down suddenly in the sand, slithered and went over. Jamie was thrown and came down heavily on his shoulder. He struggled upright, only to find he was sinking deeper every second. The horse staggered to its feet, shook itself and stood still on the hard surface nearer the dunes. The ground sucked at the soles of Stuart's feet. Now he was up to his knees. In a minute he would not be able to crawl any further. Quicksand.

A horse's hoofs pounded the sand, then halted, and a man leapt to the ground. Jamie looked up at Kennedy.

'I knew I would get you in the end, Stuart.'

He was grinning as he drew his pistol.

'You had better hurry or you'll be too late—for both of us,' said Jamie.

'It would be a pleasure to watch you sinking slowly under the sand. It would be pleasant to push you in deeper. But that won't be necessary. You are going to die, Stuart, with wet sand filling your gullet.'

'Better hurry, Kennedy. The hangmen are close behind you.'

'There will be time for everything,' Kennedy sneered. 'Say your prayers, Mr. Stuart.'

He raised the pistol and took aim carefully.

Jamie shut his eyes. It was better not to see. Then he heard a sound like a shot. He looked up again. Kennedy's face reflected a dreadful, spreading astonishment. His mouth was open. His eyes were focused on something in the distance. An arrow had struck above his left shoulder and embedded itself in his chest. With an agonising effort he squeezed the trigger of his pistol. The shot passed an inch above Jamie's head.

Then, staggering around, he set off across the sand to his horse, struggling as he went to pull the arrow from his chest. It seemed the effort of climbing into the saddle was too much for him. He began to walk along the beach, swaying as he went like a man blinded or drunk.

By this time, Jamie was up to the waist in the sand and sinking fast. He heard a shout, and looked up to see Rory and Alistair dismounting. Alistair found a tether-rope hanging from the pack-horse's saddle and threw it to Jamie. 'With us and two horses we'll have you out of there in a minute.'

'Was that your arrow, Alistair?' said Jamie hoarsely, once more on solid ground. 'God! What a shot!'

'Look, the bastard is escaping us,' said Rory.

Kennedy had reached the distant end of the bay and was climbing up a narrow path that led to a dark cave a hundred feet above the sands.

'He is making for that cave,' said Stuart.

Alistair turned to him with a thin, cruel smile.

'He won't reach it. Look!'

They followed Alistair's pointing finger. Kennedy was walking with an odd gait, like a man on a shipboard in a storm. Suddenly he pitched forward, rolled and lay still.

'Finished,' said Bannerman grimly.

'He's shamming,' said Stuart, looking from one face to the other. 'He'll get over it.'

The other men shook their heads.

'Watch, boy. Now you'll see something.' Alistair pointed to the sky above the place where Kennedy lay.

Against the shining lilac vault, a black speck grew almost imperceptibly larger. Soon it was joined by another speck. The two specks grew into shapes. Falling down through the morning air, in great curving swoops, the light shone on tawny brown breast feathers. Birds, huge birds, with a wing spread of seven feet across.

'Erns,' said Alistair.

'Eagles,' Rory nodded. 'Sea eagles. Look at the white on their tails. I haven't seen them as far south as this before.'

Alistair pointed to a massive stump of rock which rose abruptly out of the sea a few miles to the north-west.

'They'll have a nest there,' he said.

While the three men watched, the birds alighted on the slope near the prostrate man. And for a moment, while they folded their wings, they stood watching him. Then they waddled towards him. Ungainly. Majestic. Sinister. Obscene, somehow. Messengers of a dreadful death.

Stuart frowned and looked away from the ghastly scene. It was some time before Bannerman walked over to his horse and mounted to ride away. He had not uttered a word.

Now he said, 'Fare you well, James Stuart. She was not one whose end was likely to be peaceful. But it should not have happened so soon!'

'You blame me, Rory.'

Bannerman shrugged. 'You were well-matched, she and you. May you have better luck than she had.'

He turned his horse's head to the west.

The domes of Moscow

It was hours later and twelve miles further west. Two young men had ridden seawards through fields of barley beginning to turn brown with the sun and flecked with poppies and gowans. Now they were looking out to sea from the dunes above an empty beach of fine pink sand. High tide would come within the hour.

The water had a sleek and treacherous look, Jamie thought. Beyond it lay—what? If he stayed he would be hanged. That was sure. And it would be good to clear the smell of death from his nostrils.

'Strangers!' said Alistair quietly, jerking his head towards the dunes. Jamie glanced that way.

'No,' he said. 'Friends.'

Mary Beaton was riding pillion behind a red-haired young man, probably her brother, Alan. They dismounted and approached over the sand.

'Mary!'

'Don't think I have come to see you off!' she said. 'Nothing like that! But this is Alan. He is a passenger on the ship you are travelling with. He has business,' she added scornfully, 'in Hamburg.'

The red-haired young man grinned.

'Tyrone will pay good money for guns. I know where to find them.'

'And you can guess what our mother says about his goings on!'

'Why don't you travel with him?' Jamie asked her with a smile.

'Come with you? That's what you mean, isn't it. *Merci, monsieur!* That reminds me. I have a message for you from Mother.'

'Ah. That will be worth listening to. Tell me.'

'Wild oats make thin porridge,' she recited.

'Say it again.'

She did.

'What does it mean, Mary?'

'You ken as well as I do, James Stuart.'

'I expect I do,' he said doubtfully.

'Who is your Highland friend?'

'Alistair MacIan.'

'My God, he's a beautiful man.'

He looked at her in astonishment.

'He's a hideous man,' he said. 'Alistair, come here. We have company.'

But Alistair was too busy at that moment looking out to sea.

'There she comes,' he cried.

They walked down to the edge of the water. Out there, a ship came in sight from the north-west, its swollen sails catching the early sun.

Some time later, a small boat approached the shore with Sinclair standing in the stern.

'Did you catch the bastard?' he called out as soon as he was within hailing distance.

Jamie nodded emphatically and pointed to Alistair.

Sinclair stepped ashore and stood at the water's edge.

'A shot like the one that felled Orkney's sentry.'

'Magnificent,' said Sinclair. 'Are you ready to go? A navy pinnace will be along at any minute now looking for us. They know we are soon to sail.'

Mary Beaton thrust a parcel into Jamie's hand. 'From mother.'

'What is it?'

'A spare shirt.'

She threw her arms round him and kissed him. He was astonished to find her tears wetting his cheeks. He thought he heard her say, 'Come back, you wicked man.' As she turned away, he caught her.

'One moment,' he said.

Opening the leather bag that hung on his chest, he took out the jewelled clasp. 'Keep it for me, Mary. It has been for years in the family. *Au revoir.*'

'A promise is a promise,' she whispered.

He looked at her in perplexity. By the time he remembered what she was talking about it was too late to turn back. The boat was already some distance out into the firth and he was not a good swimmer.

'The domes of Moscow!' cried Sinclair, pulling him aboard the ship. 'The palace of the Tsars. Gold, jewels, loot!'

'Cold. Dirt. Slavery.' Jamie stepped on deck, and began whistling a silly tune he had known since childhood.